AN UNSPOKEN WISH

"It's a beautiful night, isn't it?" Adam said, leaning back his head to regard the moon and star-lit sky overhead.

"Beautiful," agreed Lora. "I must thank you, Adam, for giving me your company this evening. I was feeling very low when I came here, but now—now I feel quite cheerful. You can't know how pleasant this last hour has been for me."

"Yes, I think I can, Lora. You must know that it's been very pleasant for me, too," said Adam. "In fact, it's been quite the best time I've ever had at a ball. I assure you that's not the champagne talking. I am very glad I met you."

"I'm glad I met you, too," said Lora. She spoke demurely, but was surprised by the very undemure wave of feeling that accompanied the words. In all her well-behaved life she had never once encouraged a gentleman to kiss her, not even the late Lord Carroll, but now, looking into Adam's eyes, she was seized by a sudden, overwhelming desire to be kissed. Looking into Adam's eyes, she deliberately willed him to kiss her.

Kiss me, she said silently, gazing into his eyes. *Kiss me—kiss me—kiss me.*

Adam regarded her solemnly for a moment. And then, with grave deliberation, he leaned down and kissed her . . .

Books by Joy Reed

AN INCONVENIENT ENGAGEMENT
TWELFTH NIGHT
THE SEDUCTION OF LADY CARROLL

Published by Zebra Books

The Seduction of Lady Carroll

Joy Reed

ZEBRA BOOKS
KENSINGTON PUBLISHING CORP.

For J.K.

ZEBRA BOOKS are published by

Kensington Publishing Corp.
850 Third Avenue
New York, NY 10022

Copyright © 1996 by Joy Reed

First Printing: August, 1996
10 9 8 7 6 5 4 3 2 1

Printed in the United States of America

One

"Lora, my love, it's been two and a half years now since Carroll died. It's none of my business, I know, but still I can't help wondering just what you were planning to do with the rest of your life."

The speaker of these words, Lady Helen Spelbourne, raised herself on one elbow to look at her companion. She was lying atop a large plush sofa, which was decorated like the rest of the drawing room in Turkish style with crimson upholstery and a profusion of barbaric ornament. It was a striking piece of furniture, and Lady Helen made a striking picture lying upon it. She was not a beautiful woman in any sense of the word, but she had the trick of making the most of those assets she possessed, and her appearance invariably attracted second glances. She had a thin, dark, angular face with large, expressive dark eyes, a quantity of rather unruly dark hair, and a small, slight figure. At the moment, the latter of these features was sheathed in an opulent gown of gold brocade that was perfectly in keeping with the exotic splendor of her surroundings.

The other occupant of the drawing room, to whom her words were addressed, was a lady of an altogether different style. Lora, Lady Carroll, was taller than Lady Helen, with more of a feminine softness to her face and figure. Her appearance was admittedly less striking than her friend's, but it was also very much prettier, with a beauty that did not require a second glance to discern. She had soft brown eyes, hair of a dark golden blonde, and a fair, delicate complexion that colored slightly as she responded to Lady Helen's question.

"I don't know, Helen," she said in a constrained voice. "To speak truth, I hadn't made any plans for the future beyond this visit. But if my staying here is inconveniencing you and Arthur—"

"Foolish creature! You must know how glad I am to have you with me. And Arthur is glad to have you here, too. He was saying just the other day that your being here had a good effect on me; that since you arrived I've seemed less moody, and not so anxious about coming events."

With a wry smile, Lady Helen looked down at her brocade-clad abdomen, which after seven months of pregnancy was only now beginning to advertise its condition. "Indeed, Lora, I would be very glad to have you with me permanently, but I expect that's too much to hope for," she went on, smiling at her friend. "I suppose really that I have cut my own throat by inviting you here. Now that you're out of mourning and going about socially, it's only a matter of time before some gentleman falls in love with you, and then you will be lost to me once more. I only hope that this time you will choose a gentleman who lives closer to Spelbourne, so that I may see you more often than I have these last ten years."

Lora's only response to this was a quick, negative shake of her head. Lady Helen eyed her speculatively for a moment, and when she went on her voice was gentler than it had been before.

"Indeed, Lora, I don't wish to pry, but we have been friends for many years, and though other people may not notice anything amiss, I can't help seeing that you're not in spirits." In a gentler tone still, she added, "Do you still miss Carroll so very much?"

"No," said Lora. She spoke quickly and rather repressively. Lady Helen eyed her for a moment or two before going on.

"Well, then, if what you say is true, there's no reason why you shouldn't start living again, is there?" Lora made no response, and Lady Helen went on, speaking quickly as though determined to have her say now that she had begun. "What I mean is, that when we were both giddy girls, you used to love parties and dancing and music almost as much as I did, but nowadays you don't seem to take an interest in anything. Even at the opera the other night, which I felt certain you must enjoy, you looked as though you hardly heard the music."

Lora looked down at her lap. "I'm sorry, Helen," she said in a low voice. "I do appreciate all you've been trying to do for me—"

"Yes, but you see I don't want your appreciation, my love." Lady Helen leaned forward on the sofa, her dark eyes aglow and earnest. "All I want is to see you enjoying yourself again, like your old self. You need to make an effort to shake off these foolish doldrums you've fallen into. And Lora, I think you ought to consider marrying again. Not that I want to lose you, but I would rather see you happy than keep you selfishly to myself."

"Oh, no," said Lora, in such a sharp voice that her friend looked at her in surprise. She flushed. "No, I could not consider such a thing, Helen," she said in a more level tone. "After Carroll died, I made up my mind that I would never marry again."

"Oh, but that is foolishness, Lora!" In her vehemence, Lady Helen leaned forward so far she almost pitched herself off the sofa. Righting herself, she went on speaking more quietly, but with no less vehemence. "You're only twenty-six, hardly more than a girl yet, Lora. No matter how much you loved Carroll, you cannot spend the rest of your life mourning for him. I suppose you think it disloyal to think of remarrying when you cared for him so much, but—"

"No, it isn't that, Helen. The thing is. . . ." Lora hesitated, then went on resolutely. "The thing is, Helen, that I was not at all happy in my marriage with Carroll. That is the reason I don't wish to marry again, not because I feel it would be disloyal."

"Lora, are you serious?" Lady Helen's eyes were wide with astonishment as she regarded her friend. "Why, I never dreamed such a thing! I had always thought you and Carroll quite the ideal couple. You don't mean to say he mistreated you, do you?"

Lora shook her head and even smiled a little, though it was a rather mirthless smile. "Oh, no, nothing so bad as that, Helen. He did not beat me, or keep a mistress, or stint me on my pin-money, even. I suppose most people would say he was a very good husband."

"Well, and I know he thought you a good wife," said Lady Helen, still regarding her with astonishment. "Why, he often used to boast of how sweet-tempered you were. I remember him saying once that you were such an angel, it was impossible to quarrel with you."

"Did he say that?" A fleeting look of sadness passed over Lora's face, to be replaced a moment later by a look of surprising sternness. "But I wasn't a good wife, Helen. At least, I wasn't bad outwardly, but on the inside—oh, you cannot think how much I resented him. Helen, there were times when I almost hated him, and for the stupidest, most trivial reasons! It makes me quite ashamed when I think of it now."

"What reasons?" said Lady Helen with interest.

"Oh, it sounds ridiculous to tell them now." Lora gazed down at her lap a moment, then looked at her friend with a rather twisted smile. "You know that Carroll was inclined to be rather nice in his dress, Helen. Sometimes he used to ruin a dozen neckcloths before he could get one tied to suit him. And all the time he was trying to tie them, he would swear, and shout at his valet, and throw things. I used to hear him at it when I was in my dressing room, and it made me feel *sick*, Helen, actually physically sick."

Lora's voice had gradually warmed in tone, until in making this last statement she sounded downright impassioned. But she seemed to regret her passion as soon as she had spoken, for she threw Lady Helen an apologetic smile and finished in her usual gentle way. "It got so I started getting up an hour before he did, so that I might be downstairs when he was dressing and wouldn't have to listen to him."

There was a new understanding in Lady Helen's eyes as she regarded her friend. "Yes, you always did have a rather sensitive temperament, didn't you, my love?" she said. "I can see how that might have disturbed you."

"And then there was the time he got angry with the cook for over-boiling the breakfast eggs and turned her out of the house without notice, on the same day we were having guests to dinner. All this without saying a word to me, mind you, and then he went out hunting for the rest of the day and left me to deal with the situation!" The impassioned note had once more crept into Lora's voice in recounting this incident. Once more she seemed to regret it and made a visible effort to lighten it as she went on. "The only reason we managed to have a dinner to serve that night was because I went into the kitchen and cooked it myself. It took me all day to do it, and when I told Carroll afterward, he only thought it was a very good joke and said he would never have thought I could do something so clever!"

Lady Helen shook her head sympathetically, though there was a faint quirk about her lips as though she was trying not to laugh. "Poor Lora! That *was* too bad of Carroll," she said. "But of course, men don't realize what a lot of work it is to get up a dinner party."

"It wasn't the work so much that I minded." Lora looked at her friend soberly. "The thing was, you know, that it ought to have been me who dismissed the cook if she needed dismissing. I was supposed to be in charge of all the inside staff, but the truth was that I could hardly ever give an order without Carroll contradicting it, and it was he who made all the decisions about hiring or firing. Of course the servants couldn't help seeing that it was he who was in charge, not me, and so they didn't respect me. It got so bad toward the end that when Annie would go down to order my breakfast, or my bathwater, they would purposely delay bringing it to me. It was all very mortifying."

"I imagine that it was," said Lady Helen, regarding her with some bewilderment. "But didn't you tell Carroll how all this bothered you, Lora?"

"I did try to tell him once, but he only laughed and said that no one expected a pretty little goose like me to be an accomplished housekeeper."

"What did you say to that?"

"I didn't say anything. It didn't seem to me it would do any good, and I could see he would be offended if I made an issue of it. Indeed, I suppose he was only trying to help me, according to his lights. But you can see why I wasn't very happy living with him."

"Well, of course, it's difficult to live with anyone without conflicts," said Lady Helen fair-mindedly. "I know Arthur and I fought like cats and dogs the first year we were married, but since then we've settled down pretty well. We still have our differences, to be sure, but that stands to reason, for we *are* rather different, you know. A great many people predicted we would separate within the year, but though our tastes may not be exactly similar, they're compatible enough that we don't rub along too badly. And of course, it helps that we're compatible in other ways," she added with a conscious smile.

Lora nodded and looked away, trying not to show her embarrassment. She knew what Lady Helen meant, but despite a friendship of many years' standing, she could never get used to her friend's outspokenness on this and similar subjects. Mingled with her embarrassment was a kind of wonder that Lady Helen should speak of her intimate relations with Lord Spelbourne with so much satisfaction. Her own experience with such relations had been, if not invariably painful, at least invariably awkward and unsatisfying. She could only suppose there must be something wrong with her in that regard. This supposition was strengthened by the fact that in her seven years of marriage with the late Lord Carroll, she had failed to conceive a child.

This failure to conceive had had serious consequences for Lora. Upon Lord Carroll's death two and a half years before, his title and estate had passed to a distant cousin, and she had found herself suddenly reduced to the status of dowager countess, bereft alike of home and husband. Since that time she had been staying with her parents in the county of Suffolk, but Lady

Helen had begged so earnestly and incessantly for a visit that
Lora could not refuse her, little inclined for society though she
was. It was this that had brought her to London, and to the
Spelbournes' elegant townhouse where she was presently resid-
ing.

Lady Helen's thoughts seemed to have been running on
somewhat similar lines, to judge by her next remark. "I wonder
how the Lancashire Carrolls are enjoying their newfound lux-
ury! I must say, I think it was infamous of them to push you
out so soon after Carroll's death."

Lora looked pained. "Oh, but they didn't push me out,
Helen," she said. "Indeed, they urged me very kindly to stay
on as long as I liked, but of course it was awkward with all
of us in the same house. They were so anxious not to say or
do anything that would cause me pain that it got to be positively suffocating. And for their part, poor things, I'm sure
they wished me at Jericho so that they might settle down and
enjoy their inheritance. It would have been different if there
had been a proper dower house for me to remove to, but as it
was, I was as eager to go as they were to see me go."

Lady Helen nodded understandingly. "So you returned to
the parental fold," she said. "No doubt your mother and father
were very glad to see you home again."

"Yes, they were." A wistful smile played around Lora's lips.
"And of course I was glad to see them again, too. After everything that had happened, it was a great relief to be back at
Laurel Park, with my own family and my own old rooms and
everything going on just the same as always. It probably
sounds hypocritical after the things I've been saying about him,
but I really was dreadfully cut up by Carroll's death, Helen."
Lora looked at her friend earnestly. "I couldn't have felt worse
if I had still loved him as I did when we first married. Indeed,
I don't think I would have felt as badly if I had, because then
I wouldn't have felt so guilty about it."

Again Lady Helen nodded. "Yes, I can see how that would
be, and I don't doubt it was a dreadful time for you, my love,"

she said. "I only wish I could have been there with you when it happened."

"Don't be sorry, Helen. I was glad you didn't hear the news until after, because then you would have felt obliged to rush right home, and you would have missed seeing Italy and Switzerland."

Lady Helen smiled. "I'm sure Italy and Switzerland would have still been there for us to visit later on," she said. "But there's no use crying over spilt milk now, of course. And at least your family was there for you, even if I wasn't. I suppose really it's one's family one wants at such a time anyway."

Lora hesitated a moment before answering. "Mama and Papa were certainly a great comfort to me," she said carefully. "Truly, I don't know how I could have stood it without them. And I was very glad to return with them to Laurel Park and just sort of sit back and let them take charge of things for a while. Only, after a while that got to be even more suffocating than living with the Lancashire Carrolls."

"Indeed? Suffocating in what way?" said Lady Helen, regarding her with lively curiosity.

Lora gave her an embarrassed smile. "Well, you see, after I had been at home a few months, Mama and Papa seemed to forget that I was a grown-up woman who had been married for a good many years," she told Lady Helen. "By the time I had been there a year, they were treating me as though I were a little girl again. It was Mama who was the worst. I stood it as long as she limited herself to ordering my companions and my amusements, but when she started ordering my dresses, too, I knew it was time to go."

Lady Helen burst out laughing. "Oh, my poor Lora! So that explains the ladylike restraint of your wardrobe! I didn't like to say anything, but really, that dress you wore to the opera last night! You looked the most perfect little Quakeress, my love."

Lora smiled wanly. Lady Helen laughed again and got up from the sofa to embrace her.

"At any rate, you had the sense to come to me when you left

Suffolk," she told Lora. "I only wish you had come to me before. But now that you're here, we must see about ordering you some new dresses. I'll take you to my modiste in Oxford Street tomorrow. She's my own discovery, and I can vouch that she is very clever."

"I would appreciate that, Helen." Lora returned her friend's embrace affectionately. "I do need some new dresses, no doubt about it."

"Once you've been properly gowned, we'll have to see what we can do to cheer you up," said Lady Helen, her face kindling as she contemplated both these delightful projects. "If you ask me, the best thing that could happen would be for you to find some nice gentleman to fall in love with."

Lora shook her head with decision. "No, that's out of the question, Helen. I am quite determined not to marry again."

"Goose! You don't have to marry just because you fall in love, you know. Look at Lord Mandeville and Mrs. Ames. Or Sir Henry Allen and Lady Dunbury."

"Take a lover, you mean?" Lora could not hide the shock in her voice. "Oh, I could never do that, Helen!"

Lady Helen gave her an amused look. "But why not, my love?" she said lightly. "It is very often done, I assure you. More often than not, I sometimes think!"

Lora's eyes were wide and startled as she regarded her friend. "Helen! You don't mean to say that *you* ever—"

"Well, no, I don't mean to say that, my love." Lady Helen gave a little laugh, a sound both amused and embarrassed. "As I said before, Arthur and I are very compatible that way, and what with one thing and another, I have never been much tempted. I have certainly had *offers,* however. . . ."

For a moment, Lady Helen sat smiling reminiscently to herself, then shook herself and went on briskly. "But for you, why not? You've just said you don't intend to marry again. You don't want to spend the rest of your life living like a nun, do you?"

"Why not? I already have the wardrobe for it," returned Lora, with a laugh that could not quite hide her discomfiture.

Lady Helen laughed, too, and squeezed her shoulders affectionately. "Poor dear, you do at that! But we will get you to Madame LeClaire's tomorrow and outfit you fresh all around. For the Monroes' party tonight, perhaps my woman can do something about retrimming one of your old dresses. If that Annie of yours had any kind of initiative, she would have done something about it long before now—"

"Don't blame Annie, Helen. If I had asked her to, she would have, I'm sure, but it never occurred to me to ask."

"A really first-rate dressing woman wouldn't wait to be asked," said Lady Helen severely. "Annie doesn't add to your consequence, Lora, and that's a fact. You really ought to let her go and hire someone like my Chalmers, who knows exactly what's what. I doubt you would have had half the problems you did at Carrollton if your dressing woman had been able to hold her own with the other servants." Seeing that Lora was looking mulish, she continued in a milder voice, "But it's like you to be loyal, Lora, even to a losing cause like Annie. We won't argue about it anymore. Why don't you come upstairs with me now and see what we can salvage from your wardrobe for tonight?"

"Very well, Helen," said Lora. Taking her friend's arm, she accompanied her upstairs to her bedchamber.

Two

Gripping her fan and reticule in one hand, and holding up her skirts with the other, Lora stepped into the carriage behind Lady Helen. She took a seat on the banquette beside her friend while Lord Spelbourne, Lady Helen's husband, entered the coach and sat down across from them on the forward banquette. He was a large, blunt-featured man, fair-haired and slow-moving with a good-natured, rather vacuous smile: in every way the reverse of the small, dark, vivacious Lady Helen.

Lora, looking at them now, wondered for the hundredth time what could have brought two such opposites together. But she could not doubt Lady Helen's affection for her husband, or his for her. There was an ingenuous look of love and admiration on Lord Spelbourne's face as he regarded his wife across the carriage.

"By Jove, don't you look fine tonight, Helen," he said. "That's a dashed pretty get-up you're wearing. You look dashed pretty, too, Lora," he added, in what was obviously an afterthought.

"Thank you, Arthur," said Lora. She could not wonder that Lord Spelbourne should be struck by his wife's appearance. Lady Helen was wearing a dress of vivid orange and purple satin that would have looked impossibly gaudy on anyone else, but which on her managed merely to look very dashing. If, as Lora supposed, it was the work of Madame LeClaire, then she felt the modiste deserved every encomium that Lady Helen had heaped upon her. The dress was so cleverly cut that it successfully concealed Lady Helen's advanced state of pregnancy while revealing nearly everything else about her. Along with this remarkable garment, Lady Helen wore a striped orange and purple evening toque, a pair of amethyst bracelets, and a quizzing glass on a long chain around her neck.

Lora's own toilette was less eye-catching, but she was tolerably pleased with it nonetheless. Her white muslin dress had short sleeves, a white satin sash, and a couple of scalloped flounces at the hem. Although its décolletage was modest compared to Lady Helen's, the removal of a lace tucker had given it a more modish look and had rid it of the Quakerish air which Lady Helen had found so objectionable in her toilette of the previous evening. Lady Helen's dressing woman had taken charge of these alterations while Lora's maid had dressed her hair in its usual style with clusters of side curls and a topknot bound with white ribbons. To complete her toilette, Lora wore long white kid gloves, white kid sandals, and an India shawl with a deep figured border.

Although satisfied with her appearance, Lora was not looking forward to the evening ahead with much enthusiasm. She had no reason to suppose that the ball that evening would be more enjoyable than any of the other evening parties she had attended since arriving in London. This particular party was being held at the home of Sir Edward and Lady Monroe to celebrate the betrothal of their daughter to the Honourable Major Linville. Lora, to whom all of these people were equally unknown, had naturally no great interest in the proceedings; and though she had found a certain amount of relief in unburdening herself to Lady Helen that afternoon, she was still far from feeling in the mood for festivity.

The carriage arrived at length in the square that fronted the Monroes' home, a large and handsome townhouse dating from the reign of Queen Anne. Lora left the carriage along with the Spelbournes and was admitted to the house by a couple of liveried footmen, who bawled out their names for the benefit of those already inside:

"Lady Carroll. Lord and Lady Helen Spelbourne."

This impressive announcement created no great stir, being indeed barely audible over the noise of music, laughter, and conversation. The entrance hall was a sea of plumes, turbans, and jewel- or flower-bedecked coiffures, interspersed with the sleek pomaded heads of gentlemen. Two broad and constant streams of guests were struggling their way up and down the great curved staircase leading to the upper floor. When at last Lora and her companions arrived there, they found the crowd within the ballroom even denser than that in the entrance hall below.

"Lady Helen! And Lord Spelbourne, too. So glad you could come. This is Lady Carroll, I presume? Very glad to make your acquaintance, my dear. This is my daughter Althea, and this is her fiancé, Major Linville."

After Lora, Lady Helen, and Lord Spelbourne had greeted their hostess and paid their respects to the newly betrothed couple, they turned their attention to finding a place to sit down. This had no sooner been accomplished than a pair of gentlemen converged upon Lady Helen from opposite ends of the ballroom and simultaneously requested the favor of dancing with her.

"Indeed, I am much obliged to you both, but I don't mean to dance at all tonight," she told them with a smile. "It's lowering to admit, but nowadays I am not quite so light on my feet as I could wish!"

One of the gentlemen merely accepted this statement with a bow and walked off. The other, however, a very tall, thin young gentleman dressed with almost foppish nicety, turned to Lora. Having scrutinized her through his quizzing glass for a minute or two, he ventured to request an introduction. Lady Helen laughingly complied.

"Lora, this is Mr. Ferdinand Hastings: a sad, impertinent creature, I am afraid, but, I venture to say, perfectly harmless. Ferdie, this is my dear friend Lady Carroll. You must remember my speaking of her when we were at the Elmhursts' last week."

"I remember the circumstance perfectly," said Mr. Hastings, bowing gracefully toward Lora and then again toward Lady

Helen. "But it hadn't occurred to me that this could be Lady Carroll. You spoke of her as a dowager, you know, and no one looking at this blooming creature would ever suppose her to be something as prosaic as a dowager. Will you do me the honor to dance with me, Lady Carroll?"

"Yes, Lora, do go ahead and dance, my love," said Lady Helen, before Lora could reply. "No, you needn't scruple on my account. I will be perfectly all right here with Arthur. You go on and dance with Ferdie. Though you wouldn't think it to look at him, he does dance divinely, I assure you."

"Then I shall accept your invitation with great pleasure, sir," said Lora. She had not been much impressed by Mr. Hastings's appearance and was a little vexed to have him forced on her as a partner, but there was no polite way to refuse him after Lady Helen's urgings. Knowing her friend's interference to be well-meant, however, she swallowed her resentment and went out to take her place on the floor with Mr. Hastings.

Once there, she found her resentment toward both Lady Helen and her partner abating a little. Mr. Hastings did indeed dance divinely, and if his conversation was not of a very edifying sort, it was at least very entertaining. Lora and he were soon in the midst of a discussion about the Prince Regent's most recent act of folly.

"He didn't say *that*, surely?"

"Indeed he did—and right at the dinner table, too. Lady J. looked quite no-how, I assure you," said Mr. Hastings with a grin, as he dexterously swept Lora through the movements of a quadrille.

She laughed and shook her head, then stopped laughing abruptly as she caught sight of Lady Helen. Lady Helen was looking toward her and Mr. Hastings with an expression of deepest satisfaction on her piquant little face. As Lora watched, she saw her friend whisper something to her husband, then nod toward Lora and her partner.

This circumstance instantly destroyed all Lora's pleasure in the dance. She was reminded of her earlier conversation with Lady

Helen, and although she could not be certain, she felt a conviction that Lady Helen's thoughts were still running on the subject of love and lovers. The idea that Mr. Hastings had been presented to her in the capacity of a potential lover made Lora blush hotly. Her embarrassment was made all the worse by Mr. Hastings, who observed her blush and remarked upon it with surprise.

"I say, you're not feeling ill, are you, Lady Carroll?" he said. "Seems to me you're looking a bit flushed."

"No! Oh, no, I am not ill, Mr. Hastings. It is only that—I suppose it must be because—this room is really dreadfully warm, isn't it?"

"That it is," said Mr. Hastings cheerfully. "But then, discomfort of one kind or another is pretty much a given at these sort of affairs. I've never been in a ballroom yet that wasn't either heated like an oven or drafty as a barn."

Having taken up this theme, Mr. Hastings proceeded to expound on it with a good deal of humor, but he got only weak smiles and inaudible replies for his pains. The idea of Mr. Hastings as a lover was impossible, unthinkable; Lora's mind revolted rather than even consider it. Yet, having once been admitted, the idea would not go away, but continued to hover around the periphery of her thoughts in a way that was very disconcerting. She could not speak to him or even look at him without its recurring to her. As soon as possible after the dance was over, Lora excused herself to Mr. Hastings and hurried back over to Lady Helen.

It was only a few minutes later that another gentleman solicited her to dance. This time it was a gentleman already known to her: a Mr. Julian Roberts, who had been a close friend of her late husband's and had often visited her and Lord Carroll at their estate in Wiltshire. Since she was already in the habit of considering Mr. Roberts in a merely friendly light, Lora did not find herself troubled by the same excesses of imagination that had disturbed her while dancing with Mr. Hastings.

" 'Pon my word, it's good to see you again, Lora," said Mr. Roberts, smiling at her warmly as they went down the line of dancers. "I don't believe I've seen you since—well, since the funeral, you know. Poor Carroll, that was a shocking thing to happen, a very shocking thing indeed. I can't say how shocked I was by it all. But of course you had the worst of it, poor girl. You've been bearing up all right, I hope, this last year or two?"

"Yes, quite well, thank you, Julian," said Lora. Here was another subject to make her uncomfortable. But her widowhood was still so recent that condolences were inevitable whenever she appeared in public, and constant practice during the last two and a half years had enabled her to bear them with at least the appearance of composure. Summoning up a smile, she told Mr. Roberts, "I am very well, and I hope you are well, too, Julian. Do you make a long stay in London?"

"No, I'm just down for the party. Linville's a friend of mine—Major Linville, y'know, the happy groom-to-be. He looks happy, don't he? That Miss Monroe's a nice little gel. Pretty, too. I used to know her when she was a skinny little thing with freckles, all arms and legs, but she's improved a lot since then."

"Indeed, she is a very pretty girl," said Lora, looking toward the head of the room where Miss Monroe, radiant in white satin, stood beside her fiancé. The sight brought an odd pain to Lora's heart. Ten years ago she had been just such another young girl, standing beside Lord Carroll and blushingly receiving the best wishes of their friends and family. The contrast between what she had been then and what she was now struck Lora most bitterly. Averting her eyes, she hurried on in a voice of brittle gaiety: "Yes, Miss Monroe is a very pretty girl, and not just in the common style, either. One seldom sees red hair of that particular shade."

"Well, I don't know about that. You'll likely be seeing a lot more of it as time goes on, for Lady Monroe's got three more daughters with hair just as red who'll be making their bows here in another year or two."

Mr. Roberts went on talking for some time on this and similar inconsequential subjects, but Lora heard scarcely a word.

All the while she was smiling, nodding, and making polite sounds of interest, her thoughts were running on the events of ten years before. Having once been started in this direction, they proved as impossible to check as they had earlier when she was dancing with Mr. Hastings. She was feeling tired and jaded by the time she bade farewell to Mr. Roberts and resumed her seat beside Lady Helen. Lady Helen's first words, however, served to give her thoughts quite another direction.

"Ellsworth was asking about you, Lora. He was here just a minute ago when you were dancing with Julian. I think he means to ask you to dance. Yes, here he comes now. Mind you watch your step with him, my child." Lady Helen sunk her voice to a whisper as she continued. "That's one connection I'd rather not see you make, if you understand my meaning. Ellsworth is a handsome creature, but as cold-blooded as they come. It was really criminal, the way he treated poor Constance Shaughnessy last spring."

Lora murmured something in reply; she knew not what. Her eyes were on the gentleman who was even now approaching their corner.

He was a remarkably handsome gentleman, tall and well-formed with dark hair and the bluest of blue eyes. Lora had met him many years ago when she was still Miss Darlington and knew him as Lord Ellsworth, a young peer with the reputation of an avid sportsman. But it appeared now from Lady Helen's words that in recent years he had been cultivating a reputation of a different sort.

Lora had no difficulty believing that Lord Ellsworth had enjoyed as great a success with the opposite sex as on the hunting field or in the boxing ring. Early in her career, and in common with nearly every other young woman of the *ton,* there had been a time when she herself had been wont to sigh after Lord Ellsworth's blue eyes: to treasure up the memory of every word or smile he had bestowed on her, and to thrill with pleasure whenever he asked her to dance. Even now, she was conscious of a little thrill of pleasure as he took her gloved hand and bowed over it.

"Lady Carroll," he said, with the smile she still remembered so well. "I've been hearing rumors that you were back in London, but I hardly dared believe they were true. I cannot doubt the evidence of my own eyes, however. Here you are, and looking exactly as you looked at sixteen. If country living can accomplish such miracles of preservation, I'm inclined to try a course of rustification myself."

"If it did you any good, Ellsworth—which I take leave to doubt—you would only undo it again on your next visit to London," said Lady Helen. She spoke smilingly, but there was a hint of anxiety in her eyes as she looked from him to Lora. "And Lora knows better than believe your flattery, don't you, Lora? To say that she looks just as she did at sixteen, indeed! As well say she looks six and be done with it."

"Now that you mention it, I believe I may have erred in that regard," said Lord Ellsworth, regarding Lora pensively. "I should have said rather that she looks *better* than she did at sixteen."

"Incorrigible," said Lady Helen, rolling her eyes heavenward.

Lord Ellsworth laughed and turned again to Lora. "Lady Helen is doing her best to distract me, but I shall not be turned from my purpose so easily. I came here with the fixed intention of asking you to dance, and your only hope of getting rid of me is to agree. My preference would be for this next dance, which I understand will be a waltz, but I am not an unreasonable man. I will allow myself to be fobbed off with a country dance if you are already engaged for the next set."

"No, I am not engaged for the next set. I shall be happy to waltz with you, Lord Ellsworth," said Lora, trying not to show how much this speech pleased her.

Lord Ellsworth assisted her to her feet, then extended a blue broadcloth-covered arm to lead her out onto the floor. As soon as they had taken their places and the music had begun, he commenced a most desperate flirtation.

"I was speaking the truth back there, you know," he told her, gazing into her eyes. "You truly don't look a day older than sixteen. Do you remember when you really were sixteen and we used to dance together?"

"Yes, I remember," Lora permitted herself to say.

Lord Ellsworth continued to gaze soulfully into her eyes. "That was a long time ago, wasn't it? But you see, I haven't forgotten. I remember you very well when you were still Miss Darlington and I was one of your many admirers, back before Carroll dashed onto the scene and swept you off from beneath all our noses. There were a good many of us left lamenting that day, myself not less than the others. I was more than half in love with you, you know."

Lord Ellsworth spoke these words with quiet intensity and accompanied them with a look that should have thrilled Lora to the core. Yet she found herself feeling more annoyed than thrilled. Although his manner was superficially humble, beneath the surface she sensed not humility but rather a self-satisfaction so great as to verge upon arrogance. It was obvious that he expected her to be overcome by the mere notion that he had once been in love with her. Lora, normally the gentlest of mortals, felt a sudden urge to puncture a self-consequence so odiously inflated.

"Were you indeed?" she said coolly. "But that was nearly ten years ago, my lord. By all accounts, you have found plenty of consolation since then."

Lord Ellsworth looked as though he was unsure whether to be amused or offended by this speech. He eventually settled on amusement and gave her a reproachful smile.

"Are you making light of my youthful passion? I can assure you that it was very sincere. I have often thought of you these last ten years and wondered how you were—yes, and wondered what would have happened if I had pursued you rather than giving over the field to Carroll. It gave me quite a turn the other day when I heard you were back in town. You ought to have let me know, rather than find out from strangers."

This whole speech was patently ridiculous, and Lora knew

it. It had been years since she had seen Lord Ellsworth, and at no time in their acquaintance had he shown signs of any irrecoverable passion. Equally ridiculous was the notion that she ought to have informed him of her arrival in Town. "As though I made a habit of dashing off notes to bachelors' lodgings!" she told herself indignantly. Yet ridiculous or not, it was a struggle not to succumb to the appeal of those blue, blue eyes.

"If I had known you would be so much affected, sir, you may be sure I would have informed you of my arrival in town," was the response she finally settled on, spoken in a voice of ironical amusement.

If she had been searching for a way to capture Lord Ellsworth's attention, she could have hit upon no better means. He was accustomed to having his speeches received with smiles, blushes, and delighted laughter. To have them received with irony was a new experience and, by the same token, a refreshing one. As a rule, his conquests were all too easy. Lora, having proved impervious to the usual flatteries, became all the more desirable as a result, the more so because he really had once cherished a mild infatuation for the sixteen-year-old Miss Darlington. He immediately set himself to win her over in this new, fascinating adult incarnation.

Lora found this process quite as uncomfortable as anything she had yet endured that evening. She had led such a sheltered existence both before and after her marriage that she was completely unused to the kind of advances Lord Ellsworth now saw fit to make toward her. Taking his cue from her last remark, he gave her to understand that any consolation he had obtained in the past ten years had been of a transitory nature, not worthy to be spoken of in the same breath as his passion for her. And since he took it for granted that those years had worked the same changes in her as in him, and that her new sophistication of manner was accompanied by a corresponding sophistication of morals, he had no hesitation about delineating that passion in explicit detail.

Lora did her best to turn aside his words with a smile or a

laugh, but she was in truth more disgusted than amused. Her opinion of him had been falling steadily since the dance began, and by the end of it she was as eager to escape him as she had originally been to accompany him onto the floor.

"You must dance with me again," he said, taking her hand in his and holding it in his own familiarly. "Dancing one dance with you is like throwing a crumb to a starving man: it may relieve, but it cannot satisfy. You dance superbly, Lora. I may call you Lora, mayn't I? Such old friends as we are surely may dispense with the formality of titles—"

"Forgive me, Lord Ellsworth, but I don't intend to dance this next set. I must be getting back to Lady Helen," said Lora, firmly withdrawing her hand from his and pretending not to hear his question. "No, I cannot promise to dance with you later. We will probably be leaving before too much longer, for I don't imagine Lady Helen will wish to keep late hours in her condition. I would rather not make promises which I might be obliged to break."

"That's another way you haven't changed," said Lord Ellsworth, looking down at her with a musing smile. "You always were the most conscientious woman of my acquaintance. Very well, Lora, but I shall not give up hope entirely. We may yet dance again, and to that end, I shall say *au revoir* rather than good evening, my dear."

Having taken leave of Lora with these words—and having accompanied them with a perfectly killing smile— Lord Ellsworth strolled across the room to flirt with a statuesque brunette in a pearl tiara.

Lora was feeling distinctly ruffled in spirit as she sat down beside Lady Helen. Her feelings were not relieved by the first words out of her friend's mouth.

"My love, I ought to have mentioned it before. No one, but no one wears rouge anymore. It's positively *démodé.*"

"I'm not wearing any rouge," said Lora indignantly.

Snapping open her fan, she began to fan herself vigorously, meditating darkly all the while on the conceit of Lord Ellsworth and her own folly in ever having encouraged him. Across the room she could see him still flirting with the brunette; she could also see Miss Monroe and Major Linville talking to each other near the entrance to the ballroom. As she watched, she saw the Major impulsively lift his fiancée's hand to his lips and kiss it. Miss Monroe smiled up at him shyly, and there was something so sweet and speaking of affection in both their expressions that Lora found tears springing to her eyes.

Appalled by this weakness, she dragged her handkerchief from her reticule and applied it hastily to her eyes. The offending tears were easily removed, but Lora could feel others not far from the surface. It was as though the combined weight of the evening's tribulations had suddenly become too much for her. She rose quickly to her feet.

"Where are you going?" said Lady Helen in surprise.

"I must go outside for a few minutes, Helen. The heat in here—it's simply unbearable," said Lora, grasping at the first excuse that came to mind.

"You do look rather flushed," agreed Lady Helen, surveying her critically. "But you know you really ought not to go outside alone, my love. Do you want me to come with you? Or Arthur—I could send Arthur with you."

Lady Helen was already starting to her feet as she spoke, but Lora quickly shook her head. "No, there's no need for you or Arthur to come, Helen. I'll be quite all right by myself."

"Well, if you say so," said Lady Helen, settling back gratefully in her chair. "I don't blame you for wanting to get out of this heat. It's bad enough just sitting; I can imagine how intolerable it must be to dance in. Here, you'd better take your shawl with you if you're planning on going outside. Make sure you don't stay too long, Lora. I don't want you taking a chill."

"Thank you, Helen. I'll be careful," said Lora.

Draping the shawl around her shoulders, she hurried out of the ballroom.

Three

Although the Monroes' reception rooms were on an upper floor of the house, the rearmost of them opened onto a narrow balcony with a flight of stairs leading down into a small garden. Lora discovered this fact after wandering through a music room, two drawing rooms, and a state bedchamber, fearing every minute that Lord Ellsworth might appear before her and demand that she dance with him a second time.

As it happened, Lord Ellsworth was still well occupied with his brunette and did not see Lora leave the ballroom. She was able to make her way through the rooms unmolested and with relative ease, for the greater number of the guests were concentrated in the ballroom at the front of the house and in the hall downstairs. When finally she reached the small parlor at the back of the house, she found it completely deserted. Just as she was about to step out onto the balcony, however, the balcony doors suddenly swung open, and a couple of young gentlemen came into the room.

One of them, a short, stocky gentleman with a shock of bright red hair, was speaking to his companion in a voice loud, indignant, and unmistakably maudlin.

"No, my friend, I am most certainly *not* 'on the go,' as you vulgarly term it. It was the purest accident that I knocked over that table downstairs—the purest accident, I say. I am not in the least intockshicated—intoshicated—not in the least drunk; and it was wholly unnecessary for you to go hauling me away from the party as though you were my nursemaid, for God's sake. The only thing I've had to drink this evening was a glass or two of wine at dinner, a couple of glasses of port afterwards, and then that champagne we had downstairs. I am not drunk, not drunk in the least." With this definitive statement, the stocky gentleman proceeded to trip over his own feet and sprawl headlong into the parlor.

His companion courteously helped him to his feet again. He was taller than his friend, with brown hair and a rangy build: not conventionally handsome, but with a face lean, high-boned, and singularly attractive. So Lora thought as she stood waiting for the two of them to move out of the doorway. Catching sight of her, the stocky gentleman removed his hat and swept her a bow that nearly sent him sprawling once more.

"I beg your pardon, madam," he said. "I didn't shee you sanding there—see you shtanding there, I mean. My apologies if I have inconvenienced you in any way—"

His apology was cut short by the other gentleman, who took him firmly by the arm and hauled him bodily out of the doorway. The stocky gentleman strongly protested this action. His companion did not speak, but as Lora moved toward the door, his eyes met hers for a moment. They were bright with laughter and seemed both to ask her indulgence and invite her to share in his amusement.

Lora gave him a quick smile in return as she stepped out onto the balcony. She received a fleeting impression of a pair of intelligent brown eyes, a clefted chin, and a very engaging smile. It was altogether such an attractive impression that, once out on the balcony, she could not resist the urge to look back and verify it. To her embarrassment, she found that the brown-eyed gentleman had likewise turned and was looking back at her. With a blush, Lora turned away and hurried down the balcony steps.

By the time she reached the garden below, her embarrassment had passed, and she found herself smiling over the encounter. Brief though it was, it had cheered her considerably. Whether it had been the stocky gentleman's tipsy antics or his compan-

ion's friendly smile that had worked the magic, Lora could not
have said, but suddenly the world seemed a much less dismal
place and life a much less dismal business. The tears that had
threatened to overwhelm her earlier appeared now to have
passed harmlessly away. Her present mood was philosophical
rather than despondent, and after she had walked twice or thrice
about the garden and seen what there was to see of it, she went
over to a small stone bench tucked away at the foot of the stairs
and sat down to admire its beauty in the moonlight.

It was a very small garden, a mere patch of grass ornamented with a central flower bed, a statue of Apollo, and a
row of potted orange trees. On one side it was bounded by
the terrace of the house; on the others by high stone walls.
Since the houses all around it were tall townhouses like the
Monroes', these walls afforded only a token privacy, but they
gave the garden a private feeling, and with the light of the full
moon bathing everything in a silvery glow, it had rather a
magical feeling as well. Lora found it an agreeable place to
sit and relax after the irritations of the past hour. She was just
beginning to feel she ought to be going back inside when she
heard the door open on the balcony above her and the sound
of someone coming down the steps to the garden.

For a moment, Lora was seized by a fear that Lord Ellsworth
had somehow discovered her refuge and had come to plague
her with more unwelcome attentions. She held her breath as
the footsteps came nearer, but when they arrived at the bottom
of the steps, her fears gave way to relief. The intruder was not
Lord Ellsworth, but the brown-eyed gentleman she had seen
in the parlor a few minutes before.

He was alone this time, having apparently left his inebriated
companion behind in the house. He stood at the foot of the
steps, looking around the garden as though searching for something. As Lora watched him, it flitted across her mind that perhaps he was looking for her. She was just scolding herself for
this piece of presumption when he caught sight of her on the
bench. His face lit up in the same warm, engaging smile she

had noticed earlier, and he made his way over to where she was sitting.

Moved by an impulse she did not understand, Lora made room for him on the bench beside her. He sat down, and for a moment they regarded each other in silence.

"Good evening," said Lora at last, feeling she ought to say something.

"Good evening," he returned, still studying her face with his bright brown eyes. "I saw you, back in the house there."

He spoke as though this was sufficient explanation for his presence. "I saw you, too," was all Lora could think to say in reply. Another silence ensued, during which they continued to study each other.

"I do hope I'm not intruding," was the strange gentleman's next remark. "It's just occurred to me that you probably came out here to be alone. Well, it stands to reason that you did, and if you would rather I went off and left you to yourself again, you've only got to say so. I don't want to make a nuisance of myself."

"I did want to be alone earlier, but I have no objection to having company now," said Lora honestly.

The brown-eyed gentleman scrutinized her closely for a moment. Then, apparently satisfied that she was speaking the truth, he smiled again and nodded.

"That's all right, then," he said. "But if at any time I *should* start making a nuisance of myself, you mustn't hesitate to say so. I have rather a suspicion that I've had more champagne this evening than was really good for me. That's one of the reasons I insisted on accompanying my friend out here earlier. His condition was much more acute than mine, of course, but I felt a spot of fresh air wouldn't do either of us any harm."

"Indeed?" said Lora, smiling. "You didn't seem particularly intoxicated when I saw you earlier."

"Well, I don't know that I'm intoxicated exactly," said the gentleman thoughtfully. "But everything seems a little brighter and louder than usual, and my head doesn't feel quite steady.

If I were completely sober, I doubt I would be here now," he went on, in what appeared to be a burst of confidence. "You must know that in the general way, I don't make a habit of striking up conversations with young ladies I haven't even been introduced to."

He spoke so seriously that Lora could not forbear smiling. "I'm quite sure you do not," she said.

The gentleman nodded with perfect seriousness. "I assure you that I don't, in the general way, but this seemed an exceptional circumstance somehow," he told Lora. "I suppose I ought really to have waited and found a mutual acquaintance to introduce us properly. But seeing that I didn't, and that we're already in the middle of a conversation, should you have any objection to our introducing ourselves? I would very much like to know your name."

Lora hesitated. She had been enjoying the novelty of conversing with someone to whom the circumstances of her past were completely unknown. Although not averse to giving her name to the brown-eyed gentleman, she feared that doing so would put an end to the easy informality of their conversation. Once he knew that she was Lady Carroll, it was natural that he would question the existence of a Lord Carroll; she must then reveal the circumstance of her widowhood, which would oblige him to make the usual awkward condolences on her loss. Lora did not feel equal to receiving any more condolences that evening. The brown-eyed gentleman obviously took her for a young, unmarried girl who had come out to the garden for a few minutes of solitude. Why not then assume the character he gave her for the short time she remained in his company? There could be no harm in such an innocent impersonation.

All this flashed through Lora's head in the space of a moment. She hesitated scarcely longer before responding to the brown-eyed gentleman's question. "My name is Lora," she told him firmly.

His eyebrows quirked upward, and he regarded her with a mixture of surprise and amusement. "Only Laura, eh?" he said. "Well, it's a pretty name, and very poetic, too. Do you find yourself the object of impromptu sonnets from your gentlemen acquaintances?"

"No, it's not Laura like Petrarch's Laura. It's Lora," said Lora, spelling the name for him. "Short for Lorelei, I'm afraid. My mother took a Rhine cruise when she was a young girl, and it made a great impression on her."

The gentleman laughed. "So you're a Lorelei," he said. "I ought to have known it. The name suits you, you know. Yes, I should say it suits you very well."

"Do you think so? I have always thought it rather a silly, fanciful name."

"No, I think it a very pretty one, and it has the merit of originality, too. That's something that can't be said about my own name. When my parents were naming me, they showed no originality at all. In fact, you might even say they picked the oldest name in the book! Adam," he explained with a smile. "My name is Adam."

"I am very pleased to meet you, Adam," said Lora, smiling back at him.

"And I am pleased to meet you, Lora." He accompanied the words with a formal bow. "Now that we have those preliminaries out of the way, we can begin to converse in earnest. First, of course, I must ask you what brings you to London. Are you here for the Season or only making a visit, as I am?"

Lora considered. "I am making a visit, but it will probably be rather a long visit," she said. "I expect I shall be here for the rest of the Season."

"Had you ever been here before, or is this your first visit to the Metropolis?"

"No, I have been here before," said Lora evasively. "But it's been several years since my last visit."

To her relief, Adam accepted this statement without question. "Yes, it's the same for me," he said. "I don't often get to London, though there's really no good reason why not. I live near Farleigh in Hampshire, less than a day's journey away."

Lora knew the area of Farleigh well, having passed through it numerous times on her way to Lord Carroll's estate in Wiltshire. It seemed best not to mention this circumstance, however. "Are you staying with friends while you're in Town, Adam?" she asked instead.

"Yes, with John Lloyd, the gentleman you saw me with earlier. It was he who got me the invitation to this party tonight. He's some sort of cousin to the Monroes, I believe."

"Mr. Lloyd appeared to have been enjoying the party very much when I saw him earlier—perhaps a little too much," said Lora with a smile. "Did you persuade him to go home?"

"No, but I did the next best thing. I left him in one of the cardrooms with three other fellows and a cup of strong coffee at his elbow. John's a demon for whist, and I figured that an hour or two at the card-table would clear his head faster than anything else could." A sudden doubt flickered across Adam's mobile features. "Although I suppose now if he goes and loses his shirt, I'll be at least partially responsible," he said ruefully.

"Perhaps you'd better go and check on him?" said Lora. She spoke more from principle than from any overpowering concern for Mr. Lloyd's welfare, and was rather annoyed with herself for having spoken at all. Now Adam would probably feel obliged to go to his friend, and that would spell the end of their pleasant conversation. Adam only smiled and shook his head, however.

"No, I think he'll be all right now that he's at the card table. He really isn't a habitual deep drinker. That's part of the problem, perhaps. This evening was rather a special occasion, and what with all the toasts during and after dinner and then drinking the bride-to-be's health this evening, he ended up taking more than he could manage. That must be my plea, too, I'm afraid," he continued, looking at Lora seriously. "Drinking to excess isn't normally one of my vices, but an engagement party's such a happy occasion—second only to the wedding itself, I suppose. One does tend to get caught up in all the jollity."

"Indeed," was all Lora permitted herself to say. She said it rather bitterly, however, and Adam gave her a curious look.

"Now, how am I supposed to interpret that?" he asked. "I hope you aren't disgusted with me for admitting I've over-imbibed a trifle?"

"Oh, no," Lora assured him. "And in any case, I don't believe you're really drunk, Adam. You don't behave like any drunk person I've ever seen."

She smiled as she spoke, and Adam smiled, too. "No, I'm not really drunk; just a trifle on the go, to use the expression my friend so objected to earlier. Very well, then. We've established that you're not disgusted with me for being drunk. What was it, then, that prompted the disgust in your voice a minute ago? Don't tell me you're a misogynist and disapprove of engagement parties on principle?"

Lora thought this over. "I don't disapprove of engagement parties," she said. "But yes, I suppose I am something of a misogynist."

Adam regarded her with interest. "Here's a puzzle! A lady young, lovely, and charming, romantic enough to sit in the moonlight, but cynical enough to speak disparagingly of love and matrimony. Is it your contention that people should not marry at all?"

"No, you misunderstand me. I don't object to people marrying, but it always amazes me how often they do it—and how lightly. After all, it's not as though most of the married couples one sees are living examples of connubial bliss. There may be—certainly are—disadvantages to being unmarried, but they are quite as likely to be outweighed by the disadvantages of being married. I don't know why anyone would want to take the risk."

"I suppose it is a risk," said Adam thoughtfully. "But it appears to me that most of the things worth doing in life have a degree of risk about them. Travel, for instance, like that Rhine cruise your mother enjoyed so much. Think what a risk that was: a channel crossing, a long overland journey through half-a-dozen foreign countries, and then the trip down the

Rhine itself, with Loreleis and other assorted perils on either hand. And yet, I'll wager your mother doesn't regret taking the risk—in fact, I'd be willing to bet she'd do it all over again if she had the chance."

"Yes, that's true," admitted Lora. "She often speaks of returning to Germany, now that the war with France is over."

"There you are, then. To her, the benefits of traveling outweigh the risks. I could name lots of other things that are the same way." Adam paused with knit brow, considering the question. "I suppose hunting would be the extreme example," he said at last. "I'm not hunting-mad myself, but I have friends who are and who think nothing of risking life and limb on a daily basis during the season. To them the pleasure of the activity is worth the risk."

"Yes," said Lora. She could hardly keep the irony out of her voice. It was on the hunting field, while attempting to surmount a particularly ugly blind bullfinch, that Lord Carroll had met his end.

Adam, unaware that he had touched upon any sore spot, went on cheerfully. "Of course, most sensible people don't take things to such extremes as that, but at the same time, I don't see foregoing something that's important to you simply because there's a degree of risk involved," he told Lora. "Really, when you consider it, there's a degree of risk in nearly everything. To stay at home is to risk fire, or housebreakers; to step outside is to risk sunstroke, or hailstorms, or anything else the weather may throw at you; and to walk down the street is to run the risk of being hit by a runaway carriage or the contents of a slop-basin. Isn't that so?"

Lora gravely agreed that it was so.

"Why, there's even a risk in such a little thing as asking a pretty girl to dance." Adam's voice had become a trifle diffident as he made this statement. The diffidence became more pronounced as he went on, with a quick, sidelong look at Lora. "She might say she is engaged for this set—or that she is not dancing this evening—or she might be really cruel and simply laugh in your face. But then again, she might say, 'Yes, of course; I would be happy to dance with you, sir,' and then you would feel your risk had been amply repaid. Will you dance with me, Lora?"

"Oh, dear! Well, I'm not going to laugh in your face, Adam. But I'm afraid I can't say 'Yes, of course,' either. I would like very much to dance with you, only I can't quite bring myself to go inside just yet."

Again Adam gave her a searching look, as though trying to determine whether or not she was sincere. The expression on her face must have convinced him, for his own face cleared at once.

"I don't blame you for preferring to stay out here, but that needn't stop you from dancing with me, you know," he said. "Why can't we dance out here? You observe, we have adequate light and a very elegant dance floor." He gestured first toward the moon and then toward the patch of lawn in front of them. "To be sure, we're rather wanting for music, but if we listen closely I think we can catch the general drift of what the orchestra's playing. It sounds like a waltz to me, although it may be that that's just wishful thinking. I freely admit to being influenced by a strong desire to waltz with you. What do you say, Lora? I'm willing to put up with a few inconveniences if you are."

Lora laughed but rose willingly to her feet. "I believe after all you must be a little drunk, Adam," she said. "But just to show you that I, too, am capable of taking an occasional risk— yes, I would be very happy to dance with you, sir, here and now."

Adam smiled and extended his hand to her. She took it and let him lead her to the center of the little garden. They stood still a moment, trying to catch the strains of melody that came drifting fitfully toward them on the night air.

"It *is* a waltz," said Lora.

"Yes, another risk paid off!" Adam's eyes were alight with laughter as thy began to move in time to the music. "If I hadn't screwed up my courage and asked you when I did, I wouldn't be having the pleasure of waltzing with you now," he told Lora. "I might have had to make shift with a cotillion—or a mere country dance—or I might have dithered so long that you simply gave up and went inside. And then I would never have known what a wonderful—what a really super-excellent dancer you are."

"You dance very well, too," Lora told him. This was no mere politeness on her part. Adam was a most accomplished and considerate partner, guiding her deftly over the inequalities of the ground and around such obstacles as Apollo and the orange trees. If he were truly intoxicated, as he claimed, it was certainly not apparent in his dancing. It was more apparent in his conversation, which continued in as lively a fashion as before. Indeed, he made her laugh so many times that by the end of the dance Lora was completely breathless. Adam obligingly conducted her back over to the bench to recover herself.

"Yes, definitely I have had too much champagne," he said, leaning back his head to regard the moon- and star-lit sky overhead. "Everything is still spinning a trifle, even now that we've stopped dancing. It's a beautiful night, isn't it?"

"Beautiful," agreed Lora. Although she herself had drunk nothing stronger than orgeat that evening, she, too, was conscious of a giddy sensation as she sat beside Adam looking up at the night sky. Exploring it further, she discovered that the sensation was happiness. She felt young again, happy and free of restraint, as though she were truly the carefree girl her companion supposed her to be. Impulsively she turned to him.

"I must thank you, Adam, for giving me your company this evening," she said. "I was feeling very low when I came out here, but now—now I feel quite cheerful. You can't know how pleasant this last hour has been for me."

"Yes, I think I can, Lora. You must know that it's been very pleasant for me, too," said Adam. He spoke in quite a different tone than he had used a moment before, a tone both serious and reflective. His eyes, too, were serious and reflective as they rested on Lora's face. "In fact, it's been quite the best time I've ever had at a ball, and I assure you that's not the champagne talking. I am very glad I met you."

"I'm glad I met you, too," said Lora. She spoke demurely, but was surprised by the very undemure wave of feeling that accompanied the words. In all her well-behaved life she had never once encouraged a gentleman to kiss her, not even the late Lord Carroll, but now, looking into Adam's eyes, she was seized by a sudden, overwhelming desire to be kissed. It was wanton, shocking, reprehensible—but Lora could not gainsay it. What made it more shocking still was that she did not even try. Looking into Adam's eyes, she deliberately willed him to kiss her.

"Kiss me, she said silently, gazing into his eyes. *Kiss me— kiss me—kiss me."*

Adam regarded her solemnly for a moment. And then, with grave deliberation, he leaned down and kissed her.

Lora shut her eyes. It was a brief, sweet, tender kiss: quite perfect in her estimation, except that it was over much too soon. Opening her eyes, she found Adam looking down at her with a rather panic-stricken expression.

"I'm sorry," he said. "Perhaps I shouldn't have done that. The champagne, you know—"

"It's all right, Adam," said Lora, smiling up at him. He was still inclined to apologize, however, until at last she silenced him by laying one hand on his mouth and following it an instant later with her lips. This did silence him for a very considerable time. When at last he spoke again, his voice was weak and disbelieving.

"I must be drunker than I thought," he said. "Or possibly I've just passed out altogether, and this whole thing is a dream. Any minute now I'm going to wake up, and you, this garden, this whole house, perhaps, will all have disappeared into thin air."

"The Monroes would find that a trifle inconvenient," said Lora, laughing. She felt half intoxicated herself, flushed with daring and a newfound sense of power. "I assure you that I'm not going to disappear, Adam, at least not immediately. But I suppose I must be going back inside the house before too much longer. My friend will be wondering where I've gone."

"I suppose I ought to be thinking about my friend, too," said Adam, rising reluctantly to his feet. "What time is it? Good God, almost midnight. If John's still conscious, he'll be wondering what happened to me. He was wanting to leave at half past eleven to look in on an assembly over in Cavendish Square."

"Then you must go, of course," said Lora, also rising to her feet. Adam came over to assist her, and when she was standing, he stood looking down at her, holding her hand in his.

"This has been a most remarkable evening," he said. "A remarkably enjoyable evening. I would like to see you again, Lora. I hope you've no objection?"

"No, none at all. I would like to see you again, too, Adam."

"I will be in London at least another week or two. Might I call upon you at home? Or perhaps you would prefer to meet me in public first, just to make certain I'm wholly respectable. After all, you haven't known me very long, and you've no one to vouch for my character."

"I would have no objection to your calling on me, Adam, but since I'm staying with a friend, that might not be quite convenient," said Lora. It had just occurred to her that Lady Helen, a notable high-stickler, might object to having a strange gentleman appear in her drawing room. "Perhaps it would be better to meet somewhere in public first, as you say."

"Certainly, if you would prefer it so. Where will you be tomorrow night?"

"Let me see, where *will* I be tomorrow night?" Lora had taken so little interest in the plans Lady Helen had made for her entertainment that it was only with an effort that she could recall them at all. "Oh, yes, Almack's. We go to Almack's tomorrow night."

"To Almack's?" A strange, almost startled expression flickered across Adam's mobile face. When he spoke again, his voice was a little more formal than it had been before. "I have not the *entrée* to Almack's, I'm afraid."

"Oh, dear, then that won't do, will it? We shall have to wait and meet the day after tomorrow instead. I believe my friend and I are going to the theater that evening—to Drury Lane, I think she said."

"Well, as long as I've two sixpence to rub together, I ought to be able to get the *entrée* there," said Adam, smiling and sounding more at his ease. "Does your friend have a box at Drury Lane?"

"Yes, a very good one, I imagine. Spelbourne is the name: Lord and Lady Helen Spelbourne. You shouldn't have any trouble finding it."

"No, I should suppose not," said Adam. Once again his face had taken on that curious startled expression. "Your friend is Lady Helen Spelbourne?"

"Yes," said Lora, rather puzzled by his reaction. "Do you know her, Adam? She is a very dear friend of mine."

"No I don't know her, but I have heard of her . . . as nearly everyone has, I suppose." Adam was silent a moment, and Lora could see by his expression that he was experiencing some kind of internal conflict. More puzzled than ever, she waited, and at last he seemed to make up his mind to confide in her.

"Look here," he said, with the self-deprecating smile that made him so attractive. "I'm sure Lady Helen is a good friend of yours, but you must know I'm not much accustomed to dealings with the nobility. I confess I feel a little nervous about putting myself in the way of such a great lady. You don't think she would object to my coming to her box and paying my respects?"

"No, for you are coming as my friend, Adam. At least, I hope I may count you as a friend?" Tucking her arm beneath his, Lora smiled up at him confidingly.

"You may count me as anything you like," said Adam. Lifting Lora's hand from his arm, he carried it to his lips, then tucked it beneath his arm once more and began to lead her toward the house.

Four

Adam led Lora back through the parlor, state room, and drawing rooms, and from there into the crowded ballroom. He took leave of her near the chairs where Lord Spelbourne and Lady Helen were sitting.

"I shall look forward to seeing you Thursday night at the theater, Lora," he said. She gave him such a sweet smile in return that he was once more emboldened to carry her hand to his lips, as he had in the garden. He felt a little self-conscious doing it in front of the Spelbournes, both of whom were looking at him curiously, but it was an indulgence he could not deny himself.

"I shall look forward to seeing you, too, Adam," she said in her soft voice. He smiled, pressed her hand, and was just turning away when he suddenly found himself face to face with a very tall, dark-haired gentleman with very blue eyes. The gentleman gave him a brief, insolent stare that said as clearly as words could have done, "Who the devil are *you?*" before turning to Lora.

"My prayers have been answered," he said, taking her by the arm in what Adam could not help but feel was a rather possessive fashion. "You're still here, and the next set is just beginning. Now you must fulfill your promise, Lora, and dance with me a second time."

"I wasn't aware that I had *promised* to dance with you again, my lord," she said. Adam, a jealous spectator to this exchange, thought she sounded rather vexed.

"Yes, indeed you did," said the dark-haired gentleman confidently. "You promised most faithfully, and if you refuse me now, you'll end up breaking my heart a second time."

She shook her head quickly, and there was a suggestion of color in her cheeks as she replied, "That is nonsense, my lord, and you know it. But if you insist, yes, I will dance with you again." With a last, covert glance in Adam's direction, she accompanied the dark gentleman onto the dance floor.

Adam watched them until they disappeared among the crowd. He then hastened to the cardroom where he had left his friend. He found Mr. Lloyd largely recovered from his earlier excesses and inclined to be irritable over his own long absence.

"Where the deuce have you been, Adam?" he demanded, once he had collected his winnings and taken leave of his companions in the cardroom. "Not that I minded waiting, for I was having a famous run of luck back there. Picked up close to a pony in the time you were gone. But I was wanting to take a look-in on the Ramseys' assembly tonight, and we'll have to drive like Jehu to make it now."

Adam smiled self-consciously. "I'm sorry, John," he said. "I didn't mean to keep you waiting, but the fact is, I fell into pleasant company and lost track of time."

Mr. Lloyd showed no interest in following up this suggestive statement, rather to Adam's disappointment. "Oh, you did, did you? Perhaps you'll remember that next time I suggest taking in an evening party. You kicked pretty hard against coming to this one, if you'll recall."

"Yes, I did, and I owe you an apology, John—or rather, an eternal debt of gratitude. I would have been very sorry to miss this particular party."

This second hint proved more successful in rousing Mr. Lloyd's interest. He stopped dead in his tracks and swung round to look at Adam with frank curiosity.

"What's that supposed to mean? Good Lord, look at you, man! Hectic flush to the cheeks, feverish glitter to the eyes, foolish smile on the lips—symptoms unmistakable. You don't mean to tell me you've gone and fallen in love just here in this last hour or so, do you?"

"Well, yes. As a matter of fact, I think perhaps I have," said Adam modestly.

"Well, I'll be damned," said Mr. Lloyd, surveying him still with frank interest. "And here I've always thought you were such a steady, level-headed fellow. Fallen in love in the space of an hour! She must be a regular siren to have brought you to your knees as quick as that."

"Not a siren, a Lorelei," said Adam, and laughed aloud.

Across the room he could see Lora going gracefully through the figures of a reel with the dark-haired gentleman. She saw him, too, and gave him another of her dazzlingly sweet smiles. Adam smiled back, thinking how completely lovely she was and noticing with amusement that her partner's head had slewed jealously around to see whom she was smiling at. Ignoring the dark-haired gentleman's jealous stare, he gave her a smiling bow. Mr. Lloyd, observing the movement, looked also toward the dance floor.

"Who's that you're nodding to? Oh, I see—Lora Carroll, isn't it? How'd you become acquainted with her, Adam?"

"Is her last name Carroll? I only knew her as Lorelei."

"What, she's your Lorelei?" Mr. Lloyd stared at Adam incredulously. "Flying pretty high, aren't you, old man? I didn't know you were in the business of courting countesses."

"She, a countess?" It was Adam's turn to be incredulous. "You must be joking, John."

Mr. Lloyd shook his head solemnly. "I've never been more serious in my life," he said. "She's a countess, sure as I'm standing here. The countess of Carroll, all right and tight."

"But that would mean—good God!" There was consternation in Adam's eyes as he looked at his friend. "Are you saying she's *married,* John?"

Mr. Lloyd shook his head again, this time with almost a reluctant air. "As a matter of fact, I believe she's a widow now," he said. "If I remember rightly, her husband broke his neck on the hunting field a couple of seasons back. But even so, I wouldn't get your hopes up, old boy." He threw a quick, embarrassed glance at Adam. "What I mean to say is, a trifle above your touch, don't you know. She runs with Helen Spelbourne and that set—a regular high-flyer—and though I've never heard any harm of her personally, you can see for yourself who she's dancing with. That's Ellsworth, you know, the one who was involved in that business with Shaughnessy's wife last year. That ought to tell you something."

"I've heard of Lord Ellsworth," said Adam grimly.

He looked again toward the dance floor. Lora was smiling faintly and listening with apparent interest to something Lord Ellsworth was saying to her as he maneuvered her through the figures of the reel. A sharp surge of anger went through Adam at the sight. She looked so lovely—so young and sweet and innocent—and yet, if his friend were to be believed, she was a thorough-going woman of the world, and that world not even his own world but a far more exalted sphere, inhabited exclusively by the members of the upper aristocracy.

It cast a new and suspicious light on her behavior in the garden. Instead of being the young girl he had supposed her, enjoying a momentary respite from the conventions of the ballroom, she had more than likely been merely amusing herself at his expense, playing the role he had thrust upon her and finding diversion in his own dazzled reaction.

Adam burned with a mixture of rage and humiliation as he recalled how he had clung to her hand and begged to see her again. If he followed through on her suggestion and met her at the theater two days hence, would she continue the charade or take pleasure in spurning him in front of her friends? Adam resolved to find out, not two days hence, but this very evening. He turned again to his friend.

"You go on to the Ramseys' without me, John," he said. "There's some unfinished business here that will keep me a little longer. Don't worry about sending the carriage after me. I can take a hackney home later."

Mr. Lloyd's homely face wore a worried expression as he regarded his friend. "It wouldn't be this business with Lady Carroll, would it? Because if it is, I hope you won't go causing a scene, old man. She likely didn't mean any harm by flirting with you a bit. You know ladies in London give themselves a good deal more leeway in these little matters than they do in the country. Especially ladies of *her* station!"

"So it appears," said Adam grimly. "Don't worry, John. I won't cause a scene, but I must talk with her at least once more before I go."

Mr. Lloyd gave him another worried look, but finally consented to go on to the Ramseys' assembly without his friend. He continued through the ballroom, while Adam turned and began making his way back through the crowd toward Lora.

He reached her side just as Lord Ellsworth was leading her off the floor after their dance together. The gentleman gave him another supercilious stare, but Adam ignored him, addressing himself exclusively to Lora. "I wonder, ma'am, if you might be so good as to dance with me a second time?"

"Why, Adam," she exclaimed, with a smile so apparently genuine that he had difficulty not returning it. "I thought you had to leave with your friend?"

"No, I sent him on without me. Will you dance with me?"

"Yes, of course. Please excuse me, my lord," she said, turning to Lord Ellsworth. "I thank you for a very enjoyable dance."

"No, I thank *you*," returned the gentleman, bowing over her hand. "And I look forward to dancing with you again. Do you accompany Helen to Almack's tomorrow night?"

"Perhaps," she said evasively, and gently drew her hand away from him. Adam gave her his arm, and together they went out onto the dance floor.

The dance was a waltz, and Lora smiled up at Adam as they

began to circle the floor with the other couples. "I didn't expect to be waltzing with you again so soon, Adam," she said.

Once again, Adam had to struggle within himself to keep from responding to that smile. "No, I imagine not," he said dryly. "Your ladyship no doubt assumed you were done with me for the evening."

She looked surprised and a little embarrassed, but not, he thought, particularly guilty. "I'm sorry, Adam, are you angry with me for not telling you my full name? I suppose I should have, only it was so nice talking to you without worrying about titles and all. I didn't intend to mislead you."

"Didn't you?" said Adam, hardening his heart against the wistful brown eyes looking up at him. "I must confess that it gave me quite a turn when my friend told me whom it was I had been—passing time with."

He made these last words deliberately offensive. It was obvious that she understood what he meant, for her color rose, but she continued to look at him steadily and rather wistfully.

"You *are* angry with me, aren't you?" she said. "I suppose I deserve that, Adam, but I hope you don't think I make a habit of behaving as I did in the garden." Her blush deepened as she spoke, and if Adam had been less intent on her words, he might have detected a note of hurt in her voice. "And I didn't mean to deceive you about my name and circumstances," she went on, looking at him almost imploringly. "The truth is that I simply didn't think they mattered that much."

"No, I daresay you didn't," said Adam bitterly. "It wouldn't matter to you if a chance-met stranger took you in earnest when you were merely play-acting. Did you mean to tell me the truth when I visited you at the theater Thursday night? I suppose it would have been amusing to you and your friends, to see me put to the blush."

"Why, Adam, what do you mean?" With a look of mingled affront and astonishment, she took a step back from him, narrowly avoiding collision with the couple behind them. "You must know I was quite as much in earnest as you were out in the garden, Adam," she told him, once they were safely out of the other couple's range. "And I was in earnest, too, when I asked you to visit me at the theater Thursday night. You can't surely think I am such an odious person that I would take amusement in publicly humiliating you in front of my friends?"

"I don't know what I think," said Adam, a little softened by her evident indignation. "All I know is that I took you for one thing originally, and now I've just found out that you're something else entirely. It's rather thrown me off balance, don't you know."

"My being a widow, you mean?" she asked, with a quick upward glance at his face.

"That, of course, but it's more your being Lady Carroll that concerns me," said Adam frankly.

She looked honestly puzzled. "But why should that concern you, Adam? You must put a great deal more stock in titles than I do."

He laughed, rather harshly. "Yes, I suppose it's natural that I should, given the difference in our positions. But then, you don't know much about me and my position, do you?"

"No, I don't. But whatever it is, I can't believe it makes any difference, Adam," she said with spirit.

"Let me tell you about it, and then your ladyship can decide for yourself whether it makes any difference," returned Adam aggressively. "My name is Wainwright, Adam Wainwright—a respectable enough name, but not quite so exalted as your own. I haven't a single aristocratic or titled relative, unless you count my great-uncle the magistrate. I own a farm in Hampshire which I inherited from my father a few years back. It's a nice little property, somewhere in the neighborhood of three hundred acres—I would estimate it to be about the size of your late husband's pleasure park. In addition to the income from my property, I have also a small independence that came to me from my mother. It's enough so I can afford to make an occasional visit to London, as I am doing now, but I doubt it would pay a year's rent on your great friend Lady Helen's townhouse."

Adam paused. Lora was looking at him with a mixture of bewilderment and indignation.

"I don't quite understand your point in telling me all this, Adam," she said. "Of course, I am very glad to know more about you and your circumstances, but there is no need to tell me in such an offensive way. What does it signify if you couldn't afford to pay a year's rent on Spelbourne House? Neither could most other people I know, but that doesn't mean I automatically exclude them from the lists of my friends. What you've told me doesn't alter my opinion of you one bit, Adam. However, I'm beginning to wonder what your opinion of *me* must be, if you think it could!"

"It truly doesn't make any difference to you that I'm nothing but plain Mr. Wainwright?" said Adam, looking at her searchingly.

"Not a bit of difference. I would be honored to number plain Mr. Wainwright among my friends—assuming, that is, that he will rid himself of the habit he has lately acquired of calling me 'your ladyship' in the most horrid, sneering way." Lora's soft brown eyes were alight with laughter as she threw this charge against him. "I would much prefer him to call me Lora again, as he used to."

"Then he shall do so," said Adam, completely won over by the smiling sweetness of her manner. "And he apologizes most humbly for the sneer, and begs you to forgive him for speaking to you as he did just now. He doesn't normally fly into the boughs like that, but what with one thing and another, I'm afraid he's in an unusual state of excitement this evening."

"There you go, blaming the champagne again, Adam," said Lora with a reproachful smile. "The truth is, you thought I was completely unprincipled, and arrogant to boot. Didn't you, now?"

"As I said, I didn't know what to think when I found out who you really were," said Adam, neatly sidestepping this home question. "I was so bowled over to learn you were a countess that I would almost have been prepared to swear black was white, and white black. If you will forgive me for saying so, you don't look at all like a countess." His eyes traveled over her in smiling perplexity, taking in the clustered ringlets and modest white dress, and the soft flush of her cheeks that grew deeper under his regard. "You seem so . . . young. But I don't mean to excuse myself on those grounds. I ought not to have jumped to the conclusion I did when I found out who you were."

She looked down at her dress rather self-consciously as she replied, "You don't have to say anything more, Adam. I quite understand how it was. Instead of an apology, I would rather you proved by your actions that you no longer held such a dreadful opinion of me. Will you come and see me Thursday night, as we spoke of before?"

"You're quite sure you want me to come?" said Adam, looking at her searchingly once again.

"I wouldn't have asked you if I didn't," she said simply. "Will you come, Adam? Promise me that you will."

"I promise," he said, and finished out the dance in a state of exhilaration quite equal to that induced by champagne.

Five

On the drive home from the Monroes' ball, Lora sat silent and suspenseful, waiting to see if Lady Helen would remark upon her behavior that evening. She had seen her friend eyeing Adam curiously when he had brought her in from the garden and again later in the evening when he had taken leave of her after their waltz together, and she felt sure Lady Helen must presently question her about the identity of the gentleman who had paid her such particular attentions.

But Lady Helen's conversation during the drive was wholly taken up with complaining about the over-solicitude of society toward pregnant women in general and herself in particular. It was not until the following day that she made any mention of her friend's behavior at the ball. When she did, it was obvious that she was more concerned with the two dances Lora had danced with Lord Ellsworth than by the attentions she had witnessed Adam paying her.

The two ladies were *en route* to the modiste's when the subject arose. Lady Helen had been telling Lora again what a genius Madame LeClaire was: how she herself had discovered Madame working in a small, out-of-the-way shop in Cheapside and had instantly recognized the woman's inherent brilliance.

"And now she has opened her own salon in Oxford Street, and I have no doubt she will make a great success of it. I give her all my custom, and I know several other ladies of the *ton* who have begun to patronize her, too. Indeed, Madame LeClaire is quite a genius, Lora," said Lady Helen, fixing her friend with a stern eye as though she suspected her of disputing this statement. "A vulgar creature, of course, and no more French than you or I, but her gowns are charming."

"Yes, they are, if the one you were wearing last night is anything to judge by, Helen," said Lora, smiling at her friend's vehemence. "I only hope your Madame LeClaire will be able to do as much for me as she has for you. I desperately need a new dress for the theater tomorrow night."

Lady Helen cheerfully assented to this statement, but there was a shadow of concern in her eyes as she regarded her friend. "Why this sudden interest in a new dress for the theater? When I first mentioned going the other day, you seemed to think one of your nuns' dresses would be good enough for the occasion."

Lora said rather confusedly that she had been thinking of getting some new dresses for some time. "And of course, Drury Lane is such a public place. I would like my appearance to do you and Arthur credit, Helen."

"I'm sure it will do that, my love, whether you get a new dress or no. But I can't help wondering if this desire to appear well hasn't more to do with a certain gentleman I saw you flirting with last night."

"What gentleman?" said Lora, trying to look unconscious but unhappily certain that the state of her complexion was betraying her.

"Why, Ellsworth, of course," returned Lady Helen promptly. "I noticed the two of you appeared to be getting very confidential when you were out there on the floor together."

"Lord Ellsworth?" Lora gazed at her friend incredulously. "Oh, no, Helen! I may have danced with him, but I certainly did not flirt with him."

"Perhaps not, but he was most definitely flirting with you, my love," said Lady Helen, laughing. "And you seemed to like it pretty well—well enough to dance two dances with him, at any rate." More seriously, she continued, "Indeed, Lora, I don't wish to offend you, but I really don't think it wise to give Ellsworth so much encouragement. He's an attractive creature, of course, but I don't think he has much heart, or much discretion, either. If you were ever to admit him to any *closer connection*—you understand me, I'm sure, my love—I'm afraid he would only end up hurting you and your reputation."

"Yes, Helen, I do understand, and I assure you that, far from encouraging him, I was doing my very best to discourage him," said Lora warmly. "It's only that he doesn't seem to take a hint very well. And I wish you would not say such things as that—about him, and me, and 'closer connections.' I don't have any intention of admitting Lord Ellsworth to a closer connection, or any other gentleman either, for that matter. I would rather you did not speak of it again."

Seeing that her friend was very agitated, Lady Helen kindly forbore to pursue the subject and instead turned the conversation to a discussion of the latest modes. This occupied the time very agreeably until the carriage at last arrived in Oxford Street, where Madame LeClaire's salon was located.

A discreet sign over the door bearing Madame's name and a single figured lace ball dress in the window were all that distinguished her establishment from the row of other indifferent-looking shops that lined that particular quarter of Oxford Street.

Inside, however, the salon was elegant, if somewhat austere: a smallish room with a gold and cream-striped wallpaper, a Wiltshire carpet imitating Aubusson, and half-a-dozen dainty gilded chairs. A very young girl in a black bombazine dress and silk apron greeted Lora and Lady Helen with a curtsy each, and, having taken their names, promptly vanished behind a curtain that screened off the salon from the rear precincts of the shop. From this same region presently emerged a stout woman, also clad in black bombazine, who proved to be Madame LeClaire.

"Ah, Lady Helen. *Bon jour,* my lady, I hope I find you well? Ah, *très bien*—very good, very good. You will be here for your fitting, of course," said Madame, bowing deeply and leading both Lady Helen and Lora toward the same inner sanctum from which she had emerged. Having pushed aside the curtain so that they might enter, she let it fall back into place and turned to survey them.

"Yes, you look very well, my lady—*très bien*—though we're not going to be able to hide this state of things much longer, I'm thinking," she said, nodding frankly toward Lady Helen's abdomen. "But you've kept your figure remarkably well, considering how far along you are. The baby's due in June, *n'est-ce pas?*"

"Yes, late June," said Lady Helen, just glancing at Lora as she spoke. Lora had difficulty repressing a smile. Madame's vulgarity was as self-evident as Lady Helen had promised, and her French ancestry quite as doubtful. Though she sprinkled her speech with Gallicisms, her accent was pure Cockney, and her round, ruddy face and mild blue eyes likewise proclaimed her a native Briton. There was a good deal of shrewdness in those eyes, however, as she turned from Lady Helen to regard Lora.

"Madame, this is my friend Lady Carroll," said Lady Helen, observing the direction of Madame's gaze. "She mentioned to me that she needed some new gowns, and I told her that she could not do better than come to you."

"I'm much obliged to your ladyship for your good opinion," said Madame, bowing again. *"Merci beaucoup.* And I'm honored to make your acquaintance, Lady Carroll. What was it you was looking for today?"

"I need a number of things, but my most urgent need is a gown for the theater tomorrow night. Would it be possible to have something ready by then?"

Again Madame's eyes appraised Lora shrewdly. "Hmmm . . . tomorrow night don't leave much time to work in, and as luck would have it, one of my girls is out sick with the influenza right now. But I suppose . . . there's the evening gown I was making up for Mrs. MacTavish. You and her are about the same size, I'd say. I suppose I might make that over for you, and make her a new one in time for her party next week."

"Oh, but—really, Madame, that doesn't seem quite fair to Mrs. MacTavish, does it? I wouldn't feel right about taking a dress away from someone else."

"Don't be a goose, Lora," said Lady Helen cheerfully. "Madame's just told you that she has plenty of time to make another. The question is, is it a dress that will suit you? I know Mrs. MacTavish, and though she is certainly an admirable woman in many respects, I'm afraid she hasn't the best taste in dress."

"Any gown from my salon will be in good taste," said Madame, drawing herself up offendedly. "You can rely on that, my lady. When a lady comes to me, she puts herself in my hands, so to speak, and I won't make a gown that doesn't suit her. It's a matter of my own reputation."

"Oh, yes, to be sure. But just because a gown suits Mrs. MacTavish doesn't mean it will suit Lady Carroll, you know. Mrs. MacTavish is quite dark, almost as dark as I am, while Lady Carroll is quite fair. What color is the gown you were speaking of?"

"White," said Madame. "And it's my opinion that it ought to suit my Lady Carroll right down to the ground."

"Yes, you always look like an angel in white, Lora," agreed Lady Helen.

"I don't want to look like an angel," said Lora, so forcefully that both Madame and Lady Helen looked at her in surprise. She flushed. "I am a grown woman and a widow, for heaven's sake. I have been wearing white dresses ever since I came out, except for the time I was in mourning, and I think I am getting rather old for them."

"Ah, but *ma chère madame,* there is white and then there is white," said Madame, making another foray into Gallicism. "This is a very sophisticated white—*très mondain,* you know. I can tell you for a fact that this gown won't make you look like a girl just out."

"Oh, yes?" said Lora, a bit doubtfully. "Well, I suppose I may as well look at it, as long as I'm here."

"It's a very pretty gown, I assure you, but I'm afraid it's not cheap, my lady. There's a deal of handwork in it, and I must recover my costs—the cost of making the gown in the first place, you know, and then the cost of altering it to fit your ladyship at such short notice. And then there will be the cost of my own time and effort to create another one, for of course I can't just turn around and give Mrs. MacTavish an exact copy of yours."

"Let us see the gown, and then we will decide if it's worth all this cost," said Lady Helen, cutting in upon the dressmaker's speech rather impatiently. "It will have to be something truly out of the ordinary if it is," she added in a low voice to Lora, as Madame left the room to fetch the gown. "In my opinion you'd better have Chalmers make over one of your nun's dresses if you need a new gown in such a hurry. But of course, it's your money, and you must do as you choose about it."

Lora was not called on to reply to this, for Madame had already come back into the room, accompanied by the small assistant who had been in the salon when they first came in. The assistant was bearing in her arms a single white gown, which she displayed before Lora and Lady Helen with the reverent expression of a priest displaying some sacred relic. "This is the gown I was talking about," said Madame, somewhat unnecessarily. "Would your ladyship like to try it on?"

Lora, regarding the magnificent garment before her, swallowed hard and nodded. Madame and the assistant helped her remove her pink China crepe pelisse and walking dress and then set about arraying her in the white evening gown. It was of heavy silk sewn with small crystaline beads, cut low and square in front with short sleeves and a scalloped hem. To Lora, it was quite simply the most dazzling dress she had ever seen. The slightest move sent sparks scintillating from the crystals encrusting the sleeves, bodice, and lower part of the skirt.

And when she took a step, the beaded fabric made a soft, rich rustling sound very satisfying to hear.

"Is it not *magnifique?*" demanded Madame.

"It is indeed," said Lora with feeling.

"Lovely," agreed Lady Helen. "If you don't want it, Lora, I do. Even if I can't wear it until after my lying-in!"

"I *do* want it, but still I cannot like to take a gown ordered by someone else. It seems like stealing from Mrs. MacTavish."

"Indeed, your ladyship, I'll make Mrs. MacTavish one she'll like quite as well," said Madame earnestly. "It's not as though she's ever seen this particular gown. I only discussed the general idea of it with her beforehand, and she hasn't been in to be fitted with it yet. By using different beads and changing the cut of the sleeves and skirt a trifle, I can make a gown different enough from this one so it won't be an exact copy but will be just as pretty."

"I don't see how anything could be as pretty as this one," said Lora, touching the beaded skirt reverentially.

"Thank you, my lady. That's kind of you to say, and I don't say I don't agree with you, for I think myself that this one's something special. If you like the gown, I wish you'd take it, my lady. Speaking frankly, it'd do me and my business a deal more good to have you seen wearing it rather than Mrs. Mac-Tavish. Her figure's good enough, but she don't carry herself so well as you do, and she hasn't nearly such a pretty face."

"Take it, Lora, do," urged Lady Helen. "You couldn't hope to find a more gorgeous gown. And you do look like an angel in it. Like a sophisticated angel," she amended, with a laughing look at her friend.

Lora turned to regard herself long and hard in the glass; "Yes . . . yes, but that's another thing. I almost think it's *too* sophisticated for me, if you know what I mean. It's gorgeous, of course, but I'm afraid I wouldn't have the nerve to wear it if I did buy it. The neck is so low. . . ."

"It's not a bit lower than what is commonly worn nowadays," said Lady Helen. "The only reason it seems low to you is that you're used to wearing nun's dresses. And you were the one who said you wanted a change from them, don't you remember?"

"Yes, but I almost think this is too much of a change, Helen. Perhaps the neck could be altered so it's not quite so low? Or I could wear a handkerchief, perhaps."

"Fichu, my child, fichu," corrected Lady Helen. "Nobody says handkerchief anymore. And nobody wears one, either, at least not in the evening. I tell you, that neck's not a bit lower than what everyone wears nowadays."

"Indeed, my lady, if you take the dress, you must wear it just as it is," said Madame, looking alarmed. "I couldn't sell it to you under any other conditions. Like I said before, I'm just starting out in business for myself, and it's of the first importance that all my work that appears in public be slap up to the mark. I don't like to turn away custom, my lady, but you must understand I've my reputation to look out for. I hope your ladyship won't be offended by my plain speaking."

Lora took a last long look at her reflection in the mirror. It was true that she would have preferred to have a little less of her bosom on display, and perhaps a little less of her ankles as well, but having once seen that vision of herself in dazzling white, she could not bring herself to relinquish it.

"Very well, Madame. I will take the gown and abide by your conditions," she told the modiste with a smile. "And if you have any other dresses to show, I would very much like to see them. My entire wardrobe wants replenishing in the worst way."

Madame's face lit up at these gladsome words, and she at once dispatched her assistant to fetch dress samples, fabric swatches, and fashion plates. When the assistant had returned with these articles, Madame settled down to discuss them with Lora one by one, while Lady Helen looked on and contributed her own advice.

This was a delightful but trying process for Lora. So surely as she fixed upon one dress as being exactly what she wanted,

Madame would respectfully suggest that a different color might suit her better, and Lady Helen would add that no one *she* knew nowadays was wearing bishop sleeves, or tunics, or Circassian wrappers. Lora soon began to feel as though she had fallen under a thralldom only slightly less absolute than that of her mother. But her companions' taste was indisputably better than Mrs. Darlington's, as well as being very much less conservative, and in the end, after a couple of hours of discussion, several fittings, and a heated argument with Lady Helen over a certain green levantine pelisse, Lora emerged with three new morning dresses, a like number of afternoon dresses, a carriage dress, a velvet evening cloak, two ballgowns, and the beaded evening gown that had been ordered for Mrs. MacTavish.

Lady Helen was scarcely more backward in her purchases. After being fitted for the evening gown she had ordered the previous week, she proceeded to order two more, in addition to a couple of new walking dresses, a dinner dress, and a Wellington mantle of ruby velvet lined with sarcenet.

"Very good, my ladies—*très bien,*" said Madame, beaming with pleasure as the two ladies prepared to leave the shop. "Everything should be far enough along for fitting by Monday. All except for the white gown you wanted for tomorrow night, Lady Carroll. I'll have my girls do the alterations tonight and have it delivered to you at the Spelbourne House tomorrow morning, if that's quite convenient."

"Yes, that will do very well," said Lora. "And thank you again, Madame, for accommodating me at such short notice."

"It was my pleasure to be of service to you, my lady. I hope I shall see a great deal of you in the future. *Bon jour,* and remember, no handkerchiefs!" With this last smiling admonition, Madame bowed her and Lady Helen out of the shop and into their waiting carriage.

Six

Lora was conscious of a flutter of excitement in her breast as she made her toilette for the theater party Thursday evening.

She had felt no such excitement the evening before, when she had been preparing to go to Almack's, and indeed, it had been an evening quite devoid of excitement, dull and decorous as evenings at Almack's invariably were. The advent of Lord Ellsworth shortly before eleven o'clock had added to the dullness an element of annoyance, and as Lora had ridden home afterwards with Lady Helen and Lord Spelbourne, she had silently resolved to absent herself from all such assemblies in the future. She was no longer a young girl, after all, forced to show her paces on the Marriage Mart in hopes of attracting a suitable *parti;* henceforth she might choose her diversions and her companions as she liked. Lora made up her mind that in the future, her choice of both would differ substantially from what she had been subjected to at Almack's that evening.

The white beaded gown had been delivered the following morning, just as Madame had promised. The bandbox had been unpacked by Annie, Lora's maid, who had promptly fallen into raptures at the sight of its contents. Her raptures had been so great and had continued so long that when evening came and it was finally time for Lora to assume the wondrous garment, she could hardly leave off her expressions of admiration long enough to dress Lora's hair.

"Oh, 'tis beautiful, my lady! The prettiest dress I've ever seen. Fit for the queen herself, it is," said Annie, gazing at the gown with enchantment. "Are you going to wear your diamonds with it, my lady?"

"Yes, the diamonds would be very suitable, wouldn't they? I believe I will, Annie. And Annie—I was wondering if you might dress my hair in a different style tonight. Not ringlets, but something more, well, sophisticated."

Annie looked doubtful. "I could do it *à l'espagnole,*" she suggested. "Or in a Psyche knot . . . I think. Lady Helen's woman's been teaching me, but I'm not just sure I've got the way of it yet. Howsomever, I'd be happy to try if you'd like me to, my lady."

Annie's tone was not such as to inspire much confidence, but Lora acceded to her last suggestion, reflecting that Lady Helen's woman was always in the house to be appealed to as a last resort. Her assistance proved unnecessary, however. The Psyche knot was accomplished with a degree of success not always attending Annie's efforts, and when Lora surveyed her finished self in the mirror, she had no reason to be dissatisfied by what she saw.

Under the glow of candlelight, the white gown appeared even more magnificent than it had appeared in Madame's salon the previous afternoon. The crystals encrusting its skirt and bodice sent off flashes of fire scarcely less brilliant than the diamonds that hung around Lora's neck and sparkled atop her head in the form of a delicate tiara. Both necklace and tiara had been gifts from her late husband, personal gifts that were not among the entailed property that had passed to his cousin upon his death. They made a fitting accompaniment to the icy splendor of the white gown, but as Lora regarded these relics of the past, she was assailed by an unexpected sense of sadness.

It was a sadness fueled in large part by guilt. She felt guilty for having missed Lord Carroll so little since his death, and guiltier still for having dwelt so exclusively upon his faults during his lifetime, when he had also possessed so many undoubted virtues—the virtue of generosity, for instance, as represented by these diamonds. The reflection tended to dampen the mood of happy anticipation Lora had been feeling earlier. She gave a last cursory smooth to her long gloves, verified that the ribbons of her satin sandals were securely tied, and gathered up her evening cloak and reticule with a feeling more of fatalism than of anticipation.

This temporary gloom had subsided by the time she got downstairs, however. Lord Spelbourne was already waiting there, his large square figure neatly encased in a blue topcoat and buff-colored pantaloons. He and Lora were joined a few minutes later by Lady Helen, dressed with her customary dash in an evening dress of silver lamé with an upstanding plume of ostrich feathers in her hair.

"By Jove, don't the two of you look fine," said Lord Spelbourne, looking with naive pleasure from her to Lora. "I'll be the envy of every fellow in the house, sitting with the two most famous beauties in London."

Lady Helen laughed and kissed his cheek. "You know I'm no beauty, Arthur, you silly. But Lora certainly has full claims to the title. Indeed, Lora, you look magnificent this evening. It's odd to see you without your ringlets, but now that I look at you, I'm not sure I don't prefer your hair as it is."

"Thank you," said Lora, touching the low knot at the back of her head self-consciously. "Since I was wearing a tiara, I thought it better to dispense with the ringlets this once."

"Well, I should do so from now on if I were you. Are my plumes quite straight? Very well, then: let us go out to the carriage, and Arthur can pay us more pretty compliments on the way to the theater."

Lord Spelbourne gallantly offered each of the ladies an arm, and they all went out to the carriage. A short drive brought them to the theater in Drury Lane, and soon they were ensconced in the Spelbournes' sumptuous box, waiting for the play to start.

Lora was conscious once more of a flutter of excitement as she looked around the fast-filling theater. Perhaps Adam was already there, somewhere in the crowd. Or perhaps he was only now arriving, and she would see him presently when he went to take his seat. She scrutinized both the pit below and the gallery above, trying to locate his sleek brown head and lean figure among the throng of other theater-goers.

"Why are you craning your neck around like that, Lora?" Lady Helen demanded in a whisper. "Are you looking for someone? If so, I hope it's not Ellsworth, because he appears to be very much occupied elsewhere." She nodded meaningfully toward a box on the opposite side of the theater, where Lord Ellsworth stood with a crowd of other gentlemen clustered around a very pretty fair-haired lady who was obviously a member of the Cyprian class.

Lora glanced toward the box, just as Lord Ellsworth looked up from kissing the fair-haired lady's hand. Their eyes met for an instant. Lora looked quickly away with a flush of annoyance. "No, I wasn't looking for Lord Ellsworth, Helen," she said. "I was just—looking around. It's been a long time since I was at Drury Lane, you know."

After this incident, Lora took care to conduct her search in a more discreet manner, but her efforts were unrewarded. She could see Adam nowhere: not in the pit, not in the gallery, not in any of the boxes around her, not even among the unfortunates who had been unable to obtain a seat and were forced to stand at the back of the theater throughout the performance. At last, Lora abandoned the search altogether and sank back in her seat to watch the opening scene of the preliminary piece.

As she watched, she could not rid herself of a sense of disappointment. She had supposed that Adam would be as eager to see her again as she was to see him, and that he would be on hand early so that they might enjoy the maximum of each other's company. But it appeared now that he was not so eager as she, that he meant to content himself with a brief visit later in the evening, or even—horrible thought—that he did not intend to come at all.

Lora's spirits had been swinging wildly between hope and

fatalism all evening. This last idea brought the scales down hard on the side of fatalism. She immediately felt that she had been unreasonable to have expected anything to have come of that brief interlude in the garden. Likely Adam had regarded her as a mere pleasant diversion, and though he had seemed sincere enough at the time about wishing to see her again, he might well have thought better of his promise since then and decided their acquaintance was not worth pursuing.

Lora told herself firmly that it was just as well. In all likelihood, a second meeting would have shown him to be less agreeable than he had appeared at their first. This way, she might enjoy the memory of their time together without any risk of having it spoiled by an unpleasant sequel. With these and similar reflections Lora consoled herself during the opening piece, in much the same manner that Aesop's fox consoled himself for the loss of the grapes.

Yet in spite of her best efforts at self-consolation, Lora found her hopes springing up anew when the farce ended and a volley of knocking sounded on the door of the box. She looked toward the door with thinly-disguised eagerness. But alas: none of the callers seeking admission proved to be Adam, and one proved to be, what was infinitely worse, the Right Honourable Earl of Ellsworth.

Lord Ellsworth greeted Lora with the same brazen self-assurance he had shown at their last two meetings, an assurance that seemed to take for granted that she would be overwhelmed by the honor of his company.

"I saw you, and I had to come," he announced in a low, intimate voice. "When you looked at me earlier, it was as though your eyes were summoning me across the theater. And now you see—here I am."

"I am afraid you misunderstood my eyes, Lord Ellsworth," said Lora coldly. "They had no intention of calling you away from your—friends."

Lord Ellsworth regarded her for a moment and then smiled: an odiously conceited smile, Lora thought. "The fair Blanche, do you mean? She's no friend of mine, Lora, although I will confess to having some slight acquaintance with her in the past. Are you jealous?"

"Certainly not, my lord," said Lora, striving to sound amused rather than indignant. "Why should I be jealous?"

"Well, I had rather hoped you might be. As it happens, you have nothing to be jealous about, for Blanche is nothing to me, or I to her, beyond a mere acquaintance. You do believe me, don't you, Lora? I would hate to think I had done anything to forfeit your good opinion."

"My opinion of you is quite unchanged, my lord," said Lora truthfully.

Lord Ellsworth took this for reassurance, as she intended, but instead of departing on the strength of it, he sat down in the vacant chair next to hers and proceeded to make himself at home. "I think the play is about to begin, my lord," hinted Lora, much dismayed by this turn of events. "Shouldn't you be getting back to your own box now?"

"Surely you're not going to send me away already?" returned Lord Ellsworth. "I only got here a few minutes ago, and the view from this box is much better than from my own." He surveyed Lora's décolletage with bold appreciation.

Lora cast a despairing look at Lady Helen, hoping for her assistance in ridding the box of this most unwelcome visitor. Lord Ellsworth saw the look but misinterpreted its meaning. "Oh, Helen doesn't mind me staying, do you, Helen?" he said, smiling lazily at Lady Helen. "I promise most faithfully that I'll behave myself. You have my word of honor."

"I trust you *will* behave yourself, Ellsworth," said Lady Helen, eyeing him with disfavor. "If not, I shall ask Arthur to pitch you out on your ear."

"Eh?" said Lord Spelbourne, turning round at the sound of his name. "Pitch out who on their ear, Helen?"

"Ellsworth here, if he doesn't behave."

"Oh, aye, just as you say, Helen," said Lord Spelbourne cheerfully. "Better watch your step, Ellsworth. The play's just starting, and I'd rather not cause a disturbance while the lights are down."

Lord Ellsworth merely gave him a look of contempt and turned again to Lora. "How Helen can bear with that half-wit, I'll never know," he said under his breath. "I suppose it was the title that recommended him to her. Lord knows it couldn't have been anything else."

"Lord Spelbourne may not be a great intellectual, but he does not want for sense, I assure you," said Lora warmly. "I believe Lady Helen is most sincerely attached to him."

"Aye, there's the wonder of it," said Lord Ellsworth, with a crack of derisive laughter. But seeing that Lora was looking seriously displeased, he at once composed his features into a more conciliatory expression.

"Upon my word, I don't mean to speak ill of Spelbourne, for everyone knows him to be the best-natured fellow on earth," he told Lora. "But you must admit that he and Helen make an unlikely pairing. It will be interesting to see what their progeny turns out like, won't it?"

Lora gave a restrained assent to this and then fixed her eyes on the stage, indicating to Lord Ellsworth her desire to watch the play in silence. To all his subsequent attempts at conversation she merely nodded or shook her head; and when the first act finally ended, she had hopes that he had been offended enough by this discouraging treatment to go and leave her in peace. Unfortunately, Lord Ellsworth seemed incapable of recognizing discouragement even when it bordered upon downright rudeness.

"I think you should go now, my lord," said Lora, growing blunt through desperation. "You've been here for one whole act, and your other acquaintance will be growing angry with me if I monopolize your company much longer." She looked significantly toward the fair-haired Cyprian in the other box.

Lord Ellsworth laughed. "Who, Blanche? I already told you that she hasn't any claim on my company, Lora. Even if she did, I'd much rather stay here with you. You're a great deal prettier than she is."

Lora, opening her mouth to reply, was arrested by the sound of a knock on the door of the box. There had been many such knocks on the door that evening, for Lady Helen's acquaintance was large, and the box had been crowded throughout both intervals with ladies and gentlemen come to call upon her. There was, therefore, no reason why this particular knock should have attracted Lora's attention. She had, as she thought, abandoned all hope of seeing Adam that evening, but now she found that hope had remained with her nonetheless. Hearing the knock, she looked around in hope of seeing Adam—and saw Adam.

At the sight of him, Lora rose quickly to her feet, quite unconscious that she had done so. She watched as Adam bowed formally to Lady Helen and Lord Spelbourne.

"Good evening, my lord, my lady. I hope you will forgive my intrusion, but I wished to speak to Lady Carroll for a few minutes," he told them, before turning to Lora. In a hazy way she was aware of Lady Helen's surprised look; of Lord Spelbourne's bewildered smile; and of Lord Ellsworth turning to regard the newcomer with a disapproving frown. But though these things registered upon Lora's consciousness, her eyes were for Adam alone.

He was looking quite as attractive as she remembered him the other night. Indeed, she had the impression that he was more attractive than she remembered, although this might have had something to do with the care with which he was dressed. His garments at the Monroes' party had been perfectly neat and gentleman-like, but the ones he wore now had an indefinable air of distinction that proclaimed them the work of one of London's master tailors. A jacket of blue superfine and a pair of fawn-colored trousers clung close to his lean figure; his neckcloth was neatly tied, and his boots polished to a high sheen. There was in fact nothing about his appearance to differentiate him from Lord Spelbourne or Lord Ellsworth, although such comparisons did not occur to Lora at that moment. She only thought he looked very attractive and most completely the gentleman. She smiled and held out her hand to him as he regarded her from across the box.

If it had not been for that smile and that gesture, Adam would have been tempted to turn and walk out of the box again. His confidence had been running fairly high when he had taken leave of Lora at the Monroes' party, but since then it had been ebbing steadily lower. It seemed impossible that she could have been as encouraging as he remembered, let alone that she could have so far forgot their relative positions as to exchange kisses with him in the garden. The suspicion that she had been making game of him had more than once recurred to him. He had seriously debated within himself whether he ought to risk the humiliation of having her ridicule him or perhaps cut him altogether if he followed through on her suggestion to visit her in the Spelbourne's box at Drury Lane.

In the end, it had been his own conscience that had decided the matter. It was no part of a gentleman's conduct to break his word to a lady, and he had promised Lora he would be there Thursday night. Go he must, therefore, even if it was to endure coldness or ridicule at her hands.

This was a perfectly adequate reason for going, of course, and the only one Adam would admit to, but in his heart he had other, unacknowledged reasons as well. If he failed to follow up his acquaintance with Lora, he might well be sparing himself an evening of humiliation, but he would also be forever depriving himself of the chance to know whether or not she had been in earnest that night in the garden. And Adam wanted very much to know whether she had been in earnest. He felt he would rather have his image of her shattered than live out the rest of his life in uncertainty on that point.

So he had made up his mind to go, even going so far as to order a new suit of clothes for the occasion. Mr. Lloyd had raised his eyebrows at this uncharacteristic interest in matters sartorial, and had raised them even higher when he learned of his friend's sudden desire to attend the theater Thursday night. But he had given Adam the name of his tailor, purchased a couple of tickets for the performance, and accompanied him to Drury Lane with unquestioning affability.

Adam had greatly appreciated this demonstration of tact on his friend's part. When they had actually arrived at the theater, however, and were taking their seats in the pit, Mr. Lloyd had nodded toward one of the boxes above them with a rather sardonic smile.

"There's your siren up there," he said. "Do you plan to go pay your respects to her before the performance starts?"

Adam looked up, past the seats in the pit to the row of plush boxes on the wall above them. There sat Lora in her glittering white dress and diamond tiara, with Lady Helen and Lord Spelbourne seated a little behind her. The sight froze Adam with sudden dismay. She looked beautiful, even lovelier than he had remembered, but she also looked completely unapproachable. At the Monroes' she had looked like a young girl, so much so that he had found it difficult to believe she was a countess, but he had no difficulty believing it tonight. She might have been a princess, for anything he might have in common with such a dazzling creature.

The performance began then, and Adam sat through the whole of the opening piece without perceiving any part of the action onstage. He was once again arguing within himself whether he ought to risk the humiliation of being condescended to, or cut. By the time the first interval arrived, he had so far argued himself into a sense of his duties as a gentleman to actually rise from his seat with the intention of going to the Spelbournes' box. Mr. Lloyd observed the movement and stood up likewise.

"Devilish warm in here, isn't it? What do you say we go to the lounge and get a glass of wine?"

Adam hesitated and looked again toward the Spelbourne box above him. He was just in time to see Lord Ellsworth enter the box and seat himself in the vacant chair beside Lora. A mirthless smile tightened Adam's lips. Since the Monroes' party, he had obtained full particulars of Lord Ellsworth's dealings with the unfortunate Lady Shaughnessy, and with various other ladies both high and low born. None of it had been calculated to improve his opinion of Lord Ellsworth's character. But the fact remained that he and Lora moved in the same circles, inhabited the same world, perhaps even shared the same moral code, though Adam found that difficult to believe equally of the innocent-seeming girl he had met at the Monroes' party and of the celestial-looking creature he saw above him in the Spelbournes' box. There was no denying that Lord Ellsworth looked very much at home sitting there beside her, however.

"Yes, I wouldn't mind a glass of wine myself," said Adam, and deliberately turned his back on the Spelbournes' box.

Of the first act of the play that followed, Adam saw as little as of the opening farce. He was once again mentally wrestling with the question of whether or not he ought to go to the Spelbournes' box and pay his respects to Lora. By the time the second interval arrived, he had made up his mind to go and see her, if only to have the matter done with once and for all. Even the sight of Lord Ellsworth still seated beside her did not dissuade him. Whatever happened, he would have done his duty, and then, with a clear conscience, he might leave the theater and put the whole vexatious episode behind him.

It was with a feeling of grim purpose, then, that Adam had knocked upon the door of the Spelbournes' box. He had been prepared for a cool reception, and indeed both Lady Helen and Lord Spelbourne had looked a little surprised at his entrance, but neither of them had made any demur about his seeing Lora. As for Lord Ellsworth's look of disapproval, it completely failed to register upon Adam. When Lora had stood and smilingly stretched out her hand to him, he had felt such a rush of pleasure and relief that he could have endured the hostile glares of half a dozen lords without being much dismayed.

"Good evening, Lora," he said, taking her hand and bowing over it.

"Good evening, Adam," she returned. There followed a brief pause, during which they merely looked at each other and the other occupants of the box looked at them. It was Lady Helen who finally broke the silence.

"Won't you introduce us to your friend, Lora?" she said with a smile. "That would save us from standing about staring at each other in this stupid way."

Lora, with a soft flush of color in her cheeks, hastened to perform introductions. Lady Helen and Lord Spelbourne cordially returned Adam's greeting, but Lord Ellsworth merely raised his quizzing glass to his eye and regarded Adam without speaking.

"Your face looks familiar to me, Mr. Wainwright," said Lady Helen, rushing to fill the breach. "Were you not at the Monroes' party the other night?"

"Yes, I was, ma'am. My friend, Mr. Lloyd, is a relation of the Monroes."

"One meets a deal of odd people at the Monroes'," remarked Lord Ellsworth, ostensibly to Lora. "Sir Edward is a little too democratic in his choice of company to suit my taste."

Lora said nothing to this, but turned away from him with a suggestion of another flush. Smiling again at Adam, she indicated the empty chair on the other side of hers. "Won't you please sit down and keep us company for a while, Adam?" she said. "You don't need to return to your seat immediately, do you?"

"Well, no, not immediately," said Adam, accepting with some diffidence the proffered chair. "But I will have to go back to my seat before the next act begins. John will be wondering where I have got to."

"Oh, is Mr. Lloyd with you?" Lora said. "You should have brought him along with you, Adam. I would have been very glad to make his acquaintance."

She spoke with so much apparent sincerity and accompanied her words with a smile so soft and sweet that Adam found himself warming to her all over again, in spite of her diamonds and ultra-fashionable dress and in spite of the disapproving looks of Lord Ellsworth seated in the chair on the other side of her. That gentleman's next words struck a chill, however.

"I greatly enjoyed dancing with you last night at Almack's, Lora. It was an unusually pleasant evening, wasn't it?"

"Did you think so? I thought it much as usual," said Lora coolly.

"Ah, but to be much as usual is a high compliment when speaking of Almack's," returned Lord Ellsworth. "At Almack's you are guaranteed elegant surroundings, well-ordered entertainment, and the best and most brilliant of company. You must be *blasé* indeed if you can obtain no pleasure from that. Surely you will agree with me, sir," he went on, addressing Adam directly for the first time. "Wouldn't you say that Almack's assemblies are in a class by themselves?"

"I have not had the pleasure of ever attending one," said Adam stiffly.

"And you lose nothing by it, Adam," said Lora quickly. "I have always found Almack's the most tedious place. The patronesses give themselves such airs—and the rooms are so drafty—and there's never anything but bread-and-butter to eat, and lemonade and orgeat to drink. You know you yourself were complaining about it only last night, my lord," she told Lord Ellsworth.

"Was I? I don't recall doing so," said Lord Ellsworth, and quickly dismissed the subject of Almack's assembly rooms. But he was by no means ready to surrender control of the conversation. Settling himself even more comfortably into his chair, he went on to discuss the latest group of presentations at court, a *levée* which he had attended at Carlton House the previous week, and the upcoming marriage between Princess Charlotte and Prince Leopold of Saxe-Coburg.

In discussing these things, Lord Ellsworth did not again address or even look at Adam, but Adam could not doubt that the conversation was intended to make him feel his status as an outsider. Adam was not particularly thin-skinned; neither was he disposed to regard himself as inferior to any man simply because that man had a title and made a habit of attending royal *levées.* But he would have been more than human if he had not resented the tone of Lord Ellsworth's conversation. Lord Ellsworth had a way of making gently needling remarks about homespun provincials and country squires on holiday that was very hard to bear in silence; yet, since none of the remarks were addressed directly to him, he was unable to respond to them.

It was true that Lora did not concur in these remarks. On the contrary, she opposed them at every opportunity, often with considerable warmth, but as far as Adam was concerned this only made his position worse. It was mortifying to owe his defense to the woman whom, in natural circumstances, he would have felt it his duty and privilege to defend. If he could have been sure of her motives, he might have taken Lora's defense as a sign of partiality, but as it was, he could not rid himself of a fear that she was acting only out of pity. And there was an additional mortification in the knowledge that Lady Helen and Lord Spelbourne were overhearing everything that was said. Although they had personally taken no part in the conversation, Adam fancied that they would naturally side with Lord Ellsworth in the matter and must be laughing at him behind his back. He sat, dumb and resentful, growing angrier every minute.

As for Lora, she was in a state of near desperation. There seemed no way of stopping the flow of Lord Ellsworth's spite, and though she did her best to counter his more offensive remarks, she could not but feel how intolerable the situation must be for Adam. She stole frequent, anxious looks at him, trying to gauge the state of his emotions. When he had first entered the box, he had seemed much as she remembered him, but since then his manner had grown noticeably reserved, much more reserved than it had been when he had bade farewell to her at the Monroes' party two nights before. Now that Lord Ellsworth had taken control of the situation, he had ceased to speak at all. Lora felt quite sure he was only awaiting a suitable opportunity to excuse himself and go. And once he was gone, that would be that. In a few days he would return to his home in Hampshire, and she would probably never see him again.

As Lora studied Adam's face out of the corner of her eye, it brought home to her just how much she wanted to see him again. Even in the few words they had exchanged that evening, she had been conscious of the same attraction she had felt the first time she had encountered him. There was no material explanation for it. Looking impartially from him to Lord Ellsworth, she was forced to admit that Lord Ellsworth was by far the better-looking of the two, but she felt not the slightest shred of attraction for Lord Ellsworth. Indeed, after the events of this evening, her feelings for him were fast sinking into revulsion.

Neither was it a matter of superior wit or intellect. Lord Ellsworth did not lack for intelligence, and when he was not making a parade of his devotion, or trying to inspire an answering devotion in her, he was capable of being an amusing companion. But Lora had no desire for Lord Ellsworth's companionship and indeed would have been very glad to dispense with it on that occasion. It was maddening to sit helplessly by and watch her hopes for the evening rapidly ebbing away. Lady Helen might have assisted her, if she would, but Lady Helen seemed content merely to look on and let matters take their course; and of course there was no help to be expected from Lord Spelbourne. It looked as though it would be up to her to somehow remedy the situation, if it were not already past remedy. Lora was more than half afraid that it was.

She was sure of it a few minutes later. The lights in the theater were already being dimmed in preparation for the beginning of the next act. Lord Ellsworth remarked on these preparations but made no move to leave his seat. Adam, however, rose and turned to Lora.

"I must be returning to my friend now," he said. "I give you good evening, ma'am." Bestowing a formal bow upon her, and another upon her companions, he turned to leave the box.

Lord Ellsworth returned his bow with a nod and then turned to Lora with an amusing story about an amateur performance of *Romeo and Juliet* he had once taken part in. But he found himself addressing only empty air. Lora had risen from her seat and followed after Adam as he moved toward the door of the box.

"Adam," she said, in a low but urgent voice. "Adam, wait."

He paused and turned again to face her. "Yes?" he said coolly.

Faced by this discouraging monosyllable, Lora faltered for an instant, uncertain what to say, but feeling desperately that she must say something. "I am very glad you came to see me tonight, Adam," was what she brought forth at last. And then, in a voice too soft for the others to hear, "When shall I see you again?"

He looked down at her for a long moment. "I don't know, Lora," he said. "I shall be in London only another week, and it's not likely that we will meet again. I doubt I shall be attending the same parties as you."

There was an undercurrent of bitterness in his voice. Once again Lora faltered, but she now had a clue to his state of mind, and it gave her the courage to go on even in the face of discouragement. "I am sure you might attend the same parties as I, if you chose," she said, looking up at him steadily. "Next Friday Lady Helen and I will be attending a ridotto at the Randolph Rooms. It is by subscription—you can buy a ticket and come, too, if you will. Will you come?"

He hesitated. "I don't know—"

"Please come, Adam," she said, and took his hand in hers.

The gesture was wholly impulsive. As soon as Lora had done it, she was in a fever of apprehension, fearing that she had overstepped the bounds of ladylike behavior. If he refused her now, the rejection would be a personal one and all the more humiliating on that account. She looked at him anxiously, wondering if he were about to reject her and how she would bear it if he did.

For a moment Adam stood very still, looking first down at her and then down at his hand, which was still clasped between her own. When he spoke, his voice was low and uncertain. "Lora, I don't know," he said again. "Are you sure—quite sure—you want me to come?"

"Quite sure, Adam," she said, and gripped his hand all the tighter. Having risked so much already, she was not inclined to draw back now. It seemed to her that everything hinged upon this moment.

"Very well, then," he said at last. He said it almost reluctantly, but his hand returned the pressure of hers, and when she smiled at him tentatively he smiled back with more warmth than he had shown since entering the box that evening.

A bow, another squeeze of the hand, and then he was gone, leaving Lora to make her reluctant way back to her seat beside Lord Ellsworth.

Seven

On the morning following the theater party, Lora sat at the breakfast table brooding over the events of the previous evening.

She had risen early that morning, notwithstanding the late hour at which she and the Spelbournes had returned home from the theater the night before. Instead of calling for tea and toast in her room, she had rung for Annie, made her toilette, and gone downstairs to the breakfast room. Lord Spelbourne, an invariable early riser, was already there, consuming cold ham and perusing the morning paper.

" 'Morning, Lora," was his greeting, spoken cheerfully without looking up from the paper. "Good show last night, wasn't it? That Kean's a wonderful fellow. Gave me a regular turn when he did that business with the knife."

Lora expressed agreement with these sentiments and then went to the sideboard to help herself to hot rolls and honey. As Lord Spelbourne was fully immersed in his paper, she had ample leisure to reflect upon all that had passed at the theater the night before. It had been in all respects a most unsatisfactory evening and had only been saved from complete disaster by those few words she had exchanged with Adam at the last. And even the remembrance of those words was not a matter of complete comfort to Lora. His manner had been so strained, his consent to attend the ridotto so reluctantly given, that it was clear he would have let their acquaintance drop where it was if Lora had not taken matters into her own hands.

Lora could not in the least blame him. Her own blood boiled

when she thought of the way Lord Ellsworth had behaved, and she could readily believe that the situation must have been still more intolerable to Adam. It was natural that he would not care to remain long in Lord Ellsworth's company, but she was not satisfied that the blame for the evening's woes lay entirely with Lord Ellsworth. Adam's behavior had been constrained even before Lord Ellsworth had started his needling remarks. It must have been some word or action of hers that had precipitated it.

Perhaps he was still angry with her over her impersonation at the Monroes' the other night? But he had seemed to forgive her for that, once she had explained her reasons for concealing her name and title. They had parted on good terms, and if he had later grown angry at her again, there would have been no reason for him to come to the theater at all.

Lora frowned over her plate of rolls, trying to penetrate the mystery. How could a gentleman, formerly so warm and friendly, suddenly become so cool and unapproachably formal? Could it have been merely a matter of setting? A theater box in full view of hundreds of people was certainly not as conducive to easy conversation as a moonlit garden.

Or could it have been her own altered appearance? She had been anxious not to misrepresent herself a second time as a young girl, but had she, in her anxiety, gone too far in the other direction and assumed a sophistication that was not really hers? She had had doubts about the white gown from the beginning. And white by itself was such a cold, austere color, especially a white frosted over with crystals and accessorized with the icy glitter of diamonds. She had heard of color influencing people's moods. Lady Helen always swore that sitting in a yellow room made her bilious, and she herself knew well enough what the wearing of unrelieved black for months on end could do to the human spirit. Perhaps on this occasion the chilly splendor of her costume had had some unconscious effect on Adam's manner.

After considering the matter for several minutes, during which time she ate very little and frowned a great deal, Lora judged it likely that all these factors had played a role in the evening's unhappy outcome. It remained then to determine how best to avoid such an outcome a second time. If Adam had indeed still been angry at her for concealing her name and circumstances from him at the Monroes', then he must be even angrier now after Lord Ellsworth's rude conduct. But she could do nothing about that, save to apologize and to make certain that Lord Ellsworth was nowhere about when she met him at the ridotto. This might take some doing, but Lora resolved to do whatever was necessary to detach Lord Ellsworth from her side, even if it required brutal plain speaking.

The setting was another factor over which she had little control. It had already been settled that they would meet at the ridotto. But though there might have been spots in London more conducive to intimacy than the Randolph Rooms, Lora felt there were many that would have been far worse. The rooms would undoubtedly be very full, which would allow their meeting to take place inconspicuously among the crowd. And if Adam seemed interested in following up his acquaintance with her, they might sit together during the concert and perhaps dance together later on.

The one factor completely in her control was her dress for the occasion. The white gown, beautiful as it was, appeared now to have been a mistake. Very good, then: she must learn from that mistake and adopt a different style of dress for the ridotto. The great question was, what style of dress ought it to be? Lora's perplexed gaze fastened upon Lord Spelbourne, who had just laid aside his newspaper in order to stir sugar into his coffee.

"Arthur," she said suddenly, "what color do men like?"

Lord Spelbourne regarded her blankly. "I beg your pardon?" he said.

Lora repeated the question, with some embarrassment. "I just wondered if there was some color gentlemen particularly liked—in ladies' dress, I mean. I know Carroll never liked to see me in purple or green, and I have heard other ladies complaining of their husbands' disliking one color or another. Is there some color men *do* like to see ladies wear?"

With an effort, Lord Spelbourne bent his thoughts to this question. "Well, I don't know," he said doubtfully. "There was that red dress Adèle wore in the opera ballet last week. Of course, you couldn't hardly call *her* a lady—but it was a dashed pretty dress all the same. I remember the fellows at the club talking about it afterwards."

It was on the tip of Lora's tongue to inform Lord Spelbourne that she had no intention of dressing like an opera dancer. Her indignation soon gave way to amusement, however. With an inward smile, she reflected that anyone looking to Lord Spelbourne for advice deserved exactly what he or she got. Such was her first thought, at least, but when she had begun to reflect more seriously, she began to wonder whether his advice were so wholly without merit as she had originally thought it. An opera dancer must necessarily know a good deal about the art of pleasing, after all. Naturally one would not wish to take her for a model of manners, or morals, but where dress was concerned there could be no harm in following her lead, so long as one did not follow it too slavishly.

"I shall visit Madame LeClaire this afternoon and order a red dress," was Lora's inward resolution.

Lady Helen chose not to accompany her friend on this expedition. "No, my love, if you don't mind, I think I will stay at home this afternoon and catch up on my correspondence," she told Lora. "But I would be much obliged to you if you would ask after my yellow crepe while you are there. I have a recollection that Madame said it might be done today."

"Certainly, Helen," said Lora, and took an affectionate leave of her friend. Accompanied by her maid Annie, she then went out to the carriage and was conveyed once more to Madame's shop in Oxford Street. "You needn't come in, Annie," she told her maid, as the two dismounted from the carriage. "If you like, you may do some shopping of your own. I'll be an hour in here, at least."

"Thank you, my lady," said Annie happily, and made a beeline for a tempting-looking milliner's down the street. Lora entered Madame's shop, the door of which was opened to her by Madame herself, all smiles and deferential bows. The reason for her deference was made clear as soon as she and Lora were alone within her inner sanctum.

"I understand your ladyship made a great success at the theater last night," said Madame, smiling broadly and rubbing her hands together with an air of immense satisfaction. "I knew I did right to sell you that white gown. I've had no less than three ladies in this morning, looking to order gowns like it. It was good of you to mention my name, my lady."

"Oh—ah—you're welcome," said Lora, who in fact had no recollection of having done so. She could only suppose that some of the ladies who had come to call during the intervals of the play had drawn the information from Lady Helen. Certain it was that several of them had admired her gown very enthusiastically. "I wish to order another evening gown, Madame," she went on, as she seated herself in the delicate gilt chair Madame had drawn forward for her. "A red gown, this time."

"Red?" Madame scrutinized her dubiously. "I don't think you've the complexion for red, my lady. My Lady Helen, now—she can wear your crimsons and carmines and carry them off with a dash, but not you, begging your ladyship's pardon. You know it's my rule never to sell a lady a dress that don't become her. Now if you was wanting a *rose* dress, perhaps—"

"I want a red dress," said Lora mutinously. "Not rose. Red."

"Red's too strong a color for you, my lady. I won't sell you a red dress."

"Then I suppose I must go elsewhere," said Lora, rising from her chair. She spoke coolly, but inwardly she was all aflutter at her own effrontery. It was not her habit to defy people, certainly not people whose manner was as authoritative as Madame's; and having done so, she had to fight against an urge to apologize, resume her seat, and humbly assure Madame that a rose-colored dress would do very well.

Madame, however, had also risen to her feet, with an expression of dismay on her round, red face. "Indeed, perhaps I spoke too hasty, your ladyship," she said. "It's true I don't think a bright red would become you, but if you was willing to consider a *dark* red—say, a scarlet or a wine? I've a very nice claret velvet just over from France that might suit you, if you'd like to take a look at it."

"Wine?" said Lora, considering the idea. She had been envisioning something more on the order of crimson, but red was red, after all. Having gained her point so far, she felt she could afford to compromise a little. "I suppose it wouldn't hurt to look at your claret velvet," she said, resuming her chair once more.

Madame hastened to fetch the velvet, and when Lora had surveyed herself swathed in its glowing breadths, she had no hesitation about giving in to Madame's advice.

"Indeed, my lady, you look quite *ravissante* in that color," said Madame, folding the velvet carefully away. "I wouldn't have thought of putting you in claret myself, but now that I've seen you in it, I don't mind saying that it suits you something wonderful. It ought to be a pretty thing when it's made up. Now that we've got that settled, do you want to go ahead and try on some of the dresses you ordered the other day? I think there's at least a couple of them that are ready for fitting."

Lora assented happily and sat down again to await the arrival of the dresses. She felt very pleased and proud of herself for having triumphed in the matter of the red dress. It had been a small victory, perhaps, but for a woman who had never before successfully asserted herself against a superior authority, it seemed a very significant one. She was so elated by her success that when Madame and her assistant presently returned to fit her with the dresses, she was encouraged to assert herself a second time.

"I don't care for the bows on the front of this pelisse," she said, looking down at the offending garment with a critical eye. "They look rather fussy. I believe plain buttons would suit me better. And on the blue ballgown, I would prefer that those flowers around the hem be removed, please. I know it's the fashion, but I don't care for so much trimming on my dresses."

"Very good, my lady," said Madame, with unexpected meekness.

When Lora finally took leave of Madame LeClaire's salon, she took with her a greatly improved opinion of herself. She had often looked with awe and admiration upon Lady Helen, who was never afraid to speak out if a servant or shopkeeper failed to meet her expectations. Now she saw that she, too, might speak out, instead of accepting what was given her in uncomplaining silence. It was not so easy to speak out as to remain silent, of course. Lora had found it very difficult to break the ingrained habits of twenty-six years, but she had done it on this one occasion, and it seemed not unreasonable to hope that with practice it might one day grow easier.

As it happened, she had an opportunity to practice it sooner than she expected: on the very evening of the ridotto, in fact. Lora had stopped by Lady Helen's room on her way upstairs to dress and had found Lady Helen already fully attired in evening wear, desolately surveying herself in the mirror.

"Oh, it's you, Lora," she said. "Just look at me, will you? I look *pregnant.*"

"Well, you are pregnant, you know," said Lora, laughing at her friend's tragic voice. "And it really isn't as noticeable as all that, Helen. Looking at you from behind, I can hardly tell a difference."

"Yes, but you can certainly tell a difference from the front— and even more from the side," said Lady Helen gloomily. "Oh, Lora, I detest being pregnant, absolutely detest it. It's bad enough looking like this, but what's worse is the way everyone treats me. Now that I've started to show, everyone is always hovering around, asking me how I feel. As soon as anyone comes up to me, that's the first words out of their mouth. 'And how are you *feeling*, Helen?' " Lady Helen spoke the words in a saccharine voice and opened her eyes to their widest extent in an imbecilic look of concern. "I *feel* perfectly fine; it's the way I look that makes me nauseous. And then all the old cats insist on telling me horror stories about their own labors, as if I wasn't already nervous enough at the prospect."

Lora, who had laughed heartily at her friend's mimicry, sobered quickly at these words. "Yes, I think it is very inconsiderate of them to do that," she agreed. "But I don't think they realize how upsetting it is to you, Helen. It's only that they like having a chance to talk about their own experiences."

"That may be, but it *is* upsetting, and I wish they'd stop," said Lady Helen, smoothing the folds of her skirt over her abdomen with a vexed air, as though wishing to smooth it away altogether. "If Lady Ashton-Burke tells me one more time how she spent two nights and two days in agonizing pain, I shall hit her over the head with my reticule. Truly, I don't think I can stand it, Lora," she continued, in a voice suddenly serious. "Would you mind very much if we didn't go to the Randolph Rooms this evening? I just do not feel equal to facing it all tonight."

Lora thought of the red gown awaiting her upstairs, and of Adam, who might even then be preparing to depart for the Randolph Rooms. "Of course you shouldn't go if you don't feel like it, Helen," she said stoutly. "Do you need me to stay with you, or would it be all right if I went by myself?"

Lady Helen turned to regard her with astonishment. "Go by yourself?" she repeated. "You don't mean to say you would consider going alone?"

"Not if you need me, certainly. But the fact is—I have made arrangements to meet someone there, and I would not like to disappoint him."

Lady Helen regarded her fixedly for a moment, then turned back to the mirror to adjust a wayward curl. "Who had you arranged to meet there?" she inquired carelessly. "Is it anyone I know?"

"Yes, you met him the other night at the theater. Adam Wainwright." Lora made this statement with great firmness, though inwardly she was quaking. Lady Helen looked at her quickly, started to speak, then checked herself.

"Oh, of course, Mr. Wainwright," she said. "He seemed quite nice, though perhaps a little stiff and punctilious—but of course, it would be difficult for him to be anything else, under the circumstances. Ellsworth was amazingly rude to him, I thought, but no doubt he had his reasons."

"No doubt," agreed Lora.

Lady Helen regarded her a moment longer, then sighed deeply. "I suppose you know what you're doing," she said. "Go on and get dressed for the ridotto, Lora. I'll go with you tonight, but this is the last time I intend to go out in public, absolutely the last time. And before I go, I intend to fill my reticule with shot, so I can brain the first well-meaning busybody who brings up the subject of childbirth!"

Eight

Lora made her toilette carefully but in some haste, fearful that Lady Helen might change her mind yet again and decide not to go to the ridotto after all. When she stopped by her friend's room on the way downstairs, however, she found Lady Helen resigned and ready and just in the act of pulling on her gloves. They were long evening gloves of gold-colored kid, chosen to match the gold trimmings on Lady Helen's black lutestring dress. A helmet-shaped turban of gold tissue ornamented with a black aigrette sat atop her tightly frizzed black curls. Altogether it was a striking costume, though when Lora praised it as such, Lady Helen brushed aside the compliment with a wry smile.

"Black's supposed to be slimming, you know," she said, laying an ironic emphasis on the word "supposed." Having surveyed herself once more in the glass, she shrugged, smiled wryly once more, and turned toward Lora. In doing so, she received for the first time the full effect of Lora's costume. The vision held her speechless for several seconds. "Good heavens," she said weakly. "Quite a departure from your nun's dresses, isn't it?"

"Do you like it?" said Lora nervously. She felt suddenly uncomfortably exposed, although the wine-red gown had not seemed unduly revealing when she had tried it on the previous day in Madame's salon. Tonight, however, she had suffered a few qualms as Annie had buttoned her into it, and Lady

Helen's reaction only made her qualms the greater. Uncertainly, she looked down at herself.

The red velvet gown was cut very low in front and back, fully as low as Lady Helen's own gown though admittedly not any lower. It had the barest possible excuse for sleeves, worn very much off the shoulder. As a means of support they appeared wholly inadequate and indeed could hardly have remained in place had not the body of the gown been so tightly molded to Lora's figure. In style the gown was absolutely plain: no ruffles, no ruching, no trimming of any kind. Lora's maid had dressed her hair as she had worn it the night of the theater party, with a low knot in back and a few loose curls around her face. Long white kid gloves and red satin slippers completed the costume. She wore no jewelry except for her wedding ring, concealed beneath the finger of her glove.

"Yes, of course I like it, you goose. It's gorgeous, even prettier than the one you wore the other night. Only—" Lady Helen considered Lora critically with her head to one side. "I think it would look even better if you wore some jewelry with it, Lora. With so much of your shoulders showing, you need at least a necklace so you don't look so bare."

"Yes, I thought the same thing, but unfortunately my diamonds didn't look right with this color."

"No, they wouldn't, of course. I tell you what, Lora: I shall loan you my garnet necklace and earrings. That ought to be just the touch you need." So saying, Lady Helen hurried into her dressing room to fetch the garnets. After she had fastened them around her friend's neck and in her ears, she stood back to survey her a second time.

"Yes, that's just what you needed. You do look ravishing, Lora. If I didn't know better, I'd almost say you were trying to seduce somebody—"

Her voice broke off suddenly, and she looked at Lora with a startled question in her eyes. Lora could feel the telltale blush mount to her cheeks. Irritably she told herself that she really must rid herself of this foolish trick of blushing like a schoolgirl at every little thing that was said. Then and there she made a resolution to conquer it, along with her other bad habit of passively letting other people run her life.

Aloud she said, "I am *not* trying to seduce anyone," in her firmest voice.

"Of course not," said Lady Helen heartily. She tried Lora's newfound resolution very much, however, by continuing to eye her speculatively all the way downstairs.

Notwithstanding her resolution, Lora was put to the blush a second time when she got downstairs. Lord Spelbourne was there, about to go out to his club for the evening. Having no great fondness for vocal music, he had elected not to attend the ridotto with his wife and Lora. But he commended his wife's costume in high terms and Lora's in even higher, making her tremble for fear he might connect it with their breakfast table conversation of the previous week. She was relieved when at last he took leave of them, and the carriage arrived to take them to the ridotto.

Adam had made his own preparations for the ridotto that evening in a very divided state of mind. At one moment he castigated himself as a fool for voluntarily risking more of the same humiliation he had endured at the theater; at another, he would think of the way Lora had taken his hand and urged him to come to the ridotto. It was hard to refuse a lady, especially a lady so exceptionally lovely and so seemingly in earnest about wanting his company. Adam had made up his mind to go, but he did not cherish any great hopes for the evening ahead. He told himself firmly that if she seemed cool or preoccupied, or if her aristocratic friends tried to patronize him, or if Lord Ellsworth persisted in hanging about as he had the other night, he would merely pay his respects to her and go.

He delayed in dressing and got to the Randolph Rooms rather late, not wishing to arrive before Lora and find himself

alone in a room full of strangers. The first of the featured
musicians were just taking their places on the dais as he entered the concert room. He stood in the doorway with several
other late-arriving gentlemen and looked about the room for
Lora.

It took him some minutes to locate her among the crowd.
When at last he did locate her, he almost failed to recognize
her, for he had been unconsciously expecting her to be wearing
white, as she had done at their two previous meetings. His
attention was first caught by her bare shoulders, creamy white
against the deep red of her dress. He admired her for a full
minute as a perfect stranger before realizing who she was.

It was the sight of Lady Helen sitting beside her that finally
awoke him to her identity. He took another startled look at
her, observed the general resemblance in hair, height, and figure, and sagged weakly against the door frame. "Good Lord,"
he said aloud.

"Terrible squeeze, ain't it?" said the gentleman beside him
sympathetically. "Don't look like there's a hope in heaven of
getting a chair. May as well cut out and head over to Brook's
instead, I'm thinking. Like to come with me, sir? There's room
in my curricle if you care to come along."

Adam declined this generous offer and continued to stand
in the doorway, looking across the room at Lora. She and Lady
Helen were seated at the end of one of the first rows of chairs.
He observed that there was a vacant seat beside her and assumed it must be Lord Spelbourne's, until he saw Lord
Ellsworth making his way purposefully in that direction. Adam
watched the nobleman's progress with a lowering brow. He
told himself that it was no more than he should have expected.
He had been foolish to come, and the sooner he left, the sooner
he might close what had undoubtedly been the most irksome
and exasperating chapter in his life.

So Adam told himself, yet he continued to stand in the doorway, watching as Lord Ellsworth approached Lora. Upon
reaching her side, he addressed some words to her with a

smile, after which he seated himself in the vacant chair beside
her. Adam saw Lora look at Lord Ellsworth, then look quickly
away as though annoyed or embarrassed. When she looked
back, however, her face wore an unusual look of determination,
and she said something to Lord Ellsworth that made that gentleman's confident smile change to a look of astonishment. He
glanced quickly around the room, caught sight of Adam standing in the doorway, and his look of astonishment turned into
a scowl. Rising to his feet again, he made Lora a stiff bow
and stalked off.

There was a look of distress on Lora's face as she looked
after him. Then she, too, caught sight of Adam in the doorway;
and, like Lord Ellsworth, her expression underwent an immediate change. A sunny smile spread over her face. She lifted
one hand and beckoned Adam toward her. He went, hardly
conscious of how he did so. Once he had made his formal
greeting to her and Lady Helen and had had those greetings
cordially returned, Lora touched the empty chair beside her.
"I saved you a place, Adam," she said, and blushed like a girl.

Adam had no remembrance of what he said in reply, but a
moment later he found himself seated at Lora's side, listening
to the opening number of the concert. For the next hour, the
music prevented the two of them from doing more than exchanging smiles and a whispered word or two, but Adam felt
this was probably just as well. Having gone from a state of
deepest despondency to one of highest elation in a matter of
seconds, he needed an interval in which to regain his equilib-
rium.

To Lora, it seemed as though no music had ever sounded
so sweet. She listened to an English soprano, a German tenor,
and an Italian castrato with equal enjoyment, and was quite
unable to enter into Lady Helen's feelings when she compared
the castrato's voice unfavorably to the yowling of cats. When
the intermission came, Lora and Adam went to the refreshment

room together, leaving Lady Helen in conversation with several ladies of her acquaintance. As Lora and Adam were walking away, Lora overheard one of them anxiously inquire of Lady Helen, "And how are you *feeling,* my dear?"

Try as she might, Lora could not stifle a giggle. Adam looked down at her quizzically. "May I know the joke?" he asked.

"Yes, of course, Adam. That was very rude of me, but indeed I couldn't help laughing." Another giggle escaped Lora as she continued, "You see, poor Helen was complaining just before we left the house that everyone is always asking how she feels. She is increasing, you know, and I suppose people do tend to be over-solicitous on that account, though they don't mean any harm by it. But Helen has always disliked being fussed over, and she finds it perfectly intolerable. And as we were leaving just now, I overheard Mrs. Burton asking her, 'How do you feel?'—and I couldn't help laughing. Poor Helen!" Lora laughed again at the remembrance. "I hope Mrs. Burton will be careful about what she says next. Before we left this evening, Helen was saying that she was going to fill her reticule with shot and brain the next woman who told her horror stories about labor and childbirth."

"I can see I will have to be very careful inquiring after Lady Helen's health," said Adam with a smile. "Is the baby due very soon?"

Lora nodded. "Yes, quite soon: at the end of June," she said. "But I am sure it cannot be soon enough for Helen!"

They had reached the refreshment room by now, and Adam helped Lora to cakes and sandwiches and filled a glass of punch for her. They strolled through the rooms as they ate and drank, observing the preparations for the dancing that was to take place after the concert.

"This is really lovely," said Lora, setting down her plate and cup and standing on tiptoe to peer into a small ivy- and flower-covered wishing well that stood at the far end of the ballroom. "How sweet these roses smell."

Adam set down his own plate and cup and reached up to

break off one of the roses that was twined around the roof of the well. "It's just the color of your dress," he said, presenting it to Lora with a smile.

She received it with an answering smile and carefully tucked it into the coils of her hair. This done, she took up what she supposed to be her cup of punch and took a sip. "Good heavens, what's this? Lemonade?" she said, making a face.

"You must have picked up my cup by mistake," said Adam. Gravely he handed her the other cup and took back the one she was holding.

"You prefer lemonade to punch?" said Lora, eyeing him with wonder.

"I don't know that I prefer it, but I thought it better to abstain for this one evening, at least," said Adam, looking rather embarrassed. "What I mean is—I don't want you to think that I habitually overindulge. I am afraid I gave you a bad impression of me that night at the Monroes'."

He spoke so seriously that Lora was both touched and amused. "On the contrary, you made a very good impression on me, Adam," she said. "You can't think I would have invited you to meet me here tonight if I had thought you a habitual drunkard!"

"Well, no. Looking at it that way, I can see that you wouldn't, but I'm afraid my thinking lately hasn't been marked by an excess of clarity. I am very grateful for your good opinion of me, however. And indeed, after this evening, my opinion of myself will be growing by leaps and bounds. Your saving me a seat that way has quite set me up in my own esteem, especially after seeing what hot competition I had for it."

"I suppose you mean Lord Ellsworth," said Lora. She spoke the name collectedly enough, but could not quite keep a blush from rising to her cheeks. "You must not be thinking that I—that I am in the habit of *encouraging* him, Adam. Our acquaintance is really very slight, though he tries to make it out to be more than it is. And Adam—I want to apologize for the way he behaved the other night at the theater. I was extremely vexed about it, I assure you. If I had known he would make such a nuisance of himself, I would have borrowed Helen's trick and provided myself beforehand with a nice heavy reticule!"

Adam laughed. "I can see it behooves a man to tread carefully around you two," he said, taking Lora by the arm and leading her away from the wishing well. "I'll have to take care that I don't go making a nuisance of myself like Lord Ellsworth."

"Oh, no," said Lora seriously. "I am very glad you came to see me tonight, Adam. As I said, I felt so badly about what happened at the theater. I hope you forgive me?"

"There's nothing to forgive," said Adam. He spoke rather huskily, looking down at her upturned face. He was beginning to feel just as he had felt that night in the Monroes' garden. She seemed so sweet, and at the same time so alluring—even more alluring than she had been that evening. Tonight, all of her seemed aglow: her hair, her eyes, even her skin had a new radiance about it, Adam thought, discounting with masculine naiveté the effect of dress and jewels and seeing only the glamour they lent her. His eyes traveled over her admiringly, dwelling on the rich golden coils of her hair; resting on the smooth skin of her bare arms and shoulders; and touching discreetly on the gentle swell of her breast above her décolletage.

Lora regarded him in turn, her expression smiling but uncertain. "Why are you looking at me like that, Adam?" she said.

"Because I would like to kiss you," said Adam honestly.

Her eyes fell for an instant, then raised themselves to his face once more. "Then why don't you?" she said softly.

Adam stole a quick look around the ballroom. There were several other couples wandering about, but none in their immediate vicinity, and a large trellis entwined with roses stood just behind them. Taking Lora by the hand, he drew her behind the trellis, gathered her in his arms, and kissed her.

Lora shut her eyes and abandoned herself to the kiss. It

progressed by degrees from a light, fleeting kiss such as they had exchanged in the garden to something else altogether. Lora had never been kissed thus by any man but the late Lord Carroll and but seldom by him, he having been a man not given to wasting time with preliminaries. She found it strange now to experience such a kiss from another man. Her first impulse was to recoil guiltily, with a sense of having done something wrong or disloyal, but after the first minute or two this sensation began to fade. By the time another minute had gone by, it had passed from her mind completely. Adam's kiss was gentler than Lord Carroll's, but at the same time more insinuating, and when at last he released her, she found herself affected in a way no kiss had ever affected her before.

Adam seemed also to have been affected by the experience. Although he was smiling, his eyes had a feverish brightness about them, and when he spoke his voice was a trifle unsteady. "I suppose we should—ought we to go back to the concert room now?" he said.

"Yes, I suppose so," said Lora. She, too, had difficulty keeping her voice steady. Adam gave her his arm, and together they returned to the concert room.

Lady Helen looked them over narrowly as they resumed their seats, but if she observed anything different in their demeanors, she did not remark upon it. Lora was self-conscious under her friend's gaze, however, and hurried into speech in an effort to distract her.

"I hope you were comfortable while we were gone, Helen," she said. "And that you weren't obliged to hit anyone with your reticule!"

"I came near it once or twice, but I managed to restrain myself," returned Lady Helen. "Fortunately, Lady Ashton-Burke wasn't there to try me too far. Did the two of you manage to get any refreshments? I wish I had thought to ask you to bring me back something to drink."

"I would be more than happy to fetch you something now if you like, Lady Helen," said Adam, rising courteously to his feet. "I don't think the music will start for another few minutes yet. Would you prefer tea, punch, or lemonade?"

"Tea, thank you, Mr. Wainwright," said Lady Helen with a smile. After he had gone, Lora waited apprehensively, supposing Lady Helen would seize this opportunity to address her with her usual embarrassing frankness. Lady Helen's sole observation, however, was, "Your Mr. Wainwright improves on acquaintance, Lora. I like him very well."

This remark put Lora's cheeks in a glow, but she only said, "Yes, so do I," and let the matter rest there.

Adam soon returned with Lady Helen's tea, and a few minutes later the musical program resumed. If the first half of the program had been sheer bliss for Lora, the second half managed to be both bliss and torture at the same time. She could not concentrate on the music, try though she would. All her thoughts were taken up with Adam and the remembrance of that kiss in the ballroom. In remembering it, she felt its effects once more, until it seemed that her whole body cried out to feel his embrace again.

It was a new sensation for Lora, and an uncomfortable one, too. She was acutely aware of Adam sitting beside her, his shoulder brushing hers now and then as he shifted in his chair. She looked at him, seeing him as she had seen him before, lean, attractive, and intelligent; but also seeing him in a new light, as the author of the single most stirring encounter she had ever experienced. It made her feel weak and shaky inside just to look at him.

As though he felt her gaze upon him—almost as though he felt the force of her thoughts—Adam turned his head to look at her. Lora looked quickly away and then, impelled by an irresistible urge, looked back at him again. He regarded her steadily for a moment and then, slowly, casually, let his hand drop down to rest on the edge of her chair. Lora's own hand came out eagerly to meet it. He caught it tightly in his own, and for the rest of the program they sat listening to the music with seemingly perfect decorum, their clasped hands hidden by the folds of Lora's skirt.

The end of the concert was attended by a general movement of the audience in the direction of the ballroom. Lady Helen got to her feet a trifle unsteadily and accepted Adam's other arm for support as he and Lora made their way through the throng.

"I haven't yet had a chance to tell you how well you look this evening," he told Lady Helen, with a hint of a mischievous smile. "No one looking at you could possibly doubt you are in blooming health!"

"Blessed man," said Lady Helen fervently. "For that, I shall dance the first set with you. Don't be angry with me, Lora. I'm doing it for your sake as much as my own, I promise you. The first dance is only a minuet, while the second and third are waltzes, and I daresay, given the choice, you and Mr. Wainwright would prefer to spend your time waltzing rather than wasting it on minuets."

"Blessed woman," said Adam, imitating her tone so exactly that they all laughed. Having carefully established Lora on a bench nearby, he led Lady Helen out onto the floor.

Lora was not left to languish on the bench for long, for a few minutes later she was approached by another gentleman of her acquaintance, who invited her to be his partner for the first and second dances. Lora told him that she would be happy to dance the first with him but was engaged for the second, and the two of them went out to join Adam, Lady Helen, and the hundred or so other people who were taking part in the opening minuet.

The minuet was succeeded by the waltzes, for which Adam claimed Lora as his partner. They danced two waltzes together, and it seemed to both that never had dances flown by so quickly.

"I wish we might dance again," said Adam wistfully, as he

led her off the floor. "Are you sure you cannot give me one more dance? Just one more?"

She debated a moment, then gave him the shy, sweet smile that always struck him with such potent force. "Perhaps just one more," she said. "But it will have to be later in the evening, Adam. I don't dare shock everyone by dancing three dances in a row with the same gentleman."

"Are you engaged for this next set?" inquired Adam, rather jealously. She shook her head, smiling.

"No, and I would really rather not dance any more at present. Perhaps, if you are not engaged yourself, you would not mind taking me to the refreshment room to get another glass of punch?"

"There is nothing I would rather do. No, I take that back: there is *one* thing I would rather do." He shot her a sideways glance. She colored delightfully and looked away, then looked back to address him in a voice so soft that he had to bend low to hear it:

"Well—perhaps we can do that, too."

The refreshment room lay some little distance from the ballroom. It was reached by way of a short corridor that led past the room where the concert had been given. This room was at present quite deserted of company, and since most of the lights had been extinguished after the departure of the guests, it was rather dark as well. Only a single branch of candles burned at the far end of the room near the harp and grand pianoforte. The rows of chairs that a short time before had held bejeweled ladies and gentlemen in severely tailored black-and-white evening dress now stood in vacant disarray, cluttered with discarded concert bills, empty punch glasses, and a shawl that had been left behind by one of the guests.

Lora and Adam passed this room on their way to the refreshment room. They said nothing about it then or later, but both turned their heads to look at it as they passed, and on the way back, as though by unspoken accord, they turned aside and entered its shadowy recesses.

Just inside the concert room, to one side of the doorway, was a wide, shallow alcove hung with a red velvet portière. It had probably been meant to hold a statue, but at the moment it was empty, and it was to this alcove that Adam led Lora. Here, invisible to the people passing to and fro in the hallway outside, he took her in his arms and kissed her.

She made not the slightest pretense of protest. To do so, indeed, would have been hypocrisy after her brazen behavior in the ballroom. Lora had never behaved so in her life, never even envisioned behaving so, but a new and reckless spirit seemed to take possession of her with the first touch of Adam's hand. She wanted nothing but to feel his arms around her and to experience once again the intoxicating pleasure of his kiss. At least, she thought she wanted nothing more, but as the kiss progressed, growing deeper and more intimate, Lora found she did want more. There was within her a growing desire for a different kind of intimacy, a kind of aching hunger that cried out for fulfillment.

It was a moment of revelation for Lora. "Oh, Adam," she said, catching her breath with a little sob. "Oh, Adam!"

"Oh, Lora," he responded, devouring her ear, her neck, and her shoulder with hungry kisses. "Oh, Lora, you are so sweet . . . so sweet, my love."

Lora shivered at the touch of his lips on her shoulder. She pressed herself close against him, and he responded by tightening his arms around her and pressing her even closer. His hands ran up and down her back, becoming bolder as she responded fervently to his caress. They were becoming very bold indeed when a worried voice came suddenly from the doorway beside them.

"I am sure I left it in here, Tom. I know I had it during the concert. We were sitting in this row, I believe—or perhaps it was a row farther down. It's so dark in here, I can't be sure."

Lora and Adam had barely time to draw apart before the

speaker, a young girl, came into the room. She was followed by a young gentleman whose face was nearly obscured by a set of extravagantly high shirt-points. The two of them were both fortunately intent on searching the rows of chairs, so that Lora was able to give a quick smooth to her dress and recover some part of her composure before either of them noticed her or Adam.

"Oh, I beg your pardon," said the girl, catching sight of them first. Her eyes traveled doubtfully from Adam to Lora and back again as she continued, "I just came in to fetch my shawl. I didn't know there was anyone in here—"

"Here it is, Fanny," interrupted the young gentleman, presenting her with the shawl that had been lying abandoned in one of the chairs. "We'd better be getting back to the ballroom now." He gave Adam and Lora a brief, disinterested glance, then took the young girl's arm and led her out of the room. She went obediently, but continued to eye Adam and Lora in a doubtful way until she and her partner had passed through the doorway.

Lora let out her breath in a long sigh, unaware until that moment that she had been holding it. She was sure her complexion must be as red as her dress. Adam, on the contrary, was looking noticeably pale. He caught her by the hand, looking down at her with an expression of agonized contrition.

"Oh, Lora, I'm sorry," he said. "My dear, I am so sorry. That might have been disastrous, and it was all my fault. Can you ever forgive me?"

A soft laugh escaped Lora. Now that the critical moment was past, the knowledge that she and Adam had narrowly escaped disaster merely added an extra spice of excitement to an episode already incredibly exciting. She could feel the quick pulse of her heart and the blood warm in her veins, and her skin still tingled from the remembrance of Adam's touch. Deliberately she moved a step toward him and put her arms around his neck.

"I don't think it was *all* your fault, Adam," she whispered

in his ear. "But you may be sure I will forgive you most readily, if only you will kiss me again."

Drawing a deep breath, Adam complied. They kissed, and
then kissed again, and though the incident of the shawl had
made them somewhat more mindful of their surroundings and
a great deal more alert to the possibility of interruption, this
did not prevent it from being a very absorbing interview. When
the time came that they could no longer put off returning to
the ballroom, they could barely tear themselves apart.

"Oh, Lora, I must see you again," said Adam, very low, as
he took leave of her and Lady Helen later that evening. "May
I call upon you? Soon?"

"Yes, and yes—the sooner, the better. It can't possibly be
soon enough for me. Oh, Adam, how brazen I am, but I don't
care. I can hardly stand to see you go."

"I can hardly stand to go," said Adam with emphasis. "And
if you keep looking at me like that, I don't think I shall be
able to. You must turn your head away—pretend to be busy
studying that nice old gray-haired lady with the Roman nose
over there—and then perhaps I can summon up resolution to
leave. No, I'm serious, my dear. You mustn't look up until I'm
safely out of the ballroom, or like as not I'll be drawn right
back into your coils."

Lora laughed but obeyed these instructions. She did not follow them to the letter, however, for only a second later she
looked up, hoping to catch a last glimpse of Adam before he
left the room. He was standing in the doorway, looking back
at her. When he saw her looking, too, he mimed a look of
extreme horror, put his hand over his eyes, and fled the ballroom as though pursued by furies, to the wonderment of those
around him.

Nine

In after days, Lora was accustomed to look back on the night of the ridotto as a turning point in her life. The events of that night served to crystalize her feelings not only about Adam, but about several other important issues as well.

Ever since she had met Adam at the Monroes', she had felt a strong attraction toward him. It was that attraction which had led her to exchange kisses with him that very first night and which had made her so anxious about the niceties of her appearance at their subsequent meetings. In the beginning she had tried to discount the attraction she felt toward him, telling herself that he was merely a very pleasant gentleman whose company she enjoyed, but after the night of the ridotto she could keep up such a pretense no longer. What she felt for him clearly went beyond a desire for enjoyable companionship, though paradoxically it had some element of that in it, too. But there was also in her feelings toward him a very different desire—a desire strong and unmistakably physical.

This had been amply demonstrated on the night of the ridotto, and on subsequent nights, too. For from that night on, Lora found her dreams taking on an increasingly erotic character, as though those illicit kisses in the concert room had awakened a part of her that had lain dormant up till then. On occasion these dreams were accompanied by physical manifestations very embarrassing to the modest and ladylike Lora. Having existed twenty-six years without being much troubled by this kind of thing, she found it disconcerting to be beginning now. But there was enlightenment to be gained, even from this unlikely source, and she began to understand as she had never understood before the cause of some of the difficulties she had experienced in her relations with Lord Carroll. She felt reasonably certain that she would not experience those same difficulties with Adam as her lover.

For Lora had determined by this time to make Adam her lover, if he were willing, and for all her natural modesty she entertained little doubt that he *would* be willing when the time came. During those heady, stolen moments in the deserted concert room, it had been very evident that he was feeling what she felt, wanting what she wanted; it was that as much as anything that had made the whole episode so exciting. Since then, with a half-fearful interest, she had begun to reflect more and more upon Lady Helen's suggestion about taking a lover, and somehow, in a matter of a few days, it had gone from being an inconceivable idea to a very real and appealing possibility.

This change in feeling, naturally enough, had not come about without a great deal of soul-searching. Lora's birth had been relatively humble and her upbringing strongly moral, two circumstances that made the step she was considering seem far more momentous than it would have seemed to the aristocratic Lady Helen. Among such country gentry as her parents, it would have been a step to put her forever beyond the pale of decent society.

In London, of course, such things were regarded with a more tolerant eye. But Lora's early training had left its mark on her, as early training generally will, and she felt faint when she envisioned her parents' reaction, should they learn of this latest turn to their daughter's career. It was almost enough to dissuade her from taking the fatal step—almost, but not quite. For when she thought of Adam, such considerations faded into the background, and she felt she would be willing to endure even exile from her home and family for his sake.

In the week following the ridotto, Adam had come to call

upon her twice at Spelbourne House. He had also met her once at the opera, where Lora had been occupying the Spelbourne box, together with Lord Spelbourne.

Lady Helen had been absent on this occasion, for no amount of argument could persuade her to appear in public until after the completion of her pregnancy. She had been very insistent that her friend attend the performance in spite of her absence, however, and of course Lora was not loath to do so, seeing that Adam would also be present. Present he was, and early, too: Lora was still settling her skirts around her, unfurling her fan, and making all the other little preparations necessary for the evening's enjoyment when he walked into the box.

At the sight of him, her enjoyment was secure. She watched him advance across the box, wondering once again what there was about this man that made her heart beat faster every time she so much as set eyes on him.

Lord Spelbourne greeted Adam with his usual unaffected good-nature. "Evening, Wainwright; how'd-ye-do?" he said with a cheerful nod. "Come to suffer along with the rest of us, have you?"

"Lord Spelbourne is joking," said Lora, seeing that Adam looked somewhat doubtful how to respond to this form of address. "I'm afraid he doesn't much care for operatic music. I am the more obliged to him that he agreed to accompany me here this evening."

"Oh, I don't mind taking in an opera every now and then," said Lord Spelbourne in a large-minded way. "It's true I don't care much for hearing people sing away in Italian, or German, or some other dashed language I don't know a word of, but apart from that, I like opera pretty well."

"Indeed," said Adam gravely. "The same disadvantages have often struck me when attending the opera, my lord. We shall have to ask Lady Carroll to translate the songs for us." Turning to Lora, he bestowed upon her a formal bow, accompanied by a slow, warm smile that caused an answering warmth to suffuse her being. "Good evening, Lora. I hope I find you well?" was all he said, but his manner of saying it made it seem the most intimate of addresses.

"You find me very well—now," said Lora, returning his smile. "Won't you sit and keep us company for a while, Adam? The performance won't begin for some time yet."

"Aye, plenty of room to spare," said Lord Spelbourne, waving toward the half-dozen empty seats within the box. "Helen wasn't up to coming tonight, so it's just Lora and I, rattling around in here like a pair of peas in a post-chaise."

Adam bowed his thanks and took a seat beside Lora. Again she smiled at him, but any hopes she might have had of conversing with him in private were foiled by Lord Spelbourne, who appeared to be in an unusually loquacious mood that evening.

"Didn't happen to attend the last sale-day at Tatt's, did you, Wainwright?" he asked, leaning back in his chair to address Adam behind Lora's back. "Fine lot of prads on the block this time around. Not that I need any more horses, but there was a nice-looking pair of blacks there that I wouldn't have minded bidding on. Came from your part of the country, as it happened: a place down in Hampshire, it was. Tommy Everett ended up buying them, but I'm dashed if I don't have half a mind to make him a counter-offer, and see if he'll sell."

"A pair of blacks—and from Hampshire, you say?" There was a curious, half-amused expression on Adam's face as he looked at Lord Spelbourne. "The name of the seller wasn't Hinksley by any chance, was it?"

"I couldn't swear as to that, but it might have been Hinksley. Came from down in Hampshire, that I do remember. Do you know this Hinksley fellow?"

Adam coughed slightly. "Well, yes, my lord: it happens that I do. Hinksley lives in the village next to mine, and I've had some dealings with him in the past. If you do decide to buy those horses, my lord, I'd advise you to look them over pretty closely before you make an offer. The horses *may* be all right— but then again, they may be the pair he was driving the last

time he was in Farleigh. A beautiful pair of blacks, as I recall:
fast-paced and well-matched. But I do remember hearing him
complain that the near horse had a tiresome tendency to throw
off a splint."

"He said that, did he?" Lord Spelbourne's normally vacuous
face wore an unusually wide-awake expression as he regarded
Adam. "I'm much obliged to you for the tip, Wainwright. My
groom didn't like the look of the near horse, now I think of
it, but I was that taken, I wouldn't hear a word against 'em."

While Lord Spelbourne was speaking, the orchestra in the
pit had begun to emit numerous tuneful squeakings and scrap-
ings, preparatory to launching into the overture. Observing
this, Adam sought to excuse himself to Lora and Lord Spelbourne, but the two of them were so loud against the idea of
his leaving that he consented to stay in the Spelbourne box
during the opera's first act.

Although this was a matter of some satisfaction to Lora, it
was not so much as it might have been under different circumstances. Lord Spelbourne was still intent on absorbing all
Adam's attention to himself and did so with a complete disregard for what that gentleman's preferences might have been,
not to mention the preferences of Lora and of those opera-go-
ers around them who had come to hear the music and were
forced instead to hear a lengthy discourse on horseflesh.

When the first act was over, several other visitors presented
themselves in the Spelbourne box. This fortunately served to
divert Lord Spelbourne's attention from Adam, so that Adam
was able to exchange a few words with Lora in an undertone.

"Well, at least I've had a chance to *look* at you this evening,
even if I haven't had much chance to talk to you," he told her,
with a sparkle of laughter in his eyes. "And I can say with
full assurance that you look very lovely. So lovely, in fact, that
I wish I could stay and look at you longer, but I've already
used John abominably, abandoning him all this while. It will
take the rest of the evening to make it up to him, I'm afraid."

Lora nodded resignedly. "I was afraid you would have to

be going," she said. "Really, I could be quite vexed with Lord Spelbourne if I let myself! But of course he meant no harm, and perhaps next time we see each other, we will have a chance to do more than just look at each other."

"I hope we will," said Adam, in such a meaningful voice that she blushed. He laughed and took her hand in his. "I look forward to our next meeting, but I'm afraid it can't take place so soon as I would like, Lora. I find I must return home this next week to attend to some business about my farm."

"Oh, Adam! Will you be away long?"

"Not any longer than I must. A week at least: perhaps two at the outside. You may be sure I will be back as soon as I can, Lora." Adam's expression was serious now as he looked into her eyes. "I hate like the deuce to leave just now, but my affairs won't run themselves without assistance, worse luck. You do understand?"

"Of course I understand, Adam," she assured him warmly. He smiled then, kissed her hand, and took leave of her with another earnest promise to return as soon as his business was complete.

Although perfectly sympathizing with the necessity that called Adam away from London, Lora was nonetheless sorry to see him go. Life lost all its zest; London became a howling desert; and the weeks ahead seemed to yawn blankly with no hope of profit or diversion.

On reflection, however, she decided a week or two away from him might not be altogether a bad thing. It would give her time to take stock of her feelings and decide if she were really prepared to go through with the step she was contemplating. But she missed him so much within the first twenty-four hours of his leaving that her soul-searchings were soon at an end, and she devoted the remaining time of his absence to considering when and where their critical next meeting might best take place.

* * *

Adam, too, was going through a period of soul-searching about this time. Having taken leave of Lora at the opera, he had returned to his seat beside Mr. Lloyd and had spent the rest of the evening being rallied in a rather heavy-handed way about his growing predilection for the company of the nobility. The next morning, he had risen early, seen to the packing of his bags, and taken a punctilious leave of Mr. Lloyd, who had also risen early to see him off.

"I don't know how long this business with Evans is likely to take, but I shouldn't think more than a week or two," Adam said. "Once I get that settled, and see how the wheat and clover are coming along, I expect I'll be coming up to London again."

"You've spent a deal of time in London this spring," observed Mr. Lloyd. "When I first invited you up here, I remember you saying you could only spare me a couple of weeks."

His voice was perfectly matter-of-fact, but there was a certain tone to it that put Adam on the defensive. "Yes, I know I have stayed a little longer than I planned, John. But there's no harm in taking a holiday from work now and then, is there? At any rate, if I'm inconveniencing you by staying here, I can easily put up at a hotel when I come back to Town—"

"Don't be an ass," said Mr. Lloyd amiably. "You know you're more than welcome to stay here whenever you're in Town, Adam. It's no inconvenience to me, and considering the way you've been behaving lately, I'd rather have you where I can keep an eye on you. It's a question to me whether you're safe out on your own anymore."

"If you're referring to what happened the other day on Bond Street—"

"Yes, I am, and just the thought of it's enough to send me into a full-blown fit of the spasms. Any man who can miss seeing a fully-loaded dray-wagon bearing down on him is about fit for a strait-waistcoat, in my opinion."

Adam laughed and colored slightly. "I thought I saw Lady Carroll, in a carriage across the street," he said.

"Yes, Lady Carroll," said Mr. Lloyd. He paused a moment, then went on with an awkward attempt at delicacy. "You and she have been pretty thick lately, haven't you, old man? Mean to say, her letting you sit with her half the night at the opera last night looked pretty particular."

He paused again to look at Adam, who made no response. Clearing his throat, Mr. Lloyd went on, with would-be jocularity. "I've always felt you were up to anything, old man, but I never expected to see you hobnobbing with marquesses and countesses the way you've been doing lately."

Adam smiled ruefully and rubbed the back of his neck with his hand. "Truth to tell, I never expected I'd see it myself, John," he said. "There've been times these last few weeks when I wondered if I might not be dreaming it all. Perhaps that's why I've seemed so oblivious to my surroundings!"

Mr. Lloyd's response to this was an skeptical snort. "No need to go humbugging *me,* old man," he said, in his usual acerbic tone. "We agreed a long time ago that the symptoms were unmistakable!"

"I suppose they are." Adam glanced at his friend, then glanced away. "I'm afraid I haven't been much company to you this visit, John," he said, rather diffidently. "It's been good of you to put up with me and my vagaries."

Mr. Lloyd, looking embarrassed, recommended him once more not to be an ass. "No need to apologize, old man. It's the sort of thing that might happen to anybody, I suppose."

"I suppose so," said Adam. Smiling faintly, he looked down at Mr. Lloyd's troubled face. "You think I'm nine parts a fool, don't you, John?"

"Oh, not so much as that," said Mr. Lloyd judiciously. "I've known you a long time, Adam, and I've never yet seen you played for *point non plus* in any game that was going. At the same time, though, I'm obliged to say that I've never seen you harrowed up by anything as you have by this business. If you asked me, I'd say your best course would be to go back to Hampshire and stay there till you're over it—but of course, I know I'm wasting my breath to tell you that."

"Yes," agreed Adam.

Mr. Lloyd sighed and shook his head, but ended up grinning reluctantly.

"Well, then, I'll look to see you again in another week or two, old man," he told Adam. "I'll tell my landlady to have your room ready for you. Of course, if you should receive an invitation to stay at Carlton House in the meantime, I'll expect you to notify me of your change in plans!"

Adam laughed. "I'll do that, John," he said, and parted from his friend with a frank and amicable handshake.

Adam's groom Sam was waiting for him with his phaeton outside. It was a beautiful morning, cool and clear, with dew sparkling on such patches of verdure as might be glimpsed amid London's grey and often squalid streets. As always, Adam was glad to leave the city and its suburbs behind. Yet, though he welcomed the sight of the countryside with its hills and hedges, ponds and pastures, he had never left London with so unwilling a spirit as he did now. If duty had not been calling him with such a clear voice, he felt he could hardly have wrenched himself away.

The rattle of the wheels and steady clip-clop of the horses' hooves made a background for his thoughts as he drove along the road. With swelling heart, he thought of Lora and of how she had looked and spoken the previous evening; then, as was usual, his thoughts strayed further back, to recall that momentous evening at the Randolph Rooms. This occupied him very pleasantly for a considerable time. So sunk was he in thought that it startled him not a little when Sam spoke up from the seat beside him.

"Begging your pardon, sir, but I'm thinking that's our turn right there," said Sam respectfully.

"What? Oh, yes, thank you, Sam," said Adam, and gave his attention to making the necessary turn. Sam said nothing more, but Adam was conscious now of the groom's curious scrutiny and felt obliged to address to him some further remark.

"That's what comes of staying so long in London, Sam," he said, shaking his head with mock chagrin. "I seem to have forgotten the way home!"

"Aye, you've been a fair while in London," agreed Sam in a reserved voice.

Adam cast a smiling glance at him. "Not homesick, are you, Sam?" he asked. "I would have thought there was enough in London to keep a foot-loose young bachelor like you fairly well occupied. Mr. Lloyd was telling me yesterday that his landlady's maid has quite lost her heart to you and is already wearing the willow at the prospect of your leaving."

Sam sniffed. "That forward piece? If she is, I'll lay odds she won't wear it for long. The first time something in trousers winks at her, she'll be up and chasing after it as hard as she can run, with no more thought for me than if I was yesterday's street-sweepings. Take 'em all in all, I don't have much opinion of London serving-girls," he went on, crossing his arms over his chest and preparing to deliver himself of a full disquisition on the subject. "A parcel of lazy, scheming good-for-naughts they are, and the men not much better. That valet of Mr. Lloyd's is the most worthless creature I've seen in my life. And his groom is near as bad. If he spends half the time on Mr. L.'s prads as I do on yours, sir, it's more than I know."

"Not everyone is fortunate enough to possess servants as conscientious as you, Sam," said Adam, smiling.

"It don't suit me to be idle," said Sam simply. "I'll be glad to get back home, sir, and that's the truth. Make-work's a wearisome business when all's said and done."

"Yes," said Adam hesitantly, "yes, I'm not sure idleness suits me, either. It seems an odd, futile kind of life that most of these society people lead, going the rounds of balls and parties night after night and making a business out of pleasure.

And yet, I'm bound to say I've had a very enjoyable time these last few weeks." His voice softened a little, and a smile came to his lips as he reflected upon she who had been the cause of his enjoyment. "So enjoyable, in fact, that I'm planning to go up again in another week or two, once I've got my affairs at home halfway settled."

"Ah," said Sam. He spoke non-committally, but Adam fancied there was comprehension in his voice, and also a touch of disapproval.

"I know it's not the best time of year to be away from the farm, Sam, but I have already pledged myself to return," he said defensively. "Mr. Lloyd expects me—and one or two other people as well. It would be unconscionable to disappoint them. Besides, there are several social engagements that I've already committed to that I can't very well get out of. I don't plan to make a long stay of it, but then, I didn't plan to stay as long this time as I ended up doing," he added, with a smile he sought to make easy but feared was only lame. "At this stage, everything is rather . . . indefinite."

"Ah," said Sam again. "Well, no doubt you know your own business best, sir."

This sounded so much like a snub that Adam made no further efforts to justify himself, but instead wrapped himself in a dignified and injured silence. He also took care to pay greater heed to the signposts thereafter, so that the remainder of the drive was accomplished without mishap.

There was plenty at Highleigh House to keep Adam busy during the next few days. He had to meet with Mr. Owen, a Welsh cattle-breeder seeking an arrangement by which his animals might be fattened in the fields of Highleigh House before making their final journey to the London market. When the details of this arrangement had been satisfactorily hammered out, Adam had then to deal with the hundred and one small difficulties that had arisen about the farm during his stay in

London. Most of them were such very small difficulties that Adam could not help being annoyed that they had not been handled in his absence, but he did his best to deal with them patiently.

"And then, sir, there's that matter of the hedge in the south pasture," said Will Masters, looking at Adam anxiously. He was a slow, careful man, the most senior of the farming men, conscientious to a fault but possessing the annoying habit of clearing his throat after every other utterance. He and Adam had been closeted together for over an hour, going over various matters appertaining to the crops and livestock. "There's a gap three foot wide, sir, where the cattle've been pushing their way through." Will cleared his throat once more and folded his large, gnarled hands across his knee as he continued, "It's been that way nigh on three weeks, and the beasts straying through every time our backs are turned, seemingly. They got into Stubbs's cornfield t'other day and caused a rare to-do. And I was wondering, sir, what you wanted done about it."

"Why, I want it fixed, of course," said Adam, with what he felt to be pardonable exasperation. "It ought to have been fixed as soon as it was noticed. You don't need me to tell you that, Masters."

"No, sir, but, seeing as you was coming back so soon—leastways, we *thought* you was coming back at the first of May or thereabouts, like you said when you left." Masters paused to clear his throat. "And then when you didn't, we naturally supposed another day or two'd see you home and we could ask you then. None of us liked to take the liberty, sir, not knowing what your wishes might be in the matter."

"You might have known I would not wish for my cattle to be straying into Stubbs's cornfield on a daily basis!"

"Oh, aye, sir, but we didn't know whether you wanted the hedge fixed permanent-like, with another tree planted, or only fixed with stakes and brush like we did in the seven-acre field."

"Oh . . . well, I suppose another tree ought to be planted,

but it wouldn't hurt to stake it, too, until there's enough growth to fill in the gap. You see to it tomorrow, Masters, and I'll pay a call on Stubbs and make it right with him about the damage to his corn. Is that all you needed to see me about?"

"Well, no, sir." Masters cleared his throat. "There's also the matter of that big elm near the long barn. That ought to come down, sir, before the next storm brings it down and does a deal of damage."

"Then bring it down," said Adam, with thinly-disguised impatience. "Anything else?"

"Well, Simms was wondering whether you wanted the south field put down to turnips, once the wheat-shearing's done with. But I doubt not he'll ask you himself as to that, so there's no use my mentioning it." Once more Masters cleared his throat. "I don't know that I've aught else to ask you, sir, except if you was planning to stay here about the farm for the next week or so. Sam did say you was thinking of going up to London again. . . ."

"Yes. Yes, I must go back quite soon, I'm afraid. But I'll do my best to go over all the business that's pending before I go, so you won't be held up by my absence."

"That'd be kind of you, sir. We do find it awkward to get on without you, and no mistake." Though there was nothing reproachful in Masters's tone, Adam nevertheless felt reproached, both by his words and by the steady, mild gaze that was fixed on his face. "You've spent a deal of time in London this spring, sir, seemingly. I don't recall you ever being gone so long as this before."

"No, nor ever shall again, likely," said Adam, as lightly as he could. "Very well, Masters. I'll speak to Simms about the south field, and to Stubbs about his cornfield. And I'll trust you to see to mending the hedge and bringing down that elm by the long barn."

After Masters had left, Adam remained in his study for some minutes longer, not perusing any of the papers that lay on the desk in front of him but looking unseeingly out the window

at the neat hedge-bordered fields that lay beyond the garden and shrubbery. At last he roused himself and left the study, shutting the door quietly behind him. As he passed through the corridor on his way to the back door, he heard within the kitchen the sound of female voices engaged in low-toned confabulation.

"You'll find there's a young lady in it somehow," said one of the voices, which Adam recognized as that of his cook. "I've lived long enough to know the signs. You mark my words, Rose, we'll be having a mistress to rule over us one of these fine days, and then you'd best look sharp to your dusting, my girl. What passes in a single gentleman's house won't do for when there's a lady about."

Here another voice intervened, apparently that of Rose. Its general tone seemed to be one of protest, although it was pitched too low for Adam to distinguish the words.

"Nonsense," was the cook's robust reply. "I tell you, I know the signs. He hasn't hardly touched his victuals all this last week, morning or night. When a gentleman's off his feed, you can be sure 'tis love or business that's troubling him, and I shouldn't think 'twas business—though to be sure, the poor gentleman's like to ruin hisself if he goes on as he's doing. Sam tells me he's set on haring off to London again as soon as ever he can. I'll wager Sam could tell us all about it if he would, but he's that close-mouthed, there's no getting a word out of him."

Adam paused in mid-step and listened to hear what might be the reply to this interesting speech. Unfortunately, that section of corridor upon which he paused happened to contain a loose floorboard, which squeaked loudly beneath his boots.

"Hist! I'll wager that's him now," warned a third voice, recognizable to Adam as that of his junior housemaid. There was a rustle and a clatter of tea-cups being hastily set down and chairs pushed away from the table. The sound was followed a moment later by the cook's voice, upraised in a loud and artificially cheerful accents.

"Now, Rose, it's time you was finishing up your tea and getting back to your dusting, my girl. And Rachel, you'd best be nipping around to Mr. Wainwright's study and seeing if he's done in there, for you can be sure the room wants sweeping now that Masters has been and gone. He always brings half the muck of the barnyard in with him, no matter how often I remind him to wipe his feet."

With the words of his servants to spur him on, Adam passed the rest of that day in a frenzy of activity. He was equally industrious in the days that followed, attempting to set his affairs in such order that he could conscientiously afford to leave them for another few weeks. This was not easily accomplished, nor indeed was it capable of accomplishment as judged by any very rigorous standard. It was too obvious that his presence had been missed even in the short time he had already been gone. But from all evidence of neglect or mismanagement he resolutely turned his face, holding firm to his plan to return to London within two weeks at the latest.

It was on the last day of his stay in Hampshire that he had occasion to visit a grain-dealer whose establishment lay across the border in the neighboring county of Wiltshire. Adam's business there was concluded early, and as he remounted his phaeton to begin the journey home, it occurred to him that he was within a dozen miles of Carrollton, the historic seat of the Earls of Carroll and Lora's former home. Some morbid urge, akin to self-flagellation, prompted him to turn his horses' heads in that direction.

He had been once before to Carrollton when he had been a boy, and then again later when he had been a self-important youth just down from Harrow. What had impressed him most about the place on both visits was the sheer size of the property, much of it wooded parkland with game in abundance and several streams that to his boyish eye had held promise of excellent fishing.

The park was still impressive as ever, but this time Adam's chief interest lay in the house itself. He followed the long drive as it curved through the woods and over the streams until, rounding a final stand of stately oaks, he found himself confronted by Carrollton.

It lay across a long slope of green lawn studded here and there with clusters of trees and shrubbery. The effect was so striking that it was clear nature alone could not have been responsible for its arrangement, yet so skillful had man's assistance been that the whole landscape presented a most natural-seeming beauty.

The house that was set in its midst was classical in style and ambitious in scope, a long facade of pillars and pilasters against a front of pale gold stone. Although three full stories in height, the building appeared low owing to its immense length. To Adam's fancy, it seemed to stretch on and on for miles, broken only by the glass of its innumerable windows and the regular rhythm of pillar and pilaster.

For a good ten minutes he sat regarding it all, while his horses peacefully cropped the grass alongside the drive and his groom sat silent and impassive in the phaeton beside him. At last, Adam took up the reins once more, flicked his whip across the horses' backs, and returned the way he had come.

He drove straight home without pausing for rest or refreshment. Once there, Sam took charge of the horses and phaeton while he stood for a moment, looking up at the house in which he had been born and which he had always regarded with a strong though unspoken pride. The contrast between it and the gold stone palace he had viewed earlier that afternoon struck him as almost laughable, though he felt little enough inclination for laughter at that moment. He entered the house and walked through its rooms, silently comparing them in his mind with the echoing halls and lofty galleries that he remembered from his earlier visits to Carrollton.

As he was completing his tour and coming back down the stairs, he encountered one of the housemaids industriously anointing the banister railings with Italian polish. "Good day, sir," she said, curtsying, but in her glance he read a curiosity that reminded him of the conversation he had overheard earlier. It galled him, as did the sense of inferiority that had been with him since returning from Carrollton to his own modest establishment. Then suddenly he saw the humor of the situation, and a rueful smile twitched his lips.

"Good day, Rose," he said. "When you're done with the dusting, would you please see to packing my bags? I shall be making another trip up to London tomorrow."

Rose curtsied again. "Yes, sir. Certainly, sir," she said with alacrity. Adam gave her a pleasant nod, then continued down the stairs and into his study, closing the door behind him.

"She knows what I am," he said aloud. "I never made any attempt to conceal it from her, so if she continues to see me, it can only be because she really doesn't mind—or, of course, because she simply doesn't care. What a world of difference a word makes! I wish I knew which it was. I suppose I could always demand to know her intentions."

Once more a rueful smile curved his lips. "Perhaps I will. At any rate, it shouldn't be necessary to tell her how *I* feel. I have it on good authority that my feelings in the matter are sufficiently obvious!"

Ten

Lora obtained early tidings of Adam's arrival back in town from Lord Spelbourne, who observed him driving his phaeton toward Mr. Lloyd's residence in Abingdon Street.

"A nice fellow, that," said Lord Spelbourne, who had continued to be grateful to Adam for his hint regarding the Hinksley horses. "I almost stopped and said 'How-d'ye-do,' but I was in a dashed hurry to get to Meyer. What do you think of this coat, Lora? I've been going to Weston so long that I was a little leery about going anywhere else, but on the whole I think Meyer's work has more of a dash to it."

Lora said all that was proper, but at her first opportunity she excused herself to Lord Spelbourne and went to her bedchamber to write a note to Adam. This in itself was a daring act, for gentlewomen did not commonly write letters to unmarried gentlemen, at least not without the excuse of a preexisting engagement. But the writing of a simple note seemed such a minor infringement of society's rules compared to the one she was about to commit, that Lora had no qualms.

"Lord S. tells me you have just arrived back in Town," she wrote. "I hope you will call upon me at your *earliest convenience*. I have missed you very much and look forward to seeing you again."

Here Lora began to fear she sounded over-eager and started to score out the words beginning with "very much." But in the end she let them stand and continued on.

"I do not know if you have any engagement for this coming

Saturday," she wrote. "If you have not, I wish you would consider attending the Rawlings's masquerade. I shall be there early and hope I may see you there, too."

Lora hesitated a little over the closing of this epistle. Finally she wrote, "Yours, L," folded the note hastily, and sealed it with an impress of pink sealing wax.

"I shall have to buy some new wax," she told herself, as she carried the note downstairs. "Pink is such a childish color. I wish I had thought to borrow some of Helen's. I need a new seal, too. Doves and flowers may be suitable for a young girl, but not for a grown woman."

After entrusting the note to one of Lady Helen's footmen along with instructions for its delivery—and having in the process blushed very much and given that worthy no less than half a crown for his trouble—she went back upstairs to contemplate the step she had taken.

In choosing the Rawlings' masquerade as the site for her rendezvous with Adam, Lora had been influenced by several considerations. One was the simple matter of finding an entertainment to which Adam might gain admission. This was not so difficult as it would have been a few weeks ago, for Adam had been long enough now in London to be receiving invitations in his own name. A bachelor of decent birth and good appearance might be assured of finding all but the most exclusive doors of London society open to him, particularly a bachelor seen in the company of such ladies as the Dowager Lady Carroll ("whom many will recall as the former Miss Darlington: a lady celebrated as much for her beauty as for her exquisite taste in dress," ran one especially fulsome social correspondent) and the dashing Lady Helen Spelbourne (who, the gossips whispered, had taken to the floor with him to dance the minuet when she lacked but two months to her *accouchement*—some said but one month).

Lora might then be reasonably sure that Adam would have received an invitation to the Rawlings' masquerade. She was the more sure because the entertainment in question was to be such an enormous affair—it was rumored that more than five hundred cards of invitation had been sent out—and because the Rawlings' parties were notoriously heterogeneous gatherings. Sir Hubert Rawlings had made a fortune among the collieries of Newcastle, a circumstance which ill-mannered persons held to be the explanation for the knighthood that had recently been bestowed upon him. Whatever the truth of this, the newly created Sir Hubert had promptly disposed of his collieries, purchased a vast estate on the outskirts of London, and settled down with his lady to entertain in a large way.

Lora knew Sir Hubert and his wife only by sight and had never attended any of their parties. Lady Helen considered the Rawlings to be mushrooms of the most flagrant sort and had curtly declined all previous invitations that had come her way. But Lora had heard stories about the magnificence of Rawlings Court and had long cherished a secret desire to see the place. It was rumored to be a huge pseudo-Gothic manor surrounded by gardens that rivaled those of Vauxhall in size and scope: a nearly perfect place for a lovers' assignation. So Lora thought, at all events. It seemed to her almost fateful that a gathering so well suited to her purposes should have come along at that particular time. In such a place, among such a crowd, she and Adam might meet in perfect anonymity.

Lora did not allow herself to dwell on the details of that meeting. She was content to arrange matters up to that point and then allow nature to take its course. It was hypocrisy, perhaps. Lora told herself it was cowardice and tried hard to struggle against it, but her newly acquired resolution could not carry her quite that far. Her mind preferred the comforting illusion that as long as she did not openly acknowledge what she was doing, she was really not responsible for her actions.

She continued to cling to this illusion even while she made blatant preparations for seduction. The costume she had ordered the week before, on the chance that Adam might return to Town in time to attend the masquerade with her, was one such preparation. It was a costume which she herself had designed. Madame had accepted her carefully detailed instructions without disputing a single word, and when Lora went back that afternoon for the final fitting, Madame cut short a consultation with a lady of great importance in order to attend to her personally.

"It's an honor to serve you, my lady," said the modiste, as her skillful fingers put the last touches on Lora's costume. "I knew the minute I laid eyes on you that you'd be the making of me, and you have been, my lady—yes, indeed you have. From the day I sold you that white gown, my business started picking up, and it's never slowed down since. It's gotten to the point now that I've had to hire two more girls just to keep up with all the orders I've got in hand. My name's made, and I owe it all to you, my lady. I can't say how grateful I am."

"I should say you owed it more to your own exertions," said Lora, almost equally amazed and amused by this speech. "I have really done very little, I assure you."

Madame shook her head, smiling. "My work's well enough in its way, that I don't deny. But in this business, the best work in the world may go for naught if it's not seen in the right places. It was you who got my work seen where it would do most good, and I'm grateful to you."

With inward amusement but outward solemnity, Lora once again modestly disclaimed any share in Madame's success. "I'm sure, Madame, that if anyone besides yourself was instrumental in your success, it must have been Lady Helen."

"Aye, it was she who gave me my start, so to speak," said Madame with a nod. "I'm grateful to her for that, and it's a pleasure to have the dressing of such a striking-looking lady, but at the same time I'm bound to say that what suits her wouldn't suit most ladies. It wasn't until you came along that I started getting orders from Lady Irwin and Mrs. Blythe-Davies and half-a-dozen others I could name. You've got the face and figure to set off a dress proper, my lady, and a very good taste in what suits you. I was misled, to begin with, by your being dressed so plain, but I don't mind saying now that

I'd trust your taste as soon as my own." Having disposed of her pins and her praises at the same moment, Madame got to her feet, dusting her hands off. "Will you wait for this, my lady, or shall I have it sent to my Lady Helen's with the others? *Très bien*, my lady. One of my girls will finish it up in two shakes and pack it up for you to take with you."

The bandbox containing the finished costume was presently turned over to Lora, who in turn entrusted it to one of Lady Helen's footmen, who saw it carried to Lora's bedchamber when the carriage arrived back at Spelbourne House. Lora breathed a sigh of relief when at last the costume was safely stowed away behind the doors of her wardrobe. It was unlikely that Lady Helen would have remarked upon one bandbox more or less, or demanded to know its contents if she had, but the whole subject of the masquerade had assumed such immense proportions in Lora's mind that even the smallest detail connected with it seemed imbued with a strong clandestine flavor.

As it happened, Lady Helen had been engaged in clandestine activities of her own that afternoon. "I went for a walk," she told Lora defiantly, when the two were closeted alone in the drawing room after dinner. "I took the closed carriage and went to the Green Park, where nobody knew me. And I had a very nice walk, and it didn't hurt me a bit, so there's no use fussing about it now."

"I don't mean to fuss, Helen, but I do wish you had told me you were going out. Or Arthur—you know either of us would have been happy to go with you if you had asked," said Lora, striving for a non-accusatory tone. Lady Helen's solitary rambles were in fact a matter of great concern to Lord Spelbourne, who had begged Lora to use her influence to try to curtail them. Lora had been doing her best, but though she had gained considerable self-command in the past few weeks, she was still far from comfortable in the role of commanding others, particularly when those others were as stubborn and self-willed as Lady Helen. On the last occasion she had accompanied her friend to the park, she had been able to do no more than steer her toward those paths least likely to exhaust her and to plead fatigue herself when she thought Lady Helen had walked as much as was good for her.

That these strategies were transparent to Lady Helen was evident now from that lady's sardonic smile. "Well, I *would* have invited you or Arthur to accompany me, but the two of you seem to tire so quickly nowadays. I generally prefer to walk further than a quarter of a mile when I go out walking, and to move a little faster than the snail's pace you two have been affecting lately."

"Oh, Helen, do you think you should?" said Lora, abandoning pretense and addressing her friend with open concern. "You know the doctor said you ought not to take strenuous exercise in your condition."

"Yes, and I can see the sense in not riding, or sea-bathing, or doing things of that sort. But I can see no harm in taking a walk now and then, so long as I feel as well as I do. I simply cannot endure to sit at home day after day, waiting for something to happen. Yes, I know what the doctor said—but you know, Lora, in his position he is obliged to err on the side of caution. You and he and Arthur will all simply have to trust that I know what I am about."

From long experience with Lady Helen, Lora knew it would be useless to say any more. After a short pause, Lady Helen went on, in a studiously casual voice. "Arthur tells me that Mr. Wainwright is back in Town. Has he called upon you yet?"

"Yes, he called this afternoon. But I was out at the time, and so he only left his card," said Lora, also studiously casual. She did not mention that along with his card, Adam had left a short note in answer to her own, promising to meet her at the masquerade.

Lady Helen nodded. "When you see him again, you must give him my regards and tell him that I am looking forward to dancing with him again when I am recovered from my lying-in. Do you expect to see him soon?"

Against a question so frank and direct, Lora had no choice

but to be frank and direct in return. She knew the subject of the masquerade must be broached sooner or later, and on the whole she preferred to get it over with sooner. "Perhaps," she said hesitantly. "I think—I believe he intends to attend the Rawlings's masquerade Saturday evening."

"The Rawlings's masquerade! But surely you don't mean to attend that great rout, Lora?"

"Yes, I do," said Lora stoutly.

"You cannot be serious! To hobnob with a set of vulgar Cits, and rub shoulders with every mushroom and shabby genteel in Town—it's not to be thought of."

"But you see I *have* thought of it, Helen—and I intend to go. I have a great desire to see Rawlings Court."

Lady Helen paused. "There's that, of course," she admitted, in a milder tone. "I hear it is a spectacular place and very well worth seeing. Indeed, after all the stories I've heard, I wouldn't mind seeing it myself. But still I cannot like the idea of your going there, Lora. It will do you no good to be seen in such company."

"You forget, it is to be a masquerade," said Lora. "I will be wearing a costume, and if I leave before the unmasking at midnight, no one will ever know I was there."

Lady Helen regarded her fixedly. "And Mr. Wainwright will be there, too?"

"Yes, I have reason to believe he will be," said Lora. She could not prevent her color from rising a little, but she spoke with gentle dignity and steadily returned Lady Helen's gaze.

Lady Helen sighed deeply. "You know, Ellsworth is more than half in love with you, Lora," she said. "I've never seen him so smitten with anyone. Several people have told me that he went storming out of Randolph's like a wild man after you snubbed him that evening at the ridotto. I really think you might marry him if you played your cards right."

"I care nothing for Lord Ellsworth," said Lora calmly.

Lady Helen sighed again. "No, I didn't think you did," she

said sadly. "I suppose you're really determined to go through with this thing?—with the Rawlings's masquerade, I mean.

"Yes . . . yes, I am, Helen. Quite determined."

"Well, then, I shan't tease you any more," said Lady Helen. With a rather false gaiety, she added, "But I shall quite depend on your giving me a full description of Rawlings Court the next day. Make sure you look at the Italian garden in the court-yard. I understand it is spectacular."

Touched by her friend's loyalty, Lora promised to do so, and the entrance of Lord Spelbourne and the tea-tray a minute later put an end to the conversation.

Eleven

To Lora's relief, Lady Helen, having once expressed herself on the subject of the masquerade, showed no inclination to refer to it a second time. Equally to Lora's relief, she showed no interest in what Lora would be wearing for the occasion. Her sole comment, spoken as Lora was on her way upstairs to dress, was, "I suppose, as you mean to leave early tonight, you are only wearing a domino?"

"Yes, I will be wearing a domino," said Lora evasively. This was true as far as it went, for she had judged it best to conceal her real costume beneath a voluminous domino cloak until she was safely within the bounds of Rawlings Court. Even then, she was not sure she would have the courage to take it off. But of course, she must take it off if Adam were to recognize her, she reminded herself, as Annie helped her remove her dinner dress and began to array her in her costume. Although Adam had called twice more at Lady Helen's house during the past few days, he had never once managed to find her at home. In the end she had been reduced to writing him a second time to tell him what she would be wearing and when and where he might look for her when he got to Rawlings Court.

It had been a disappointment not to see Adam when he called, of course. And yet, at the same time, Lora was rather relieved that she had not seen him. As Saturday approached, she found herself in such a state of fluctuating nerves, such a state of fear, worry, and remorse one minute, and of fevered anticipation the next, that she was unfit company for anyone.

Once Saturday was behind her, she trusted her nerves might settle down, but until then, she thought it best to avoid all excitement, and that included the excitement of Adam's company. It was enough to know that she would be seeing him at the masquerade—doing considerably more than seeing him, if all went according to plan. Her heart had beat uncomfortably fast even as she wrote the short note instructing him to look for her dressed as the Roman goddess, Ceres.

It was as Ceres that she was to go. Venus might have been a more appropriate choice, under the circumstances, but Lora felt this would be a little over-obvious and perhaps a little vain as well. Yet, she did not wish to go to the opposite extreme and impersonate a chaste goddess such as Diana or Minerva. Ceres seemed like a good compromise. While appearing much more modest, the Goddess of Agriculture's classical draperies might be every bit as flimsy and revealing as the Goddess of Love and Beauty's—and on this occasion, they certainly were.

The white muslin of which Lora's costume was fashioned was sheer enough to reveal the outline of her body beneath it, though not sheer enough to expose her completely. It had taken long consultation with Madame to decide upon the exact degree of sheerness necessary to accomplish this effect. In style it was very simple, a sleeveless tunic bound with a flowing sash of green, gold, and scarlet. A plain gold diadem and armlet added a further classical touch. On her feet Lora wore flat gold sandals, and in her arms she carried a sheaf of grain mingled with wildflowers, which in London had been more difficult to obtain, and considerably more expensive, than an equivalent quantity of orchids.

When Lora had been arrayed in this toilette and her golden hair dressed appropriately *a l'antique,* she walked over to inspect herself in front of the long cheval glass. What she saw made her fall back a step and cross her arms over her bosom in an instinctive gesture of modesty.

"It's a lovely costume, my lady," said Annie enthusiastically. "You'll turn heads tonight, you will."

"I shouldn't wonder," said Lora faintly. Summoning up all her resolve, she uncrossed her arms and regarded herself long and unflinchingly in the glass. Did she really have the courage to appear in company looking like an expensive lightskirt? Yes, if she were masked and Adam were of the company, Lora thought she did have sufficient courage—just barely. The costume was a flattering one, after all, and in ordinary light it would probably seem less revealing than it did now, under the direct glow of several lamps and half-a-dozen candles.

"Yes, I think that will do, Annie," said Lora aloud. "Please bring me my mask and domino. And I suppose I must wear gloves, too, even if they're not exactly classical."

Annie gave her a scrutinizing look, then turned to a drawer of the commode. "How about these, my lady?" she asked, producing a pair of white elbow-length kid gloves. "You wouldn't want 'em any longer than this, I wouldn't think. They'd cover up your pretty what-d'ye-call it—that bracelet thing you're wearing on your upper arm."

"Yes, thank you, Annie. Those will do very well," said Lora with an approving nod. As she donned the gloves, she added in a casual voice, "I wonder, Annie, if you would mind just slipping downstairs to see if Lady Helen has already gone to her room? If she has, be careful not to disturb her. I only wondered if she—that's to say, I thought that perhaps she might like to see my costume if she is still up."

Fortunately for Lora's plans, Annie returned a minute later to report that Lady Helen had already retired for the evening. Greatly relieved, Lora wrapped herself in her domino, slipped quietly downstairs, and went out to the carriage that was waiting to take her to Rawlings Court.

It was a drive of nearly an hour from the West End of London to Rawlings Court. This left Lora with plenty of time to experience all over again the conflicting doubts, fears, and desires she had been feeling all that week, and a few new ones as well. She felt the coachman and footmen must be wondering at her going out at such an hour, alone and in such a dress;

it seemed to her as though the purpose of her errand must be stamped on her forehead plain for all to see.

Nervously she bent her gold half-mask back and forth between her fingers and wished Adam were in the carriage with her. If he had been there, she felt certain she would not have been so fearful as she was now about the prospect of going to Rawlings Court. But then, if he *had* been there, there would have been no point in going to Rawlings Court at all, she reminded herself. The thought made her smile, and helped relieve the nervous feeling in the pit of her stomach. Leaning back against the upholstered squabs, she settled down to enjoy the long drive as best she could.

After what seemed an eon, the carriage turned off the main road and passed between a pair of massive stone gateposts spanned by a wrought iron arch. Lora, peering out the window, could just make out the letters "R" and "C" amid the ornate wrought iron tracery.

Rawlings Court was approached by way of a broad avenue lined with over-arching lime trees. The avenue led straight from the road to the house without a single curve or rise of ground to heighten the drama of its approach. Subterfuge was not the style at Rawlings Court, as Lora very soon perceived. The house itself was a vast, dark crenellated pile set uncompromisingly in the center of an expanse of smooth-mown lawn. From the wide, curving wings thrown out at either side, to the mock drawbridge that formed its entrance, to the fanciful turrets that crowned its roofline, it was a house that boldly shouted, "Look at me!" rather than seeking to call attention to itself with an aura of mystery or reserve.

Inside the house, it was the same story. Lora gazed about her wide-eyed as the Rawlings's footmen bowed her into the cavernous entrance hall and thought she had never seen so much oak, armor, and Gothic embellishment in one room before. She went first to the ladies' cloakroom to divest herself of her domino. Having entrusted it to the cloakroom maid, she gave a last touch to her hair, made sure her mask was firmly in place, shouldered her sheaf of wheat and wildflowers, and stepped resolutely out into the hall again, where a troop of noisy revelers were engaged in a rowdy country dance.

The "court" in Rawlings Court was not merely descriptive of its palatial style, but referred also to the design of the house: an open square surrounding an inner courtyard. Lora had learned as much from talk gleaned among her acquaintances, and she had heard from Lady Helen and others that this court-yard contained an Italian garden of unusual beauty. In all respects it had sounded an ideal place to meet one's lover. And so when Lora had written to Adam, she had suggested they meet there, at ten o'clock, near the garden's central fountain.

Finding the courtyard proved more difficult than Lora had anticipated, however. The house was huge, with a bewildering number of rooms, and every one of them was so jammed with people that it took her several minutes to make her way from one end to the other. Her progress was further hampered by a series of gentlemen who sought to engage her in conversation, particularly one gentleman costumed as a Moor, who persisted in addressing her as Cecelia and was most insistent that she dance with him.

"Indeed, sir, you are mistaken. My name is *not* Cecelia," snapped Lora, driven nearly to distraction by his importunings.

"Ah, Cecelia, you are cruel," returned the gentleman, not in the least discomposed. Happily for Lora's sanity, however, a pretty girl in a Gypsy costume chose that moment to sashay past with a provocative sway of the hips. The Moorish gentle-man immediately abandoned his pursuit of Lora to chase after this new quarry, and she was able to continue on her way un-molested.

She wandered through several more rooms, each larger and showier than the last. They were all very full of people, but in none of them could Lora locate any entrance to the court-yard. She could not even locate Sir Hubert or Lady Rawlings, her host and hostess for the evening. At last, in desperation, she asked directions of a jolly-looking lady in a red and gold

Tudor costume, whom she chanced to encounter on her passage through the rooms.

"Aye, to be sure, my dear: it's only a step from here. Just go back through the saloon and blue drawing room, and from there cross into the little red parlor. There's a door there that'll take you to the courtyard, sure enough. Or if you'd rather, you could go all the way back to the ballroom, go through the music room and conservatory, and go out that way."

Lora thanked the lady profusely and then set about retracing her steps through the saloon and blue drawing room. With the lady's instructions to guide her, she had no difficulty locating the red parlor, a small, square, plush-upholstered room like the interior of a jewel case.

Nor did she have any difficulty locating the door that led into the courtyard. But when she opened the door, she found herself confronted by an unexpected dilemma. The Italian garden had been usurped by a group of young gentlemen who were clustered about the central fountain, cheering on two of their number who were attempting to hang their hats on its topmost figure. Though several of them cordially invited Lora to stay and watch, she thought it best to decline their invitation and retreat from the courtyard as speedily as possible.

"Oh, dear, what shall I do now?" she said aloud, shutting the door behind her and laying a distracted hand to her flaming cheeks. Overall, it seemed to her best to wait where she was, so that she might catch Adam before he went out to the courtyard. Then she recalled that the lady had spoken of another entrance to the courtyard through the ballroom and conservatory. It was quite as likely that Adam would use that entrance as this one—likelier, really, since the ballroom was nearer the front of the house.

Lora immediately set off in the direction of the ballroom. She had by this time a much better idea of the house's layout and found the ballroom with no more difficulty than was obtained by struggling through eight or nine large and immensely crowded rooms. It seemed to her that the five hundred cards of invitation of which she had heard so much must have been an exaggeration on the side of understatement. There appeared to be more than that many people in the ballroom alone, and when she got to the conservatory she found that it, too, was crowded, filled with couples strolling about enjoying the warm, flower-scented air.

But there was no sign of Adam. A cautious peep into the courtyard likewise revealed no sign of him, but only confirmed, as she had feared, that the young gentlemen were still in possession of the Italian garden. After a moment's indecision, she decided to go back to the red parlor on the chance that Adam might take that route to or from the courtyard.

On this trip through the rooms, however, Lora found that her appearance was once again attracting unwanted attention. Several gentlemen who had only stared at her before, now accompanied their stares with audible remarks, and one or two even went so far as to address her directly. In an effort to elude one especially persistent gentleman, Lora veered from the route she had taken before, lost her way, and soon found herself on unfamiliar ground, with the red parlor nowhere in sight.

At first this did not greatly distress her, for she felt that if she kept moving she must eventually encounter Adam among the crowd. But it was not long before she saw the futility of this idea. The house was enormous; the crowds bewildering; and though she had at least the advantage of knowing Adam's costume—a black domino—the crowd included such a number of black dominoes in all shapes and sizes that this was hardly an advantage at all.

Lora told herself that Adam would be sure to find her eventually. When he went to the courtyard in obedience to her instructions, he would see the young gentlemen at their sport and realize what had prevented her from meeting him there. He then need only look for her elsewhere in the house, and if he would but ask among the other guests, he ought to be able to locate her with relative ease. *His* costume might be a common one, but hers was certainly conspicuous enough, if one might judge from the reactions of those around her.

So Lora told herself, but at the back of her mind lurked an uncomfortable fear that when Adam found her absent from the courtyard, he might simply abandon the search, call for his carriage, and leave Rawlings Court then and there. The idea made her quicken her pace as she hurried through the crowded rooms. Anxiously she scrutinized each black domino she saw, trying not to be conspicuous about it, but it was inevitable that her search would attract some attention.

"Madame was perhaps looking for me?" inquired one black-dominoed gentleman, who had noticed her look and had returned it with an appreciative one of his own. He moved toward her, a slow smile spreading across his face—a wide, bewhiskered face with large mustachios, not Adam's face at all.

"No, I beg your pardon," murmured Lora, edging past. "I was looking for someone else—a friend."

"I would like to be your friend," said the gentleman encouragingly. Lora pretended not to hear, but further quickened her pace. In her haste to get away from him, she made for the nearest door and pushed it open, not realizing until she was through it that it was an outside door leading onto a terrace at the rear of the house.

Too late did she realize that she had passed from the frying pan into the fire. The terrace was occupied by a group of gentlemen, all clad in the picturesque attire of Italian banditti, who had gathered there to lounge and smoke. "I beg your pardon," said Lora again, and turned to go back into the house.

She was barred from doing so by the nearest and largest of the banditti, who had thrown down his cigar and come over to stand deliberately in front of the door. He was wearing a black half-mask, and through its slits a pair of very blue eyes surveyed her with dawning recognition.

"Well, well, well," he said, in the familiar but unwelcome accents of Lord Ellsworth. "Well, well, well . . . what have we here?"

Twelve

Lord Ellsworth was drunk; Lora could see that at a glance. The smell of liquor was strong on his breath, and though his speech was still clear enough to be understandable, it was also noticeably slurred.

"Well, well, well," he said again. "This *is* a surprise. I wouldn't have thought this was your kind of party, my lady."

"I don't know what you mean," said Lora boldly. A quick glance around the terrace had shown her that Adam was not among the gentlemen gathered there. And, she was not really afraid of Lord Ellsworth, who, with all his failings, might at least be depended on to conduct himself as a gentleman. So Lora thought, at any rate, and the thought gave her confidence. "I don't know what you mean," she repeated. "Please pardon me, sir. I really must go back into the house now."

Lord Ellsworth hesitated, swaying slightly on his feet as he looked down at her. Lora felt sure he would move aside in the end, and in fact he might have done so, if left to himself. Unfortunately, at that moment, one of his fellow banditti staggered over and slapped him resoundingly on the back.

"No luck, eh, Ellsworth?" he said, with a wink toward Lora. "I wouldn't have thought you were the man to give up at one try, old fellow."

"Devilish pretty gal," said another to his companion in an audible whisper. "What's she supposed to be, some kind of nymph?"

"She's Ceres, you boob," said the other contemptuously. "Roman goddess of agriculture."

"Whoever she is, she don't want anything to do with poor old Ellsworth," said another, with a guffaw of laughter.

Lord Ellsworth's jaw tightened. Lora could read his thoughts as clearly as though she had been privy to them. If he let her go now, it would appear that he had been bested in the conflict, and he would lose face in front of his friends. In a lightning-swift movement, he reached out and plucked the sheaf of wheat and wildflowers from her arms.

"Forgive me, dear goddess, but now that I've found you, I cannot let you slip away from me so easily," he said, holding the bouquet tauntingly over her head. "If you would have me return your bounty, you must first pay me the price of a kiss."

The banditti loudly applauded this speech. Lora felt her color rise, but it was a flush of anger, not embarrassment.

"Indeed, no," she said bitingly. "Keep the bouquet if you like, sir. I can hardly compel you to return it. All I ask is that you let me pass." So saying, she drew her draperies around her and attempted to push past him.

Lord Ellsworth left off dangling the bouquet and made a grab for her arm. She wrenched it away from him, so that he caught the drapery of her tunic instead. The flimsy material gave way under the pressure and tore from shoulder to waist. If Lora had not caught it with her hands, the whole of her bosom would have been exposed.

Lord Ellsworth looked as appalled by this turn of events as was Lora herself. "I'm sorry—" he began.

He got no further. Even the gentlest of creatures will lash out when tried too far, and Lora had been tried to the utmost that evening. She had been in a nervous state to begin with, which had been exacerbated by the circumstance of missing Adam at their meeting place. Now her costume was in ruins; all her hopes for the evening irretrievably lost; and it was too much, entirely too much to be borne.

Clutching her bodice to her bosom with her left hand, Lora

lifted her right and struck Lord Ellsworth hard across the face: not an open-handed slap, but a close-fisted blow that made his teeth rattle.

"By Jove, she hits out like a right one," said one of the banditti in surprise.

Lord Ellsworth said nothing, but rubbed his jaw with his hand. On his face was an ugly look, such an ugly look that Lora began to be rather frightened and to repent of what she had done.

"Let me pass," she said in a voice that trembled slightly. She made another effort to push past him. Even then he might have let her go, but unfortunately the banditti were not willing to see the scene pass off so tamely.

"Go on, Ellsworth, ain't you going to collect your kiss?" one called. "Don't say you're afraid of a lady!"

"She ought to be dressed as Minerva, not Ceres," said the knowledgeable one to his companion. "Quite a warlike spirit."

Again Lord Ellsworth's jaw tightened. He took a step toward Lora, who braced herself for she knew not what unpleasant retribution.

Suddenly, the terrace door swung open, and a gentleman in a black domino thrust himself between her and Lord Ellsworth. His back was to Lora, so that she could not see his face, but she knew him even before she heard his voice—a very angry voice, but Adam's voice beyond all possible doubt.

"What the devil is going on here?"

The question was addressed to Lord Ellsworth, but neither he nor anyone else answered it. Adam regarded him coldly for a moment, then turned to Lora. One glance at her torn dress and frightened face appeared to give him all the answer he needed, for he turned back to Lord Ellsworth with an epithet that made a dull flush roll over that gentleman's face.

"*Here's* a development," remarked one of the banditti with relish.

"Aye, a regular drama," agreed another. "What will you do

now, Ellsworth? Are you going to stand there and let that fellow call you names?"

"I tell you what it is, Ellsworth: he's trying to take your gel away," said a third. "Don't let him do it, Ellsworth. You had her first, square to rights. We'll all vouch for it. Go on and mill him down, Ellsworth."

"Aye, mill him down!"

Lord Ellsworth had not waited for this counsel. Before the last gentleman was done speaking, his fist shot out toward Adam's face. Adam saw the blow coming in time to duck most of its force, but it caught him on the temple and sent him reeling backward. The banditti cheered.

"Hit him again, Ellsworth," urged one. "Hit him again and finish him off."

Good though this advice might have been, Lord Ellsworth was in no position to take it. Adam had made a quick recovery from the blow, and before Lord Ellsworth could land a second one, his own fist shot out, striking Lord Ellsworth full in the face. Lord Ellsworth stood swaying on his legs for a moment, then went down heavily, to the astonishment of the banditti.

"Well, I'll be damned," said one. "First time I've seen Ellsworth bested in a mill. Wouldn't have believed it if I hadn't seen it myself."

"I told him he was overdoing the brandy and water at dinner," said another, shaking his head. "Wasn't in his usual form."

"Still, it was a neat piece of work," said a third, looking Adam up and down with an appraising air. "Very scientifically done. Hi, you there, fellow: that was a neat shot you made there. Well hit, I say."

Adam made no reply, for Lora was pulling urgently on his sleeve, drawing him toward the terrace steps. "Let's go, Adam," she said, in a voice vibrant with anxiety. "No, not that way—out into the gardens. Let's just get away from here as quickly as we can." Behind Adam, she could see Lord Ellsworth already struggling to his feet.

Adam followed her gaze, and though not seeming to share her apprehension, he did apparently see the expediency of their quitting the terrace. Turning again to Lora, he caught her round the waist, slung her over his shoulder, and started down the terrace steps. His action was greeted with cheers and applause from the fickle banditti.

"To the victor the spoils," shouted one hilariously.

"Puts me in mind of that business of the Sabine women," said the knowledgeable one.

"Watch your step, though, fellow. She's got a mean right on her," advised another.

Adam paid them no heed but continued down the terrace steps until he reached the lawn. From there, he set off at a lope toward the wilderness that lay beyond the lawn and gardens. The banditti raised a final cheer as he vanished among the trees. By lifting her head a little, Lora could see them clustering around to console their fallen comrade. After one brief glance, however, she let her head drop back down and gave way to hysterical laughter.

"You can put me down now, Adam," she said, between gasps of laughter. "I don't think they mean to follow us."

Adam slowed his pace to a walk, but continued to carry her until they reached a summerhouse within a small clearing, some few hundred yards from the house.

Like the rest of Rawlings Court, the summerhouse was designed in a vaguely Gothic style with unglazed lancets opening to the outside and a peaked roof ornamented with wrought iron curlicues. Inside, however, it was comfortably furnished with wicker chairs and tables, and a settee with striped moreen cushions.

Adam deposited Lora on the settee, then dropped down beside her. He was breathing hard, and there were beads of perspiration on his forehead. Throwing off his domino, he leaned back wearily against the cushions while Lora, beside him, continued to be shaken with fits of hysterical laughter. At last, when he had regained his breath and Lora's laughter had subsided into an occasional giggle, he turned to look at her.

"What a memorable evening this is turning out to be," he said. "All my evenings with you have been memorable in some wise, but I believe this one has taken the palm."

"Oh, Adam, I am so sorry," said Lora, sobering immediately. She was still obliged to clutch her bodice to her bosom with one hand, but with the other she reached out timidly to touch Adam's shoulder. "I ought not to laugh, Adam, for indeed it was a serious enough situation. I hope you were not badly hurt?"

Adam put a hand experimentally to his forehead. It came away with a small smear of blood upon it. "No, nothing serious. The skin's broken, but it's not bleeding much, and there's no pain to speak of. I doubt I'll have more than a scratch to show for it. Thank heavens Ellsworth was half seas over with brandy and water. I've seen him working out with Jackson, and I am quite sure that if he had been sober, he would have laid me out in no time."

"If he had been sober, he never would have behaved as he did," said Lora warmly.

Adam gave her a rather quizzical smile. "Oh, well, as to that I don't know," he said. "I can see how you might present some temptation, looking as you do tonight." In a more serious voice, he added, "Did he really try to tear off your dress, Lora? I find it hard to believe even Ellsworth could behave as badly as that."

"Oh, but he didn't, Adam. The tearing part was all an accident. I was trying to go back inside the house, you see, and he stole my flowers and said I couldn't have them back unless I kissed him. Oh dear, and I suppose that means he still has them. I lost track of my poor bouquet in all the confusion of me hitting him, and him hitting you, and everything that happened after that."

"You hit Ellsworth?" said Adam, regarding her with surprise.

For answer, Lora held out her hand. Her glove was torn over the knuckle, and the skin beneath was chafed and bleeding. Adam examined it in silence, then kissed it tenderly and folded it between his own. After a minute, Lora went on in a subdued voice.

"Yes, I did hit him, Adam, and I'm so ashamed. I have never in my life hit anyone before, but when he tore my dress I just lost my temper completely. Do you know, I don't think I ever *have* lost my temper before—lost it completely, I mean, as I did back there on the terrace. And I wish I hadn't done it there, either. I'm quite sure it was my hitting Lord Ellsworth that made him so angry, and that's why he tried to hit you. In a way, it's all my fault that you got hurt."

"I am not *much* hurt," said Adam reassuringly. "No worse than you are, at any rate. If anyone was hurt this evening, it was our friend Lord Ellsworth, and I'm not inclined to waste much sympathy on him. I do wish I had got there sooner, however, so that I might have spared you the unpleasantness of having to go through all this."

"It seems to me quite miraculous that you got there when you did, Adam. Had you been looking for me long?"

"Yes, in a manner of speaking. I think I've been about three steps behind you all evening. Some fellows out in the courtyard told me you had been there and left, and after that I had only to follow the trail of dazed male faces to find you. If the rooms hadn't been so crowded, I'm sure I would have caught up to you long ago."

Lora, not knowing what to say to this, looked away in some confusion. "I'm sorry," she said, with averted face. "I'm afraid I have caused you a great deal of trouble tonight, Adam."

"Oh, I don't know," said Adam comfortably. "It's not every day a man gets a chance to play knight errant and rescue a damsel in distress. I abhor violence in principle, but in practice I must admit there's something rather stirring about it—gets the blood flowing, so to speak. I'd been wanting to floor

Ellsworth for a long time, but I didn't suppose I'd ever get the chance to actually do it."

"Oh," was all Lora could think to say. She stole a quick look at Adam and saw that he was smiling at her.

"And then, too, there's something very elemental and satisfying about carrying off the lady of one's choice over one's shoulder," he went on, in what Lora could only think a very meaning kind of voice. "That's another thing I've been wanting to do for a long time. And so, when the opportunity arose, I decided I might as well take it. I hope you will forgive me if my conduct was somewhat . . . high-handed."

Lora thought again of herself, her costume in shreds, being carried off across Adam's shoulder while the banditti shouted encouragement. An involuntary laugh escaped her. "It *was* rather high-handed, but I shall not hold it against you, Adam. In fact, if I am to be perfectly honest, I must admit that there is also something very elemental and satisfying about being carried off by the gentleman of one's choice."

"So you do not class my attentions in the same category as Lord Ellsworth's?"

"You know I do not, Adam," said Lora. Her voice was low, but she regarded him with unwavering steadiness as she spoke.

He smiled, rather self-consciously. "Yes, I suppose I do know. But I wanted to make sure of myself, before I did this." Leaning forward, he kissed her gently on the lips.

Lora sighed and put her free arm around his neck to draw him closer. He in turn put both arms around her and crushed her tight against his chest. "It feels so good to hold you again—to kiss you again," he whispered in her ear. "Oh, Lora, you can't know how I've missed you these last few weeks."

"I've missed you, too," she whispered back. Her heart beat fast within her, and she felt again the sensation of mingled fear and excitement that always accompanied their embraces. Tonight, the sensation was heightened to a nearly unbearable degree. All that had passed earlier in the evening seemed now as insubstantial as a dream. All that was real was the warmth and strength of Adam's arms and the feel of his mouth on hers.

It was a close, humid night, with a breathless hush in the air that hinted at the approach of rain. From time to time flashes of lightning lit up the eastern sky, but these were as yet very faint and far away. The sky overhead was still clear and lit by the glow of a gibbous moon.

In the shrubbery around the summerhouse, crickets and cicadas kept up a monotonous serenade, and the scent of lilac and honeysuckle hung heavy in the air. It was in all respects a night to stir the senses. Certainly Lora's senses were stirred, and stirred beyond what she had imagined possible as Adam's mouth traveled from her lips to her ear, from her ear to her neck, setting her whole body aflame with desire.

In the beginning, she had continued to hold up the bodice of her dress with one hand while clinging to Adam with the other. But as she fell more and more under the spell of his embrace, her hold gradually loosened, and at last she let go of her dress entirely and put both arms around him. It was a kind of unspoken surrender, and Adam clearly took it as such. His kisses grew more fevered as his hands roamed over her bare back and shoulders.

Lora made no effort to resist his advances. Indeed, she positively encouraged them, while countering with advances of her own. The touch of her hands seemed to affect Adam profoundly. His kisses became progressively more urgent and aggressive, and he began to bear her back on the settee. Lora acceded to this as to all else, willingly. She lay back, drawing him with her until he was lying atop her on the settee.

This was a position Lora recognized. She lay tensely, her hands clutching Adam's shoulders and her breath coming fast as she waited for what he would do next. What he did next came as a surprise, however. One moment he was lying atop her, kissing her with a passion that made her shudder with an answering passion; the next, he drew back abruptly, almost roughly, leaving her lying alone and exposed upon the settee.

Lora's eyes fluttered open in surprise. Adam was looking down at her, and even in the darkness she could see that something was very much amiss. There was an expression on his face that was not anger, nor yet anguish, but something in between. He turned his face away quickly, however, and when he spoke, his voice was calm and controlled.

"I think perhaps we've been out here long enough," he said.

Lora pulled herself to a sitting position, regarding him with bewilderment. Adam glanced at her briefly, then looked away again. With his face still averted, he picked up his domino from the back of the settee and tossed it to her. "You can wear my domino," he said. "I won't be needing it any more tonight."

"Adam, what is wrong?" said Lora in a voice near tears. "Have I—did I do something wrong?"

He shook his head. "No, nothing," he said, but there was no conviction in his voice.

He got to his feet and began to pace nervously back and forth across the summerhouse while Lora struggled into the domino unaided. When at last she was enveloped in its folds, he took her by the arm and began to lead her back toward the house. But his touch was impersonal, with nothing of the lover about it, and he walked so quickly that Lora, hampered by her skirts and the too-long domino, could hardly keep up. As they retraced their steps through the wood, she stumbled over a tree root and would have gone sprawling if it had not been for Adam's arm. He paused to let her regain her footing, then led her on as inexorably as before.

Never in her life had Lora felt so humiliated. She did not know whether it had been the brazenness of her conduct that had disgusted Adam, or merely the clumsiness, but she could not doubt that she had disgusted him somehow. Perhaps there was something lacking in her that other women possessed. She had often suspected as much in the past, although since meeting Adam she had begun to wonder if perhaps that something might have been lacking in Lord Carroll instead. It was therefore particularly crushing to be rejected tonight, when she had felt as though she were so close to finally possessing it.

Tears filled Lora's eyes and blinded her as she walked, so that she stumbled again and again. Adam assisted her to her feet each time, but he did not even look at her as he did so. His eyes were fixed straight ahead and his face set in hard, cold lines like the face of a stranger.

At last Lora could bear it no longer. "Adam, stop," she said, and then, "Stop," in a louder voice, wrenching her arm away from him. He turned to look at her then. For the first time he seemed to notice the tears glistening on her cheeks, and his face softened.

"I'm sorry, Lora," he said in a low voice. Taking her arm again, he led her over to a rustic bench situated near the edge of the wilderness. Having seated her on it, he stood looking down at her with an expression both searching and sober. Lora, looking back, felt a wrenching conviction that what was coming was going to be even more painful than what had gone before.

"What is it, Adam?" she whispered.

He went on looking at her, and she saw by his face that he was experiencing a strong conflict of emotions. Self-reproach struggled with anger, and hope with fatalism, and for a moment he seemed almost as though he was going to turn away without speaking. Then a look of resolve came over his face, a resolve almost desperate in its intensity. He came a step nearer, addressing her in a voice that struggled for calm in the midst of obvious emotion.

"Oh, Lora, I can't go on like this," he said. "I'm a presumptuous fool, perhaps, but you must know how I feel about you. Lora, will you marry me?"

Thirteen

Whatever Lora had expected, it was not that. Her mouth fell open, and for a moment she regarded Adam with silent incredulity. "Oh, no," she said, finding her voice at last, and then, in a more agitated voice, "Oh, no, no, indeed. Indeed, I cannot, Adam."

Adam turned away, trying not to show how her words hurt him. "I understand," he said flatly. Lora, however, jumped to her feet and caught him by the arm.

"Wait, Adam. Oh, Adam, I didn't mean that the way it sounded. Indeed, I am very honored that you would ask me to be your wife, but I can't marry you, Adam. I can't, I simply can't."

"I know you can't," said Adam in a tired voice. "I've been telling myself that all along. I'm not rich; I'm not noble-born; I can't begin to give you all the things you're used to. John was right that first evening when he said you were above my touch. I had no right even to think of it."

"Oh, but Adam, it's not that. Those things would not weigh with me if I felt I could honestly accept your proposal. But I can't, Adam. I simply can't, that's all."

"Why not?" said Adam, looking at her soberly. "If it isn't the difference in our positions that's stopping you, what is? You must know how I feel about you, Lora. I think I've loved you almost from the first moment I saw you. And I thought— God help me—I thought you loved me, too."

"I do love you," said Lora, and found that it was true. A

fresh flood of tears welled up in her eyes as she continued. "I love you, Adam, but I can't marry you. Oh, it's all so difficult, so impossible to explain. I wish I could make you understand."

Adam looked at her hard for a moment and then sat down upon the bench. "Then make me understand," he said. "I'm here, and I'm listening; I can stay all night if necessary. Explain it to me so that I understand why you can't marry me."

Lora sat down, too, but found the words did not come easily to her lips. "You know, of course, that I was married before, Adam," she began haltingly at last. "What you do not know—what scarcely anyone knows—is that I was very unhappy in my marriage to Lord Carroll. After he died, I made up my mind that I would not marry again."

"I see," said Adam. "That's natural, I suppose, and I can certainly understand your feeling that way, Lora. But at the same time, if what you're saying is true, then that would mean you've never had any serious intentions toward me at all, wouldn't it? In fact, it's pretty much what I suspected that first night at the Monroes'. I was only a diversion to you, something to pass the time when balls and banquets began to pall upon you."

Lora winced at the bitterness in his voice. "No, no, indeed, Adam. Truly it wasn't like that at all. When I said I loved you just now, I meant what I said. That night at the ridotto—and then here tonight, in the summerhouse—I would never have behaved as I did, if I didn't love you. In a way, it's because I do love you that I won't marry you."

"You're right: I don't understand," said Adam, after a moment's silent cogitation. "You won't marry me because you love me?"

"I knew you wouldn't understand," said Lora desolately. "It does sound like a contradiction, I know. But you see, Adam, I've already been married. I know what it does to people, even people in love. I was very young when I married Lord Carroll, but I married him of my own free will, because I thought I loved him." Lora raised her eyes fleetingly to Adam's face, then lowered them again as she went on. "And he always swore that he loved me, too, right up till the end—but it wasn't enough, Adam, it wasn't enough. There were always so many conflicts between us. Never big, earth-shattering conflicts, but just ordinary little day-to-day irritations that seemed to grow and grow until I could hardly bear to look him in the face. I started out loving him, and I ended up almost hating him. And then, when he died, I felt so guilty about it!" With a pleading expression, she raised her eyes to Adam's face once more. "You must see, Adam, that I could never marry again after that. I would be afraid that I might end up hating you, too, and that I could not bear."

Adam was silent for a moment. Finally he spoke, roughly, as though the words cost him an effort. "Am I like him?"

Lora shook her head and even managed a ghost of a smile. "No, Adam," she said. "You could scarcely be more different."

"Then why assume our marriage wouldn't be different, too? You were how old when you married Carroll—sixteen? Seventeen?"

"Sixteen when I became engaged to him," said Lora reluctantly. "I married him when I was seventeen."

"And how old are you now?" pursued Adam ruthlessly.

"Twenty-six," said Lora, more reluctantly still.

"You will admit there to be a difference between seventeen and twenty-six, surely?" demanded Adam. Lora bit her lip and finally nodded, unwillingly. "And you've just said that I am different from Lord Carroll," he said, his voice becoming eager as he perceived signs of yielding in her demeanor. "Two different people, an entirely different situation, Lora. Why should the outcome be the same?"

Lora shook her head slowly. "I am sure it would not be exactly the same, Adam," she said. "But still there would undoubtedly be conflicts of one kind or another. Little things, perhaps, but it was the little things that caused all the trouble between Carroll and me."

There was a brief pause as Adam digested this. "What kind of little things?" he said at last.

"Oh, it sounds so foolish to speak of them now. Things like the way he used to lose his temper when his neckcloth wouldn't come right." With a weary smile, Lora lifted her eyes to Adam's face. "That sounds very petty, doesn't it? And yet, it used to make me feel absolutely ill when I heard him swearing at his valet and throwing things around his dressing room every morning."

Adam, who had been looking singularly grim up to this point, began now to look more cheerful. "Ah, but that's a conflict you'd never experience with me, Lora," he said. "I don't aspire to anything too ambitious in the neckcloth line, as you can see." He touched the low knot at his throat with a deprecating smile. "And I couldn't swear at my valet if I wanted to, because I don't happen to possess one. My butler does for me at home, and when I'm away I'm accustomed to dress and shave myself. A shameful confession, I know. John is always criticizing me for not taking enough pains with my dress. But I believe he has had cause to revise his opinion these last few weeks."

Lora smiled but shook her head. "Oh, Adam! Perhaps that particular issue would not be a cause of conflict, but I'm sure there would be plenty of other things that would be. There always were with Carroll and me. The servants, for instance. I was supposed to be in charge of the indoor staff, but Carroll was never satisfied with the way I ran the house. He would fire servants without consulting me, and criticize the ones I hired to replace them, and he was always contradicting my orders. It often made things very inconvenient for me, but I could hardly complain, for of course they were his servants, too."

"If it caused you inconvenience, I don't see why you shouldn't complain," said Adam, looking at her rather strangely. "Lora, did you ever tell him how all this bothered you?"

"No—no, I never did. Perhaps I should have told him. But then, if I had, it would probably have caused a quarrel, and I would have hated that worse than having my orders contradicted. And Carroll would have hated it, too. He always said how glad he was that I wasn't a shrew or a scold, like some wives."

"Even so, I think he might have preferred a wife who quarreled with him occasionally to one that hated him," said Adam gently. "Mind you, I'm not trying to lay all the blame in your dish, Lora. It sounds as though Carroll probably left something to be desired as a life companion, but if you never tried to set him straight, you can hardly blame the poor fellow for not changing his ways."

In a more cheerful voice, he added, "If you were to marry me, now, we might easily prevent any difficulties of that sort by putting a few apposite clauses in the marriage articles beforehand. You, for instance, would be bound to sit down and speak your mind about anything that bothered you at least once a quarter, and I would be bound not to interfere in your running of the household. And both of us would have to get the written consent of the other before hiring or firing any of the servants. How does that sound?" He paused, smiling hopefully at Lora.

"Oh, Adam, I wish it were that easy," said Lora unhappily. "But I can't believe it would be, and—there's another thing you ought to consider. You say you want to marry me, but have you realized that in all probability I could never give you children? I was married to Carroll seven years without ever having a child—without ever even becoming with child. It was a terrible disappointment to him, I know. Not that he ever reproached me for it, but I know how much he wanted an heir, and he died without ever having one.

"That's a consideration, certainly," admitted Adam, after a brief pause. "But you know, Lora, it's not such a consideration with me as it would have been with Carroll. What property I possess is entirely my own. There's no entailment to worry about, and no title, either. The matter of having a direct heir need not influence me in my choice of wives." He paused again, then went on with an air of diffidence. "And then, too, perhaps there's something *you* haven't considered, Lora," he said. "With all due apologies to your late husband, it doesn't seem to me a certainty that you couldn't bear children, only because you didn't bear any in the time you were married to him. Those kind of difficulties don't always rest with the woman, you know."

Lora shook her head slowly. "No," she said, "no, I suppose not, Adam. But in this instance there's no way of knowing where they do rest. If you were to marry me and then find that I couldn't bear your children, either, I'm afraid you would always regret it."

"I should regret it even more if I didn't marry you," said Adam, reaching over to possess himself of her hand. "I like children, mind you. I've often thought I wouldn't mind having some of my own someday, if fate allowed. But I would rather marry you, Lora, with the certainty that I could never have them, than marry any other woman with the certainty that I could."

Lora was silent for some minutes. At last she drew a sigh. "It's no use," she said. "I can't marry you, Adam. You've answered all my objections very neatly, but—still it's impossible. Please don't ask me any more."

"But I will ask you," said Adam, tightening his grasp on her hand. "Why is it impossible, Lora? If you've other reason for refusing me, then I think I have a right to know it. Why is it impossible that you marry me?"

Lora started to speak, hesitated, and then nodded. "Very well, Adam," she said. "This is going to sound dreadful, I'm sure, but I've got to make you understand. When Carroll died, I felt guilty, as I told you—but I also felt as though I had suddenly been released from prison, a prison where I had fully expected to spend the rest of my life." Her voice quavered slightly but she went on, her eyes never wavering from Adam's face as she spoke. "I was completely at sea. I didn't know what to do, or how I wanted to live the rest of my life. But one thing I was perfectly, positively certain about was that I never wanted to risk being imprisoned again. And I still feel that way, Adam." She made the statement simply, her eyes still fixed on Adam's face. "Marriage is such a serious, such a *permanent* thing. I would do anything else for you, but I can't do that."

"In other words, you would be my mistress, but not my wife."

"Yes," said Lora simply.

Adam sat quietly for a moment, looking down at her hand where it lay in his. "I suppose I ought to be flattered," he said at last. "Most men would be, I'm sure, but I'm afraid it wouldn't satisfy me only to be your cicisbeo, Lora. I have too much—not pride, exactly—call it rather self-respect. I have too much self-respect to be happy with such an arrangement as that. The plain fact is that I don't come from the level of society where that kind of thing is an accepted practice."

Lora found herself in the curious position of having to defend what she herself had once condemned. That she could not honestly do so made her angry, and she was made angrier still by the latent sense of shame which Adam's words had awakened in her. " 'That kind of thing,' " she mimicked fiercely. "You make it sound so ugly, Adam. If we love each other, what does it matter if we choose to disobey a few stupid social conventions? I hadn't realized you were such a puritan, Adam. Do you mean to say you've never made love to a woman before?"

This was a low blow, and Lora knew it, but she was too angry to care what effect her words might have. Adam did not grow angry in return, however, but only answered quietly, "No, I don't mean to say that, Lora. What I do say is that I have never felt about any woman the way I feel about you—and I never expect to feel so about any other. What we have is very special, I think. Call it puritanism if you like, but I would not have it cheapened to a mere affair."

His words touched Lora, even in the midst of her resentment. She had already begun to feel ashamed of her outburst. "Then does that mean—do you mean, then, that you don't want to see me anymore?" she said, in a voice that would choke in spite of itself.

Adam sighed. "It would probably be better if I didn't," he

said. "It's obvious that we don't agree—probably never shall agree—on that particular subject. But though I pride myself on having a fair amount of self-control, Lora, I'm afraid I don't have quite as much as that." He smiled wryly as he pressed her hand in his. "If we do continue to see each other, however, it must not be like this. What I mean is—from now on, we'd better see each other only in formal situations where there are other people around. At the risk of sounding like one of Richardson's heroines, I don't quite trust myself and my virtue alone in your company!"

Lora could only nod. It was a relief to be granted even such a concession as this. She had been prepared to have him eschew her company altogether.

The flashes of lightning in the east had been growing more frequent while they had been speaking. Now a low rumble of thunder broke the stillness. Adam glanced at the sky and rose to his feet. "I suppose it's time we were getting back to the house," he said. "I just felt a drop of rain. The storm must be getting pretty close."

"I cannot go back to the house," said Lora, drawing the domino around her in some agitation. "Not like this—not after all that's happened."

"Would you rather stay here and have me call your carriage?"

"Yes," said Lora, and then suffered a sudden reversion of feeling. "No. I don't know. Yes, call the carriage, Adam, but I will come with you." They might already be separated in mind, but Lora felt she would rather put off the actual physical separation as long as possible.

Adam silently gave her his arm, and they set off through the wilderness once more, this time directing their steps around the house rather than toward the terrace.

Inside, the party still appeared to be going strong. Bursts of laughter and snatches of music came clearly to their ears as they rounded the house, and here and there they encountered a straggling group of revelers, though Lord Ellsworth and his

friends were not among them, Lora was relieved to see. At
last they reached the footman on duty at the front entrance.
To this individual, Adam quietly gave the order for Lora's carriage to be brought around. He and Lora then took shelter in
the portico while the message was relayed to the stable.

The rain was falling steadily now, and every few minutes
the sky was illumined by a flash of lightning. Lora shivered
and drew the hood of Adam's domino further over her face.
It occurred to her as she did so that her own domino was still
hanging in the ladies' cloakroom, but she brushed the thought
aside. The loss of a domino seemed a minor thing after all
that had happened that evening, and she felt in any case a
childish reluctance to part with the garment she was wearing.
It was a comfort to have something of Adam's which she might
keep with her, even if that something were only a domino.

The carriage arrived at last, with lamps lit and liveried servants once more ranged in state upon box and perch. The footman who opened the door repressed an obvious yawn as Adam
helped Lora into the carriage. Adam held her hand tightly in
his own for a moment, but did not kiss it.

"Good night, Lora," he said. "I'll call upon you next week,
if I may."

Lora nodded. There was a lump in her throat that prevented
her from speaking. Once she was seated inside the carriage,
Adam stepped back. The footman slammed shut the door and
remounted his perch, and the coachman whipped up the horses.

Lora, suddenly desperate for some more personal word of
farewell, let down the window glass and leaned out. Adam saw
her and raised his hand just as the carriage swept her out of
sight. Lora returned the salute, futilely, then sank back on the
squabs and for the third time that evening dissolved into tears.

Fourteen

"It must have been quite the party at Rawlings's last night," said Lady Helen. She and Lora were sitting in the Turkish drawing room, where the servants had just brought in the after-dinner tea tray. Lora made no answer, but a faint flush rose to her cheeks as she took a sip of tea. "It must have been quite the party," repeated Lady Helen. "You said, as I recall, that you were going to leave early, but I understand you got home very late last night—or rather, I should say, this morning."

Lora flushed deeper. "I hope I did not wake you coming in, Helen," she said.

"No, I never heard a thing," said Lady Helen cheerfully. "I wouldn't have known what time you got home if I hadn't asked Annie this morning. You really ought to get yourself a better ladies' maid, Lora. That girl is perfectly worthless. I'll admit she's coming along where dressing hair is concerned, but she still can't sew to speak of, and she hasn't an idea of discretion. Only imagine her giving out the hour you got in last night, as innocently as a lamb! A real ladies' maid would have put me properly in my place for asking such an impertinent question, but not Annie. 'Oh, my lady, I couldn't say exactly, but I know 'twas very late, for I sat up till two waiting for her before I finally fell asleep. Very late, it was, and the strangest thing, my lady. When I looked in on her this morning, I found she'd come home with someone else's domino instead of her own and her dress torn something shocking. 'Twill be a proper job of work to fix it, if it *can* be fixed, which I take leave to doubt.' "

Lady Helen's mimicry was nearly perfect. Lora blushed all the deeper as she said, "Annie knows you are my friend, Helen. I'm sure she would not speak so openly to anyone else."

"I'm sure I hope so, for *your* sake, but I wouldn't place any dependence on it. For all you know, she's entertaining the servants' hall with the same story right now. You really ought to get rid of her, Lora. A ladies' maid should have discretion, if nothing else, and Annie has none."

Lora merely shook her head. Lady Helen poured herself a second cup of tea and then settled back on the sofa, eyeing her friend with curiosity. "Well, and am I not to hear any of the details?" she asked. "I am very interested to hear how the exchange of dominoes came about, not to mention the torn dress!"

"It was an accident, Helen. Not what you're thinking."

Lady Helen looked politely incredulous. "If you say so. Very well, then, you can at least satisfy my curiosity about Rawlings Court. Is it as magnificent as everyone says?"

Lora, with an effort, stirred herself to describe such of the splendors of Rawlings Court as she had observed. Lady Helen listened with interest, drinking her tea and nibbling at sweet biscuits. "It does sound enchanting. I may have to break down and visit the place myself one of these—oh, dear, there's another one." With a pained look, Lady Helen set down her teacup and clutched both hands to her abdomen. Lora regarded her with concern.

"What is it, Helen? Do you think the baby is coming?"

"No, it's only a cramp. I've been having them on and off for this last week or so. As you love me, Lora, I beg you won't say anything about it to Arthur. He always wants to call in the doctor every time I hiccough."

Lora nodded, but for the rest of the evening she watched her friend narrowly and twice more observed Lady Helen wince and fold her hands over her abdomen. Lady Helen said nothing about it, however, so Lora likewise said nothing, and the two of them went up to bed without exchanging any more confidences.

Alone in her bed that night, Lora tossed and turned from side to side. She had scarcely slept the night before, which ought to have insured a quick and easy descent into sleep tonight, but the same thoughts that had troubled her then had returned to trouble her now.

Once more, in her mind's eye, she relived all that had passed at the Rawlings's masquerade. This naturally served to revive all the emotions she had felt during the evening: the frustration of her search for Adam among the crowd, her anger at Lord Ellsworth's ungentlemanly behavior, and her relief at Adam's timely rescue. And then there had been that abortive but incredibly exciting episode in the summerhouse, followed by the pain of Adam's seeming rejection and the shock of his subsequent proposal of marriage.

The thought of that proposal alone was enough to drive all hope of sleep from Lora's couch. The idea of marrying again had been so far from her mind that in all her acquaintance with Adam, she had never once considered marriage and him in the same connection. When she went to consider it now, however, she found the idea held a strong, seductive appeal. It was so easy to picture her and Adam living happily together in perfect conjugal harmony. But against that picture she had to set the picture of married life as she had known it, a life of anything but happiness and harmony.

"I can't do it," said Lora aloud. "I can't risk it. Oh, Adam, why do you ask it of me?" It seemed to her ironic that of all the men of her acquaintance, most of whose morals would not bear scrutiny on such a point, she should have fixed upon one who insisted on marriage as a prelude to physical intimacy. "But of course, he didn't understand my situation when he asked me to marry him," she told herself. "Once he has had time to think about it, surely he will come around to my point of view. And in the meantime, I still may see him and talk to him. It's not as though he has broken off our acquaintance altogether. It will all work out somehow, I'm sure of it."

In spite of her certainty that it would all work out somehow, it was long before Lora slept that night. She slept late the next morning as a result, but rose and made her toilette in great haste with the idea that Adam might come to call upon her that day. He did not come, however, although Lora lingered about the house all afternoon, putting off a fitting at Madame LeClaire's and refusing an invitation to drive in the park with Lady Helen and Lord Spelbourne.

Neither did Adam call upon her the following day, nor the next, nor the day after that. It was a full week from the date of the masquerade when he finally appeared in Lady Helen's drawing room. When he did appear, unfortunately, it was under conditions that were less than ideal. Lady Hartman and Mrs. Blythe-Davies, two ladies of Lady Helen's acquaintance, had been ushered into the drawing room only a few minutes before, their avowed purpose being to inquire after the state of their friend's health.

"Good afternoon, Lora," said Lady Hartman, the elder and statelier of the two ladies, as she seated herself on the Turkish sofa. "We have come to find out how Helen is feeling."

"Yes, dear Helen," chimed in Mrs. Blythe-Davies, seating herself beside Lady Hartman. She was a small, birdlike woman with bright black eyes and a restless manner. As she spoke her eyes wandered here, there, and everywhere, taking in all the room's appointments and every detail of Lora's toilette. "That's a pretty cap you're wearing, my dear," she told Lora. "Caps are my especial aversion—I look so dreadfully dowdy wearing one, I always feel. But of course with your face, you can wear anything and look well."

"Thank you," said Lora, touching the trifle of lace and muslin atop her head with a deprecating air. "I don't much care for caps either, but since the hairdresser was coming this afternoon—"

"Mr. Wainwright," announced the butler, swinging open the

drawing room door at this inopportune moment. Lora put her hand to her cap once more and mentally cursed the fate that had brought Adam here on this particular afternoon, when she was looking her absolute worst and could not even have the comfort of receiving him in private. It would have been an awkward meeting in any case, after what had happened between them the night of the masquerade, but the awkwardness was definitely compounded with Lady Hartman and Mrs. Blythe-Davies looking on.

"Good afternoon, Adam," said Lora, miserably certain that she was blushing.

"Good afternoon, Lora," said Adam. He was wearing the usual gentleman's afternoon costume of blue topcoat, light pantaloons, and Hessian boots. Lora thought he looked very handsome in this dress, but the expression on his face made her heart sink: it was the same cool, aloof expression he had worn the first night he had called on her at the theater, when Lord Ellsworth had made such a nuisance of himself. Knowing Adam as she did, Lora was not surprised that he should be diffident in the company of strangers, but she was grieved and a little vexed by it. If she could have made Lady Hartman and Mrs. Blythe-Davies vanish with a snap of her fingers, she would have done so, and sent her cap along with them.

Fortunately, Mrs. Blythe-Davies had also taken note of Adam's appearance, and she was not a woman to stand upon ceremony with an attractive gentleman. "Good afternoon," she said, smiling at him brightly. "Do pray take a seat, sir—yes, this chair by me, if you please. Have you come to ask after dear Helen, like us? I seem to remember seeing you in her company before—ah, yes, I remember, at the Randolph Rooms a few weeks ago. You danced with her, did you not?—yes, I thought so, a minuet. I knew I could not be mistaken. I remember remarking on it to Lady Hartman at the time, for we had both agreed that she was past dancing, and it greatly surprised us to see her walk out with you. I suppose you must be a very *close* friend of Helen's, mustn't you?"

Lora thought it well here to put in a word of her own, the
more so as Adam was looking rather displeased by the tenor
of Mrs. Blythe-Davies's speech. "I don't think either of you
ladies have been introduced to Mr. Wainwright, have you?"
she said, and hurried into introductions before either of them
could respond. "Lady Hartman, Mrs. Blythe-Davies, this is
Mr. Wainwright. Adam, this is Lady Hartman, and this is Mrs.
Blythe-Davies. They have very kindly called this afternoon to
ask after Lady Helen's health."

Adam bowed to both ladies and expressed himself gratified
to make their acquaintance. Mrs. Hartman favored him merely
with a cool "Good afternoon," accompanied by a dignified
nod, but Mrs. Blythe-Davies was more forthcoming. With a
gracious smile, she extended her hand to him, and while he
was saluting it, she was all the while studying him with her
usual birdlike air of inquiry.

"About you and Helen," she began.

"Yes, how is Lady Helen bearing up these days?" said
Adam, addressing himself to Lora. "I would not dare ask her
to her face, but to you I may apply for information without
fear of reprisals!"

The light tone of the question made Lora relax. This
sounded more like the old, familiar Adam, and she was encouraged to hope the night of the masquerade had not done
any lasting damage to their relationship. Before she could answer his question, however, Mrs. Blythe-Davies broke in once
more.

"Yes, how is Helen?" she said. "I do feel for her in this
heat. Such very sultry weather for May, isn't it? Even if it is
late May. I wonder Spelbourne doesn't take her into the country to escape it. But of course gentlemen never think of anyone's convenience but their own. I'm afraid your sex does tend
to be rather selfish, Mr. Wainwright," she said, wagging her
finger at Adam playfully. "Though of course we ladies bring
it on ourselves by catering so assiduously to your every whim."

"Oh, no, not *every* whim," said Adam gravely. Lora could

not tell if there was a personal meaning to his words, but rather feared there was. In an effort to change the subject, she rushed into speech once more.

"Oh, but you must not be thinking Lord Spelbourne is self-ish, ma'am," she told Mrs. Blythe-Davies. "Indeed, the only reason he is staying on in London is so that Lady Helen may be attended by Dr. Gilcrest. You know he is considered the finest *accoucheur* in England—"

Mrs. Blythe-Davies was not interested in Dr. Gilcrest and showed it by her summary dismissal of the subject. "Yes, to be sure nothing is too good for dear Helen," she said, and then went on, addressing Lora confidentially. "By the by, I must compliment you on the lovely dress you were wearing the other night at the Danvilles' reception. By Madame LeClaire, I sup-pose? Yes, I thought so. You know Lady Hartman and I have begun to patronize her, too—in fact this very dress I'm wear-ing now is one of hers."

"It is very pretty," said Lora politely.

"Ah, you are very kind to say so, my dear. But of course poor me will never look as good in my clothes as you do in yours. I am so dreadfully plump, you know." Mrs. Blythe-Davies laid her hands on her hips as though to mourn their ample proportions. It struck Lora that her manner was rather flirtatious, however, and this was emphasized by her next lay-ing her hand on Adam's knee and addressing him with a co-quettish smile. "You must know that Lady Carroll throws all of us other ladies in the shade, Mr. Wainwright. No gentleman will give us so much as a glance when *she* is around."

"I am sure you exaggerate, ma'am," said Adam with a polite bow.

This conversation was as little to Lady Hartman's taste as to Lora's, and she showed it by changing the subject. "I do hope Helen is well," she told Lora. "One cannot but feel for her, so close to her time."

Lora opened her mouth to assure her that Lady Helen was very well, but Lady Hartman had not waited for an answer.

"Indeed, I feel for Helen very particularly, for it was not so long ago that I was in the same situation, you know," she told Lora, with a solemn nod to emphasize her words. "I well remember when I was confined with my Geoffrey. Though to be sure, that was as nothing compared to what I endured with my dear Catherine, or with poor little Harriet."

At this ominous beginning, Lora closed her mouth and braced herself for what she was pretty sure would follow. What followed was a detailed disquisition of the sufferings Lady Hartman had endured during each of her several pregnancies. Lora could only be glad that Lady Helen was not present to endure it along with her. She herself was the only listener, for Lady Hartman had judged the topic to be an unsuitable one for gentlemen's ears and had pitched her voice so low that it was audible only to Lora. Adam was not neglected during this time, however. Mrs. Blythe-Davies had taken him firmly in hand and was regaling him with a gay account of her last rout-party.

"I do hope you will be able to attend my *next* party, Mr. Wainwright," Lora was in time to hear her say, as Lady Hartman finished her catalog of obstetrical horrors and sat back to enjoy a well-earned cup of tea. "This coming Friday, at my house in Berkeley Square. I would certainly have sent you a card of invitation had I been acquainted with you earlier, but as it is, I hope you will come anyway and not wait upon the formality of a written invitation."

Adam was looking rather amused. "Well, I don't know," he said, glancing at Lora. "It may be that I have plans for that evening, ma'am."

"Then you must change your plans, Mr. Wainwright. I really must insist that you come to my rout-party—yes, I really must insist. I shall take it as a personal affront if you do not, you know."

Mrs. Blythe-Davies accompanied her words with an arch smile and another wag of her finger. "Would you care for a cup of tea, Mrs. Blythe-Davies?" said Lora in a loud voice.

"And you, too, Adam?" She had always rather liked Mrs. Blythe-Davies, preferring her at any rate to the stiff and ponderous Lady Hartman, but now she found herself reversing her opinion. Lady Hartman had at least a dignity becoming to her years; it was disgusting to see a middle-aged woman behaving so kittenishly. No wonder Adam was looking amused. Certainly it could not be the woman herself he found amusing—or could it? Lora was astonished to find she was jealous of Mrs. Blythe-Davies. The thought held her transfixed until called to attention by the sound of Adam's voice.

"No, no tea, thank you, Lora," he told her, and then turned again to Mrs. Blythe-Davies. "Certainly I would not want to affront you, ma'am, but you see I have already pledged myself to Lady Carroll for the evening of your party. Friday was the night you spoke of going to the theater, wasn't it?" he said, looking at Lora.

She saw that he was giving her a chance to accept or decline the invitation for them both, just as she pleased, and her feelings for Mrs. Blythe-Davies settled down once more to their proper proportions. Mrs. Blythe-Davies was a generous, good-natured sort of woman after all, and if she, Lora, attended her rout party along with Adam, the two of them might there meet and converse with more privacy than was to be obtained on the present occasion.

"No, that was *next* Friday, Adam," she told him with a smile as warm as she dared make it. "I myself am attending Mrs. Blythe-Davies rout-party this coming Friday, and I would advise you to do the same if you are able. Her parties are quite justly famous."

Mrs. Blythe-Davies preened herself at these words of praise. "La, my dear, you put me to the blush! You mustn't be expecting *too* much, Mr. Wainwright, but you may be sure I'll do my best to make you welcome if you come. Indeed, I hope you *will* come. It will make up for my disappointment about poor Ellsworth being unable to attend."

Lady Hartman sniffed. "No great loss there, in *my* opinion," she said acidly. "It hasn't come to the point yet where I am forced to cut Ellsworth's acquaintance altogether, but it won't be long at the rate he's going."

"Now, I won't hear a word of abuse against my dear Ellsworth, Maria. You must know Lord Ellsworth is a great flirt of mine," she told the others with a smile. "I was very vexed to hear he had been called out of Town so suddenly.

"Oh, did he have to go out of Town?" said Lora, striving to look and sound only politely interested. Adam's eyes met hers for an instant, and she thought she saw a flicker of laughter in their depths, but she could not be sure. The rest of his face remained perfectly impassive.

"Yes, he had business to attend to at his estate in Kent—I think it was the Kent estate he said."

Lady Hartman sniffed again. "Possibly he had business," she said darkly. "But I have it on good authority that he hasn't been near the Kent estate this past decade, unless it were to bring down a party of wild friends to tear the place apart. I'm more inclined to put my credence in the story I heard from Tom Westicott, which was that Ellsworth attended that bacchanalian affair at Rawlings Court last week and got in a fight over some vulgar woman with her still more vulgar swain. According to him, Ellsworth got trounced quite soundly in the battle—a good deal of damage sustained to his face, and even more to his pride. No wonder he doesn't care to be seen in public!"

"Indeed," said Adam politely, and this time Lora was sure she saw a flicker of laughter in his eye.

Mrs. Blythe-Davies shook her head. "I don't believe a word of it," she said decidedly. "Not but what I shall quiz him about it all the same, when next I see him! But I ask you, is it likely Ellsworth would have let himself be bested by some vulgar City buck? You, Mr. Wainwright, you must agree with me at least. *You* are acquainted with Lord Ellsworth and his prowess in the boxing ring, I am sure."

"Slightly," said Adam, with a composure Lora could not but

admire. "I don't know him very well, however, Mrs. Blythe-Davies. No more than that vulgar City buck you were just speaking of, I daresay."

Mrs. Blythe-Davies received this as a joke and let out a trill of laughter. "Ah, don't tell me your relations have been *adversarial,* Mr. Wainwright," she said, leaning over to lay her hand on his knee again. "Not quarreling over a lady, I hope! Which reminds me, I haven't yet inquired after dear Helen." Turning again to Lora, she bestowed upon her a sparkling smile. "You must tell me all about how my dear Helen goes on. I missed her sadly at my last party—though to be sure, most people did think it a fair success all the same. I was immensely gratified, I assure you."

She would undoubtedly have gone on to give another triumphal account of her latest assembly, had not Adam then risen to his feet. "The conversation has been so fascinating that I've lost track of the time," he said, addressing all three ladies generally. "I'm afraid I've already overstayed my welcome." Turning to Lady Hartman, he bestowed upon her a formal bow. "I am very pleased to make your acquaintance, ma'am," he said politely. To Mrs. Blythe-Davies, he repeated the words, with a smile and another bow. "And you may be sure I will be looking forward to your rout-party on Friday, ma'am," he told her.

"And you may be sure I shall look forward to seeing you there, Mr. Wainwright," she replied, batting her eyes at him shamelessly.

To Lora he turned next, taking her hand and bowing over it. "Please give my regards and best wishes to Lady Helen," he told her. "Your very devoted servant, ma'am. I suppose, as you mean to attend Mrs. Blythe-Davies's party Friday, I may look to see you then?"

"Yes," said Lora. She was distressed to see him leave so soon, for she had been hoping he might stay on until after Lady Hartman and Mrs. Blythe-Davies left, so that they might have an opportunity to speak privately. But a glance at the drawing room clock showed her that more than a half-hour had elapsed since his arrival. Of course, it ought really to have been the two ladies who left first, since their arrival had preceded his, but it was obvious they had no intention of leaving anytime soon, and Adam could hardly outstay them without giving rise to the kind of gossip that would be very damaging to her reputation. Nevertheless, there was a very just resentment in her heart toward Lady Hartman and Mrs. Blythe-Davies as she watched Adam walk out of the drawing room.

The other two ladies watched him leave also. Before the door had quite shut behind him, Mrs. Blythe-Davies turned to Lora. "What a very charming young man," she said. "Wherever did Helen meet him? Oh, *you* met him first—and at the Monroes', you say? Well, you and Helen and the Monroes mustn't think you can keep him to yourselves, my dear, only because you made his acquaintance before the rest of us. Upon my word, I have half a mind to set him up as one of my flirts." Again Mrs. Blythe-Davies' finger wagged forth playfully.

"A very pleasant young gentleman," agreed Lady Hartman with more tepid enthusiasm. "What is his family, Lora? The name Wainwright is not familiar to me."

Lora carefully described Adam's family and background, not neglecting to mention his magisterial great-uncle. "Ah, a gentleman farmer," was Lady Hartman's dismissive summing-up. "Well, he seems gentlemanly enough, at least, which is more than can be said for some I could name, in higher positions."

"Now, Maria, I hope you're not referring again to my dear Ellsworth. I've already told you I won't hear a word against him."

"Would anyone like another cup of tea?" said Lora, rather wearily.

Lady Hartman declined this offer with a shake of her bonneted head. "No, my dear, we really must be going soon. Our only purpose in coming by was to pay our respects to you, and of course to ask after poor Helen."

"Yes, poor dear Helen," Mrs. Blythe-Davies said. "Do tell

her we called, Lora, and that we are thinking of her in this most trying time. I'm sure it must be very difficult for her, with the weather so dreadfully sultry."

As before, Mrs. Blythe-Davies gave Lora no time to respond, but continued to rattle on as she and Lady Hartman assumed their shawls and scarves and prepared to quit the drawing room. Lora personally accompanied them to the door, exchanged farewells with both ladies, and then closed the door behind them.

"Lady Helen is feeling *very well,*" she informed its unresponsive panels, then went up to her room to await the arrival of her hairdresser.

Fifteen

Although the presence of Lady Hartman and Mrs. Blythe-Davies had kept Lora from having any very satisfactory converse with Adam during his call, the few words she had exchanged with him had been enough to set some of her fears at rest. His manner had been more formal than it had previous to the masquerade, to be sure, but that might easily be attributed to the presence of the other two ladies. Overall his behavior had been perfectly friendly and approachable. And since he had agreed to meet her at Mrs. Blythe-Davies's party, she might have the comfort of conversing with him again, only a few days hence.

It seemed to Lora that Friday was a very long time in coming that week. It did come at last, however, as Friday invariably does, and immediately after dinner she went upstairs to dress for Mrs. Blythe-Davies' rout-party. She felt enough lingering resentment toward that lady to make herself very fine indeed in a dress newly commissioned from Madame LeClaire: a figured blue silk, cut low in back and front and worn with an ornate *parure* of sapphires in gold.

Adam was engaged in conversation with his hostess when Lora made her entrance thus attired. But he excused himself to Mrs. Blythe-Davies with praiseworthy promptitude and came over to greet her with a faint smile quirking up the corners of his mouth.

"You are still bent on my subjugation, I see," he said in a low voice. "Bringing out the heavy artillery, as it were." His eyes rested briefly and rather wistfully on the décolletage of Lora's dress. "But it won't answer, my lady: it will not answer, I say. I am, as I mentioned before, a man of iron self-control, and I have no intention of falling victim to your wiles to-night—at least, I don't think I do. Just to be on the safe side, perhaps we'd better not stray too far from the crowd."

"How can you, Adam?" said Lora, blushing. Yet she was not displeased to see him in this mood, so much more propitious to her purposes than his earlier, more formal one. It seemed to her that if he could joke on such a subject, he could not be far from conceding her point, and that the whole matter might yet resolve itself as she had hoped. To this end, she accepted his invitation to dance, looking forward to the opportunity of more private conversation on the same subject.

The opportunity did not answer so well as she had hoped, however. After his initial essay into playfulness, Adam seemed determined to keep the conversation on strictly impersonal subjects. "How is Lady Helen bearing up these days?" he inquired. "I had every intention of asking after her when I called the other day, but your other callers managed to circumvent me at every turn. She must be fairly near to the crisis now?"

"Yes, I keep expecting every day that something will happen, but nothing ever does. She keeps going on just the same. Poor Lord Spelbourne is on pins and needles, and so am I, but Helen herself is very cool about it. She just says that when it happens, it will happen, and she sees no use worrying about it beforehand." Lora sighed and smiled ruefully up at Adam. "I suppose that's true, but still I can't help worrying about her, especially since she still insists on going out walking almost every day. Every time she leaves the house, I wonder if something won't happen while she's out, and I go to bed every night wondering if tonight isn't going to be *the* night. All the waiting is starting to get on my nerves." She flashed Adam another rueful smile. "I can't imagine how poor Lord Spelbourne must feel."

Adam nodded, rather absently. "Has the doctor seen her?"

"Yes, and he says she is doing very well," said Lora, more cheerfully. "I asked him in private about the walking, but he seemed not to think it was of much concern. He said he has known of countrywomen who worked in the fields right up to the day of their delivery and weren't a bit the worse for it. But Helen is so small and delicate—although, to be sure, she has always had very good health and a great deal of energy. I hope it will all go well with her."

Adam expressed the same hope and went on to speak of other matters in which he and Lora were nearly concerned. But he made no mention of the matter uppermost in Lora's thoughts, and she did not dare mention it herself. He did not even renew his proposal of marriage, although she had half prepared herself for such a possibility. When he took leave of her and the party soon after, she was left feeling rather snubbed, in spite of the fervent kiss he pressed on her hand at parting.

This scene was repeated a number of times during the next few weeks. Adam came to call upon her; met her at parties or at the theater; danced with her, talked with her, even flirted with her on occasion, but nothing more. Lora did not know what to make of it.

It was almost as though he were trying to return to an earlier, merely friendly period in their relationship—except that their relations from the start had been marked by something more than mere friendliness. She could only conclude that Adam was still firm in his resolve not to indulge in marital intimacies without the preliminary of an actual marriage. And since she was equally firm in her own resolve not to venture into matrimony a second time, there seemed no point in even mentioning the subject.

The early days of June were already past. The King's birthday had been celebrated with the usual round of festivities, in spite of his increasing debility. The Season was officially over, and most of the members of the *ton* had already left or were making preparations to leave London to pass the summer at country houses or watering places.

Lady Helen and her husband were among the few that stayed on, in order to remain close to the *accoucheur* entrusted with Lady Helen's delivery. This meant that Lora, too, stayed on, and stayed on willingly, both for her friend's sake and for her own. For Adam also stayed on in London, although he spoke often of the necessity of returning soon to his home in Hampshire. As long as he remained in Town, however, Lora could assure herself that he had not lost interest in her entirely. If it had not been for the circumstance of his remaining, she would have begun to wonder if his feelings for her might not be dwindling; even as it was, she found herself wondering now and then.

It was on a balmy evening in mid-June that Lady Helen's labors finally began. Lora had just gone upstairs to undress for the night when she heard the sound of hasty footsteps pounding up the stairs and down the hall toward her bedchamber. The steps were followed an instant later by Lord Spelbourne, who came bursting into her room without so much as a knock to give warning of his entrance. As it happened, Lora had only got as far as removing her jewelry and so was perfectly presentable, but it was doubtful whether Lord Spelbourne would have noticed if she had been completely unclad.

"It's the baby," he gasped, looking back apprehensively over his shoulder as though that entity might materialize there at any moment. "The baby—Helen says she thinks it's time."

"I *know* it's time," said Lady Helen, appearing in the doorway behind him. "My waters broke," she explained to Lora. "It happened just as I was getting into bed, worse luck. Arthur, you shall have to sleep in your own room tonight."

"I'm not going to *sleep*," said Lord Spelbourne hotly. "Dash it, you're having the baby, ain't you? How could I sleep at a time like this?"

"The baby probably won't be here for hours and hours yet.

You might just as well try to get some sleep. And you, too, Lora. If I have Doctor Gilcrest with me, I won't need either of you to sit up with me."

"The doctor," said Lord Spelbourne, catching at these words and disregarding all the others. "I'd better drive over and fetch him right away. You get into bed, Helen. Lora, you watch her and make sure she doesn't go having the baby until I get back with the doctor. I'll take the curricle and bays and be back in a trice. Harness up my bays," he bellowed to a maidservant passing in the hall, who looked at him as though he had gone mad. "The baby's coming, demmit. There's no time to be lost."

With a resigned smile, Lady Helen watched him rush off down the hall, still shouting for his curricle and bays. "I hope he won't kill anyone on the way to the doctor's," she said. "Perhaps I ought to send word to the stables to have him restrained while one of the footmen rides over to fetch the doctor."

"Are you feeling much pain, Helen?" inquired Lora anxiously. "I quite agree with Arthur that you ought to be in bed. Is there anything I can do for you?"

"The best thing you could do is go to bed yourself, as I suggested before. But if you insist on staying up, like Arthur—"

"I do insist, Helen."

"Then I suppose you might as well come into my room and read to me. I must do something to pass the time. If I've learned nothing else from the old cats and their horror stories, it's that first babies take an unconscionable amount of time to get here. And there really isn't much pain yet: just a cramp now and then like before, only stronger."

Lora accompanied Lady Helen to her room and saw her comfortably tucked into bed, before taking up the marble-covered volume that was lying on the bedside table. She had read only a few pages, however, when Lord Spelbourne burst into his wife's room with as little ceremony as he had Lora's, closely followed by the doctor and monthly nurse.

"Well, well, and so we've reached the point at last," said

the doctor, smiling genially as he approached Lady Helen's bedside.

"Yes, it appears that we have," agreed Lady Helen. She looked impatiently at Lord Spelbourne, who was pacing up and down the room in a frenzy of nervous anticipation. "Doctor, isn't there something you could give Arthur—a nice strong dose of laudanum, perhaps—that would put him out of his misery for the next twenty-four hours or so?"

Doctor Gilcrest laughed merrily. "A very good joke, my lady. The poor husbands do suffer, too, there's no doubt about it. Laudanum, indeed—ha, ha, ha, ha. It's good to see you're keeping your spirits up, my lady. If you would allow me to examine you, just briefly for a moment—ah, yes, very good. Everything seems to be proceeding splendidly."

"I wasn't joking," Lady Helen told Lora.

"Yes, everything seems to be proceeding splendidly," the doctor repeated. "Cramps, you say, but not regular or strong as yet—yes, still some hours away from *partus*, no doubt, though of course it's difficult to be certain about these things. If I might venture to suggest it, your lordship would undoubtedly be much more comfortable in the next room. Ladies do often become nervous during these ordeals, and we've a long way to go before we'll have anything to show for it."

"Thank God," said Lady Helen, as Lord Spelbourne reluctantly withdrew into the next room. "Now read to me, Lora."

Lora read. She read on and on, past midnight and into the small hours: on and on, until her voice grew hoarse and the words began to blur together on the page. At last Lady Helen stopped her.

"Thank you, Lora; you're an angel," she said, taking the book from Lora's hand. "You'd better ring for a pot of tea and some sandwiches to recruit yourself. I suppose I can't have any?" she asked the doctor.

The doctor shook his head regretfully. "I'm afraid not, my lady. Afterwards you may have anything you like in the way of food or drink, but for now it would be better if you took nothing except perhaps a little wine and water."

"Very well," said Lady Helen. "Get yourself some tea and sandwiches, Lora, and order me some wine and water. Now *I'm* going to read for a while."

Taking up the book, Lady Helen began to read from it in a loud, clear voice. Her style of reading was very singular, however, for every few minutes she was seized by a cramp that made her voice speed up and rise an octave or two above her normal tone.

"And though the Gypsy's words . . . seemed but of little moment . . . Isabella-found-her-heart-disquieted," read Lady Helen determinedly. "In vain was her resolve to . . . think-of-it-no-more."

For an hour and more she kept this up, to Lora's mingled amazement and distress. At last she laid down the book with a grimace. "I can't read any more," she said. "It hurts so I can't make sense of what I'm reading. How much longer do you think it will be, Doctor?"

"At least another hour, my lady; perhaps two. But your ladyship ought really to stay in bed and rest—"

"I *can't* rest. I feel as though my insides were being put through a clothes mangle. If I get out of bed and walk about a bit, perhaps it will help me to keep my mind off the pain." Throwing off the bedclothes, Lady Helen got out of bed with surprising nimbleness and began to walk up and down the room.

She managed to keep this up, too, for nearly an hour, steadfastly ignoring the doctor's, Lora's, and the monthly nurse's pleas for her to return to bed. Most of the female staff, by now alerted to what was going on, found excuse to come to the room to offer their services. Maidservants peeped wide-eyed around the door, while Lady Helen's dressing woman bustled importantly to and fro with basins and towels, and every few minutes Lord Spelbourne's valet appeared discreetly in the door to make inquiries on behalf of his master, who was waiting anxiously in the adjoining bedchamber.

Finally, after being doubled over by a particularly severe cramp, Lady Helen meekly consented to return to bed. "Oh, Helen, I am so sorry. Is it very bad?" said Lora, hovering helplessly at her side.

"Yes," said Lady Helen with emphasis. "I must have been mad to consent to this business." A moment later she said suddenly, "Arthur. I want Arthur. He got me into this, he can damned well come and keep me company now!"

"My lady's husband had much better remain in the next room until your delivery is over," said the doctor hesitantly. "He is liable to find the process somewhat upsetting—"

"Get him," said Lady Helen, her voice rising dangerously close to a shriek. "Get him, now."

The monthly nurse glanced at the doctor, who shrugged his shoulders and nodded resignedly. The woman vanished into the adjoining room and returned a few seconds later, followed by a very pale and scared-looking Lord Spelbourne.

"Arthur, you may hold my hand," said Lady Helen, smiling wanly at him from the pillows. "I will try not to scream, but if I do, you must not let it disturb you. At the moment I am not feeling particularly brave."

"Don't you worry about that, Helen," said Lord Spelbourne stoutly, taking his place beside the bed and gripping her hand in both of his. "You go on and scream if you want to."

"Thank you, I believe I will," said Lady Helen, and proceeded to do so. Lora, the monthly nurse, and the doctor all clustered around, the latter assuming a position of authority at the foot of the bed.

"Yes, yes, very good. It won't be long now, my lady. That's right, that's right. No, your ladyship must assist me, if you please. Yes, very good. Again, if you please."

"Oh, God," said Lady Helen in a long-suffering voice, but did her best to comply with these instructions. Lord Spelbourne, Lora, and the monthly nurse joined voices to encourage her.

"You're doing very well, my lady. It's all but over now."

"That's right, old girl—you're doing fine."

"Oh, Helen! Oh, Helen, I can see the baby! I can see it, Helen." And a moment later a thin wail was heard, as Lady Helen completed her labors with a last herculean effort and fell back exhausted on the pillows.

"That's the baby?" said Lord Spelbourne, surveying the small, wailing bundle in the doctor's arms with fascinated horror. "Good God! Is it . . . all right?"

"Yes, they're always a bit messy when they first arrive, my lord. Once Mrs. Larkin has cleaned him up a bit—yes, there you go. Your son, my lord! And as fine, healthy a boy as I've ever seen."

Lord Spelbourne looked down at the blanket-wrapped baby which the doctor had just placed in his arms. The baby had by now ceased to cry. It lay quietly in its cocoon of blankets, looking up at him with a wide-eyed, inscrutable stare.

"Oh, Arthur, he's beautiful," said Lora, almost overcome by the pathos of the moment. "He's beautiful, Helen, just beautiful."

"Not too bad," agreed Lord Spelbourne. With one finger, he reached down gingerly to touch the baby's hand. The baby's fingers promptly closed around his own. A bemused smile spread over Lord Spelbourne's face. "I say, Helen, he's holding my finger! Got a good grip on it, too. You ought to see this, Helen. Look here, ain't he a fine little chap? That's right, sir, you know your old dad when you see him, don't you?"

The doctor and monthly nurse had been attending to Lady Helen meanwhile, straightening the bedclothes and discreetly disposing of the after-effects of birth. Lord Spelbourne turned to her now, seating himself on the edge of the bed beside her.

"Here, Helen, you can hold him for a bit," he said, depositing the baby in her arms. "Not bad-looking for a baby, is he? I'd say he's about the best-looking baby I've ever seen. I tell you what, Helen: you made a good job of this business. Cleverest thing you've ever done, 'pon my word."

"Well, you did have some share in it, too, I suppose," said

Lady Helen magnanimously. She surveyed her newborn son with satisfaction. "He looks more like you than me, Arthur, which is all to the good."

"D'you think so? I was thinking myself he looks a bit like my grandfather. Bald as an egg, you know, and got that same way of looking at you, as though he didn't half believe what you was saying."

"Oh, but he is not bald, Arthur! See, he has the loveliest hair—so fine and fair and soft, just like silk. But he does have a rather skeptical look on his face, doesn't he? No wonder, poor lamb, after all he's been through. I wonder what he makes of us all?"

Lora, watching them, began to feel rather out of place in this family scene. "I believe I'll go to my own room now and try to get some sleep," she said.

No one paid her the least heed. "We shall call him Arthur, of course," Lady Helen was saying fondly as Lora quietly withdrew from the room. "Arthur Edward? No, Arthur Edmund, after your grandfather that you were just talking about. And Vincent, after mine. Arthur Edmund Vincent Langley, Earl of Westbrook and heir to the marquisate of Spelbourne. That sounds rather well, doesn't it?"

"Oh, aye, just as you say, Helen."

Lora shut the bedroom door gently behind her, then turned and went down the hall. When she reached the staircase, however, she found she had not much inclination to go up to bed. It was already mid-morning, with the sun shining brightly in at the windows, and though she felt a little light-headed from lack of sleep, the excitement of the last hour or two had more than made up for it. On the whole, she thought she would rather go down and get some breakfast, if such a thing were to be had in a household so disorganized. Those of the servants she had encountered thus far had been more intent upon celebrating the arrival of the heir to the house of Spelbourne than upon their regular duties, but it seemed reasonable to hope that she might obtain something downstairs by applying directly to the cook.

And so, rather than going upstairs to her room, Lora began to descend the broad square staircase that led to the entrance hall on the ground floor. As she rounded the last turn, she looked down into the hall below and saw Adam standing near the foot of the stairs, looking up at her.

Sixteen

Adam had been waiting in the hall for some time. The flurried-looking maidservant who had admitted him had vanished immediately after without taking his hat, coat, or card, and he had stood uncertainly in the vestibule, waiting for her or some other servant to appear and rectify the omission.

This they had been very slow to do, however. Five minutes had passed, then ten, and then fifteen, until at last, growing tired of waiting, Adam had left the vestibule and made his way into the hall with the idea of finding someone to carry a message to Lora. But the house seemed completely deserted. The distinguished-looking butler he remembered from his previous visits was nowhere about; neither were any of the footmen; and if it had not been for the Spelbourne coat of arms laid out in mosaic upon the floor beneath his feet, he would almost have supposed that he had stumbled into the wrong house.

As he neared the foot of the stairs, he caught the sound of voices somewhere overhead. He paused, looking upward, wondering if he ought to go and investigate their source. Undoubtedly something out of the ordinary was taking place in the household. If his thoughts had not been running so much on Lora, he might have guessed what the something was, but all he could think was that she might be lying ill or injured upstairs and be in need of assistance, perhaps. He had just put his hand on the newel post to start up the stairs when Lora appeared on the landing above him.

"Adam," she said, surprised but pleased. In her light-headed condition, it did not seem extraordinary that he should be there. She had been thinking of him only a moment before, reflecting that she ought to write him and tell him of Lady Helen's successful *accouchement*. "Oh, Adam, I am so glad to see you," she said, coming down the last flight of stairs in a rush. "Have you been waiting long? I did not know you were here."

She smiled as she spoke and held out her hand to him. Adam could not refrain from taking it, though he would not allow himself to return the smile. "Yes, I have been waiting for some time. Is there somewhere we could go to be private, Lora? I must talk to you for a few minutes."

Lora gave him a surprised look but led him to a small parlor off the entrance hall. "We can be private here, Adam," she said, closing the door behind them. "Although I doubt the servants would disturb us much in any case. They have too much else to think about right now."

"Yes, where are the servants? The girl that opened the door to me didn't take my name, and I've been waiting here twenty minutes, wondering whether I had suddenly become *persona non grata* to you all and you were taking this way to inform me of it."

Lora laughed happily. "No, it isn't that, Adam. Helen has been having her baby! Has actually had it, in fact, less than an hour ago. I think the servants are all off celebrating somewhere."

"Is that so?" exclaimed Adam, momentarily diverted from his purpose. "Of course, I ought to have realized what was going on when I found the house so disorganized. Lady Helen and the baby are both well, I trust?"

"Yes, very well. The doctor says it was a very easy, straightforward labor, although I'm not sure Helen would agree with him! You must forgive me for the way I look, Adam. Everything happened very suddenly last night, and I haven't had a chance to sleep or even change my dress since then."

Looking at her more closely, Adam could see that there were dark smudges under her eyes and that her hair and dress were not quite in their usual order, but she still looked very beautiful to him. "Perhaps this isn't the best time to call," he said uncertainly. "I wouldn't have called so early, except that I was leaving Town and wanted to see you before I went."

"Oh, are you going out of Town again?" said Lora in a disappointed wail. "Today, Adam?"

"Yes, I hope to reach home early this afternoon if all goes well."

"And when will you be returning to London?"

Adam drew a deep breath. "I will not be returning to London, Lora," he said. "I've already spent more time here than I can afford this year, and I can't afford to spend any more. It's vital that I be at home this summer to supervise the haying and wheat-shearing, and to attend to all the business that's been neglected in my absence."

Lora looked at him in growing dismay. "But surely that won't take all summer, Adam! I hadn't supposed you would stay in London too much longer—indeed, I don't suppose I'll be staying much longer myself, now that Helen has had her baby. I think we will all be removing to Spelbourne as soon as they are able to travel. Perhaps you could come and visit us there, Adam? Somerset isn't so far from Hampshire, and I know Helen and Arthur would be glad to have you."

Adam shook his head. "It's no use, Lora," he said in a low voice. "I've been thinking about it these last few weeks, and I don't see going on like this, with both of us feeling as we do. I think it would be best if we didn't see each other any more."

Lora stared at him. "Not see each other any more?" she repeated. "You mean, not *ever?*"

"I think it would be best, Lora," he said, avoiding her eyes.

A wave of sick, dizzy feeling swept over Lora, much stronger than the mere physical dizziness she had felt coming down the stairs. She sat down abruptly on one of the parlor chairs. "Lora, I'm sorry," said Adam, looking down at her worriedly. "I know you've been under a strain. Perhaps I should have waited to tell you, only I wouldn't have had another chance to speak to you in person. Ought I to ring for your maid?"

"No, I'll be all right in a minute," said Lora. Her voice had hardened perceptibly since her last speech, and it hardened further as she continued. "Indeed, Adam, I ought to have been prepared for something like this. I have seen you so little these past few weeks. And when I have seen you, it's been almost as though we were strangers—not as it was before that night at the Rawlings's. Is it that you don't love me anymore, Adam? You needn't be afraid to say so. I don't intend to make a scene, but if I am never to see you again, I would like to know the truth before you go."

An expression that was like a smile, yet indescribably painful, passed over Adam's face. "No, it isn't that I don't love you anymore, Lora," he said gently. "How could you think it? When I told you before that you're the only woman I've ever loved or expect to love, I was telling you the truth, and it's as true now as it was then. If I've seemed cooler to you lately, it isn't any reflection of what I've been feeling, but rather of what I wish I felt. You can't know how difficult these last few weeks have been for me."

"You're saying you would rather not love me," said Lora in a flat, accusatory voice.

"I'm saying that loving you is tearing me apart." Adam's voice was suddenly impassioned. "Look at me, Lora. I'm not a rich man. I can't afford to spend months on end in London, living in idleness. All the time I've been here, I've had duties, responsibilities, commitments waiting for me at home, and yet I've thrown them all over so I could be with you. Do you think I would have done that if I didn't love you?"

"You don't act as though you love me," was all Lora could think to say.

"Because I don't make love to you? But you must know the reason for that, Lora." Adam held her gaze steadily, and there was a caressing note in his voice as he added, "If only you would marry me, you would have no cause to complain on that score, I assure you!"

"But *do* you still want to marry me, Adam?" Lora gave him a hard, searching look. "You haven't said anything about it since that night at the Rawlings's. Say what you will, I think your feelings must have cooled a little, or you could not abandon me so easily."

"Do you think it has been easy?" Adam's voice shook slightly as he spoke the question. "It's been the hardest thing I've ever done in my life. I would give anything in the world if you would change your mind and marry me, Lora, but don't you see why I can't urge you to do so?"

Lora thought, and thought she could see. "Because you think I would be making a sacrifice to marry you," she said reluctantly. "But that's not true, Adam."

"Yes, it *is* true," said Adam, almost angrily. "Even if that were the only reason, it would be enough to keep me from pressing my suit. But that's not the only reason, Lora. It's not even the main reason. Don't you see that after what you told me the other night, I can't in conscience try to make you change your mind?" In a softer voice he continued, "Marriage is something of a gamble, even under the best of circumstances. If I convinced you to marry me and then it turned out later that you were unhappy—as unhappy as you were before—it would be all my fault. I wouldn't want that burden to bear the rest of my life, Lora."

Lora nodded. "I understand," she said. The tears were flowing down her cheeks, but she made no effort to wipe them away. After a moment Adam went on, rather painfully.

"It is your happiness that I want more than anything, you know. If I thought it would make you happy, to have me on the terms you suggested originally, then I would do it, even in spite of how I felt about it all." He grasped Lora's hand tightly in his own. "But in this case, I think I know you better than you know yourself, Lora. I would like to think so, at all events. It seems to me better in every respect that we should part now as friends, rather than put it to the test. If we were to continue to see each other, I'm afraid one of us would give way to the other in a weak moment and then resent the other ever after."

"I understand," said Lora again. She got to her feet and began to move blindly toward the door, but Adam stopped her.

"Goodbye, Lora," he said, and folded her tightly in his arms. Lora lay her face against his chest and wept, equally without shame and without restraint.

"Goodbye, Adam," she managed to whisper at last.

Adam tilted up her face and kissed her, a kiss at once bitter and sweet, mingled with the salt of her tears. At that kiss, Lora broke down entirely. She turned away, covering her face with her hands.

So it was that she heard but did not see Adam leave the parlor; heard the sound of his steps crossing the hall, and then, very softly, heard the sound of the front door opening and closing.

Seventeen

After Adam had gone, Lora drifted back upstairs as though in a dream. She had forgotten all about being hungry and about going downstairs to get something to eat from the cook. When she did remember, some minutes later, the thought of food was nauseating, and there was a constriction in her throat that would have precluded swallowing anyway. At the moment, her most urgent need was solitude. She reached the first landing and started up the second flight of stairs toward her room, only to be called back by Lady Helen, who had heard her step on the stairs and sent her dressing woman to summon her to her bedchamber.

"My Lady Helen's compliments, and she would be very glad if you could come to her room for a few minutes, my lady. Her ladyship would like very much to speak to you."

Like a leaf borne by the wind, Lora changed course and drifted through the door of Lady Helen's bedchamber. She found her friend sitting up in bed, in the act of nursing her newborn son for the first time. This sight was sufficient to shock Lora out of some of her abstraction. "I thought you were having a wet-nurse, Helen?"

Lady Helen looked both embarrassed and defiant. "Well, yes, I was. In fact, I had actually hired one, but when she got here just now I changed my mind and told her I wouldn't be needing her after all. Not but what she looked a perfectly decent sort—I wouldn't have hired her in the first place if she hadn't—but still, one hears so many dreadful stories about wet-nurses. Drinking, you know, and neglect, and all that sort of thing. So I let her show me what to do, and then I gave her twenty pounds and sent her away again."

In spite of her own overpowering state of affliction, Lora was rather amused. "But weren't you concerned about nursing ruining your figure?" she asked.

"Well, I don't suppose nursing *one* baby will much damage it. And then, Sylvia Townsend was telling me the other day that she nursed all three of hers, and *her* figure certainly hasn't suffered for it. And then, too, I am getting rather old to be thinking so much about my appearance. In short, I have made up my mind to nurse young Arthur, and there's an end of it. Isn't he adorable?"

Lora agreed that he was and went away, marveling at the effect childbirth had had on her prosaic friend. Once more she drifted toward the stairs, only to be called back again, this time by Lord Spelbourne, who wanted someone with whom he could discuss the day's great event.

Lora let herself be drawn into the library and sat listening quietly as he rapturously expounded on the joys of fatherhood and the beauties of his newborn son and heir. The act cost her nothing, for she had much rather listen than talk just then. Indeed, there was something almost soothing about Lord Spelbourne's discourse, repetitive and ungrammatical though it often was. When he ordered up a bottle of champagne to celebrate the occasion, she was able to accept a glass and drink it along with the butler, the monthly nurse, Lady Helen's dressing woman, and two or three other servants who happened to be within earshot and accepted with alacrity his invitation to join him in a glass. When she finally left the library, Lora felt as though she might, after all, be able to bear the shock that had come upon her so suddenly.

All through that day she drifted, taking no part in the jubilation that was going on throughout Spelbourne House but finding diversion enough in it all to keep her from dwelling on the fact of Adam's departure. When she retired to bed late that evening, however, it was with a feeling of trepidation. She feared that the hour of reckoning had come at last, and that she would be forced to finally face the thought she had been avoiding so long. But contrary to her expectations, she fell asleep almost instantly, and her dreams were untroubled by any reference to the events of the day. It was only in the early hours of the morning, before the light of dawn had begun to steal into her bedchamber, that she awoke and found the thought bearing down on her like an actual weight pressing on her heart.

Adam was gone. By now he would have certainly reached his home in Hampshire and would be settling down to stay. Lora had been hoping and praying for some last-minute miracle to detain him: some word from him that he had relented and would be returning to London after all. But no word had come, no miracle had intervened, and she was forced to face the facts. He was gone, and the only way she could call him back was to betray the promise she had made to herself two and a half years before and sworn never to break.

It seemed to Lora eminently unfair. Amid all the other emotions that were tormenting her at that moment was a strong feeling of resentment. She felt resentment toward Heaven for not having averted this crisis; resentment toward society, whose foolish rules had precipitated it; and most of all, resentment toward Adam, who had put her in the impossible position of having to choose between her painfully acquired freedom and her love for him.

"If only someone would tell me what to do," fretted Lora aloud. "*He* won't. All he has done is to throw the decision into my lap, and oh, I don't want it, I don't want it. How I wish I had someone who would tell me what to do."

Lora had several times expressed this wish, both aloud and in her thoughts, before it occurred to her what an irony it was. She had spent most of her adult life meekly doing what other people told her to do and resenting it hotly all the while. Undoubtedly, it was easier to follow the path of least resistance rather than forge one's own way through life, but her recent experience seemed to show that in the latter way lay the greater happiness. The decision she was struggling with was one on which the entire future course of her life would depend. It followed, then, that it was a decision she must make entirely on her own.

By now thoroughly awake, Lora got out of bed, put on her dressing gown, and sat down in a chair beside the window to think. She thought first of her resolution never to remarry. That had been a resolution solidly based on her own previous experience with the marital state. But just because she had experienced unhappiness in her marriage to Lord Carroll, it did not necessarily follow that she would be equally unhappy married to Adam. There was a great deal of truth in what he had said about their being two different people in an entirely different situation. Indeed, Adam himself could not know the extent of that difference. She had told Adam that she had loved Lord Carroll, which was true as far as it went, but she knew now for a certainty what she had suspected even then, that it had not been the right kind of love.

The mistake had been an easy one to make. Lord Carroll had been young, handsome, and to all appearances madly in love with her. He had courted her in the most lavish style, showering her with flowers and gifts and sworn testimony of his devotion. Lora, always soft-hearted, had found it very easy to love someone who was so good to her, but at the same time she had wondered whether that kind of loving were really the same as being in love and whether she did in fact love him enough to legitimately accept his proposals of marriage. An honest and conscientious girl, she had expressed these doubts to Lord Carroll on more than one occasion, but he had been so sanguine in his temper, so confident that he could make her return his love in all its fullness, that she had let herself be persuaded.

Of course, it had not been his persuasions alone that had been to blame. Her mother, and to a lesser extent, her father, had been in favor of the marriage. Yet Lora knew that if she herself had really opposed it, her parents never would have insisted. It was her own weakness that had been at fault. She had let her own real concerns be overruled by those closest to her—and perhaps, too, she had been swayed by the idea of becoming a countess and enjoying all the benefits of exalted rank and nearly unlimited wealth. Lora hoped she had not been influenced by such worldly considerations, but at sixteen, she felt she would hardly have been human if they had not held a certain allure.

She had not been married long before it had become clear to her that she had made a mistake. The love that she had felt for Lord Carroll had not stood up very well under day-to-day living with that gentleman, and though he had continued to swear he loved her right up until the day of his death, Lora's grief at that untimely event had been mixed with a considerable degree of relief. This had so shocked her when she realized it that she had straightway resolved never to marry again; never to risk seeing love undergo such an ugly, unnatural transformation. Now she stood in a position to risk it again, with untold heartache in the offing if she refused and perhaps an even greater heartache if she accepted. Was it worth the risk? Lora simply did not know.

One thing which she did know was that she loved Adam. There could be no question at all about that. Most sincerely might she have echoed Adam's words, when he had spoken of having never experienced such a feeling for anyone else. Yet she knew, intellectually at least, that it would be possible for her to give him up and go on living as she was. Whether such an existence were worth living was another question. Almost Lora felt she would sooner marry him with the positive assurance of unhappiness in the offing than face the emptiness of a future without him.

"But that's weakness," she told herself sternly. "You mustn't give in to it, Lora. You know very well what a hell an unhappy marriage can be."

"But there's no guarantee that you *would* be unhappy, if you married Adam," countered a small, persuasive inner voice. "Remember what he said that night at the Rawlings's. You're two different people in an entirely different situation. Why should the outcome necessarily be the same?"

Lora shook her head in an effort to clear her thoughts. She felt as though she were stumbling through a dark room filled with elusive obstacles, seeking for something solid upon which she might rest. "If I were to marry Adam, I think it would be different," she said slowly. "Or rather, I *feel* it would be different. But feeling isn't enough in a decision as important as this. What cause have I to think that it *would* be different?"

Lora thought. She thought again of Adam's words, "two different people, an entirely different situation." That was true at any rate. She was not the same girl who had married Lord Carroll years ago. She might never be a truly assertive person like Lady Helen, but she had proved she was capable of standing up for herself if need be. If she were able to go back and live her married life with Lord Carroll over again, she felt she would have made a better job of it. That could never be now, of course, but if she had learned her lesson since then, might she not have greater success with her second attempt at matrimony? Lora shook her head doubtfully.

"It's possible," she said. "But by itself, I don't think it's enough."

She thought next of her love for Adam, a love so very different from what she had felt for Lord Carroll. That was another difference, and an important one, too. But Lora was not quite romantic enough to believe that love alone would make all the difference.

"After all, Carroll claimed to be devoted to me," she reminded herself. "And yet, I could never see that it made the least difference in his behavior. Of course, Adam is different from Carroll. I could never see him losing his temper over the things that used to vex Carroll, and I don't believe he would ever trample over me and my feelings as Carroll did. But how can I be sure? I never knew how overbearing Carroll could be until after I married him."

Lora sighed and shifted in her chair. Outside the window, she could see a faint glow in the east where dawn was just beginning to break. Soon it would be day, and the city would be illumined by the sun's radiance. Lora wished her mind might similarly be illumined. "If only I knew what to do," she fretted. "Oh, Adam, how could you leave me and make me puzzle all this out by myself? I don't think you really can love me. If you did, you would have simply carried me off to Hampshire, married me out of hand, and spared me all this miserable uncertainty."

"As Carroll did," whispered a small voice somewhere deep inside her.

"As Carroll did?" Suddenly alert, Lora leaned forward in her chair, her eyes widening as she took in the significance of the words. "As Carroll did," she repeated. "Yes, I suppose it was something like that. He didn't actually carry me off, but he was so confident, so insistent, so perfectly sure we would be happy together that I let myself be carried away just the same. It made the decision easy for me—oh, yes, it was an easy decision, but it was not the *right* decision. And now Adam has given me the same decision to make for myself, and I am resenting him for not doing as Carroll did! What a fool I am! Yes, a fool, but not so big a fool as I was, I hope. I shall have to think this through."

For the next hour Lora did think, while the sky outside turned from violet to rose, and from rose to gold, and at last gave way to the clear untroubled blue of a spring morning. Lora's thoughts were not quite so clear and untroubled, but a ray of hope had begun to illuminate the darkness in which she had been stumbling.

"I think it might answer," she said aloud. "Yes, I think I can see my way clear now. We began differently; therefore it's reasonable to suppose we would go on differently after we were married. Of course, it's still something of a risk, as he said himself. But somehow the thought of risk doesn't frighten me as it used to. The thing to do is to face the risk, and then, if the object still seems worthwhile, one simply draws a deep breath and—goes ahead."

Rising from her chair, Lora went over to her writing table. Taking up pen and paper, she began to write a letter to Adam. It was a very short letter, and Lora's pen never once slowed or hesitated until it was done. She folded, sealed, and addressed it, then took another sheet of paper and began writing to her parents. Over this letter she did hesitate, and several times grimaced to herself as though the writing of it cost her no little difficulty. But she did not lay aside her pen until it, too, lay sealed and addressed on her blotter. Lora made a hasty toilette, then picked up the two letters and carried them downstairs, where she gave them to one of the footmen with instructions to have them posted as soon as possible.

Lora then gave orders for the carriage to be brought around. When it arrived, she instructed the coachman to drive her to Madame LeClaire's in Oxford Street. Madame's assistants were just taking down the shutters from the shop windows as she arrived. She was shown to Madame's private sanctum, where Madame appeared a moment later with a look of inquiry on her round, red face. Lora smiled and stretched out her hands in a gesture of entreaty.

"Madame, I need a wedding dress," she said.

Eighteen

The nuptials between Mr. Adam Wainwright and the former Countess of Carroll took place late in June, just a few days before Midsummer. Owing to the bride's widowed status, it was a very quiet, private ceremony, but no less joyous for all that, as was agreed by those who had been present.

Adam had lost no time in responding to Lora's letter. He had received it on his return home from a long and dirty ride across a mired field and had hardly paused to pack a few essentials in a portmanteau before setting off for London, still in his mud-spattered boots and breeches. By changing horses recklessly and driving with a marked disregard for the convenience of the other travelers on the road, he had reached that metropolis in a matter of hours, thereby beating (as he later assured Lora) the Regent's celebrated record for fast travel along a similar route.

When he arrived at Spelbourne House, he had been fortunate enough to find Lora alone in the drawing room. The butler, who had apparently taken his measure at a single glance, announced him to "my lady" with a knowing smile and then took himself off, closing the door thoughtfully behind him. Adam and Lora had been left to regard each other across the empty drawing room.

Lora rose to her feet at his entrance, but remained standing where she was. He went to her and took her hand in his. "Did you mean it?" he asked, looking down at her. "What you wrote in your letter—did you mean it, Lora?"

She merely looked at him, smiling faintly. He answered his own question with a rueful laugh. "Of course you meant it. You would think I would know better than question your word by now. The fact is, I simply can't believe my own luck. Oh, Lora, now that you've said you'll marry me, I feel as though I ought to turn around and try to dissuade you from doing such a mad thing. Will you think me *very* selfish and inconsiderate if I don't?"

"No," said Lora, laughing tremulously. He promptly enfolded her in his arms. Having squeezed her nearly breathless and kissed her at least a dozen times, he loosened his hold so that he might look down into her face.

"When will you marry me, Lora?" he asked eagerly. "Soon, I hope? But there, I don't mean to rush you, my love." He checked himself with a look of self-reproach. "If you would prefer to wait a month or two, until you've had a chance to think this thing over—"

"I have nothing to think over, Adam," said Lora, breaking in upon this speech with smiling firmness. "My mind is made up, and I am quite willing to marry you as soon as you like. In fact, I might almost say, as I said on another occasion, 'the sooner, the better!' "

"Then we shall be married tomorrow," swore Adam recklessly. "Well, perhaps not quite so soon as that, but just as soon as I can arrange matters with a clergyman and get hold of a special license."

Lora agreed to this proposition, although she shook her head at its extravagance. "Banns would be much cheaper than a special license, Adam," she pointed out prudently. "And I know you said you had already been put to a great deal of expense this year on my account—"

"Damn the expense," said Adam, and folded her once more in his arms.

The plans for the wedding went forward with great dispatch after that. They did not go forward quite so quickly as the principles would have liked, for strong opposition to the match had arisen in some quarters, most notably from the county of Suffolk in the person of Mrs. Walter Darlington. Alerted to the impending disaster by her daughter's letter, she had paused only to dash off a hysterical letter in return before posting down to London to deliver her objections in person.

Lora had found it very hard to withstand the maternal pressure that was applied to her on this occasion. Nonetheless, she had held firm during the first few critical hours until Adam, who was staying in Abingdon Street with the good-natured Mr. Lloyd, had arrived on the scene to support her. Faced by an unusually recalcitrant daughter, and a future son-in-law whose manner and appearance were far superior to what she had expected, Mrs. Darlington's hysterical opposition had abruptly given way to philosophical resignation.

Mr. Darlington, arriving in London a few days after his wife, had been more reserved in his judgment both before and after meeting Adam. He had made no opposition to the match worth mentioning, however, and when Lora came upon him and Adam a couple of days later earnestly discussing the Norfolk four-crop system, she knew the day was won.

Mrs. Darlington admitted that Adam was "quite presentable, taken all in all. A very pleasant, well-mannered young gentleman." But she still continued at intervals to lament that her daughter was throwing herself away upon a man without title or fortune. It remained for Mr. Darlington to put an end to these sorrowings, which he did with his usual economy of speech.

"Pshaw, Sophy, the fellow's not a whit worse off than I was when you married me, and I don't see you regretting your bargain," he told his wife. "Wainwright seems an up-and-coming young fellow. I'll wager in ten years' time he'll stand as well with the world as I do now."

Lady Helen, naturally, had been informed of Lora's intentions before anyone else. Lora had expected her friend to respond with an outcry equaling or surpassing that of her mother, but in fact Lady Helen received the news in almost total silence. Her only comment, spoken in a wistful voice, was, "Oh, Lora, are you *sure?*"

"Quite sure," returned Lora. Lady Helen had studied her in silence a moment longer and then smiled, with a trace of her old spirit.

"Well, I always said you ought to marry again! If I am not to have the comfort of having you with me at Spelbourne this summer, at least I may have the pleasure now of saying 'I told you so!' "

It was Lady Helen who attended the bride at the altar. This was very much contrary to custom, as Mrs. Darlington, the minister of St. George's, and Lady Helen herself all took it upon themselves to inform her. "I do not want bridesmaids. I want Helen," Lora had told them, and such was the determination in her voice that no further opposition was put in her way.

For the ceremony, Lady Helen wore a saffron yellow wrapping dress, a flowered Lyons shawl, and a chimney pot hat ornamented with a flourishing wedding favor of lace, flowers, and silver ribbons. She looked very dashing in this ensemble, and it was generally agreed that motherhood had not damaged her figure in the least.

The bride herself went to the altar in a dress of violet-blue silk, worn with a matching pelisse and a straw bonnet trimmed with forget-me-nots. "There's a pretty face for you," had remarked one appreciative onlooker, who had been lounging near the entrance of the church as the wedding party came in. "A very pretty face, by Jove. Looks like one of the angels on the altarpiece." It is to be supposed that the bridegroom agreed with him. At all events, Mr. Wainwright seemed to have trouble taking his eyes off his bride during the ceremony and would have entirely neglected to receive the ring from the clergyman's hand had not his friend Mr. Lloyd, who was acting as groomsman, thoughtfully elbowed him in the ribs.

Both gentlemen wore light trousers, white waistcoats, and jackets of blue superfine ornamented with wedding favors like

Lady Helen's. When the ceremony was over, Mr. Lloyd did not depart with the other guests but stayed on to attend the next wedding, which by the strangest of coincidences happened to be that of his cousin Miss Monroe and the Honourable Major Linville.

There was no wedding breakfast after the ceremony. Instead, the bride and bridegroom bade farewell to their guests at the church door and then entered the carriage that was waiting for them there. A few more last minute farewells were exchanged, then Sam, newly promoted to the position of coachman, whipped up the horses with a flourish and the wedded pair set off for the bridegroom's home in Hampshire, to the accompaniment of cheers, clapping, and the wails of the infant Earl of Westwood, who had attended the ceremony along with his mother and father and had behaved like a perfect cherub up till that moment.

The carriage in which the newly-wed couple were to make their wedding journey was a spanking new traveling chaise drawn by a fine pair of blooded chestnuts. Both chaise and horses had been a gift from the bride's parents, and a number of other wedding gifts were stowed in the chaise's capacious boot. Among them was a handsome silver tea service, which had arrived at Spelbourne House bearing the card of Lord Ellsworth. This gift had given rise to some mild dissension between bride and bridegroom, but in the end they had decided to look upon it in the light of an apology and keep it.

The party on the church steps kept up their cheers and applause until the carriage was out of sight. Lora, who had been waving her handkerchief out the window to her mother, father, and Lady Helen, now settled back on the cushions of the chaise and smiled at Adam. He smiled back, a trifle ruefully.

"Well, that's that," he said. "As weddings go, I think ours was a pretty decent effort, don't you? But it seems a bit of an anticlimax, only to be taking you home to Highleigh House. I wish I could take you on a proper wedding trip to Scotland, or the Lakes."

"I've already been to Scotland and the Lakes. I would much rather see my new home," said Lora firmly.

"I hope you will like it." Adam's expression was dubious as he looked across the chaise at his bride. "It's a nice place, *I* think, but then I'm admittedly partial. You know I don't live in a very grand way, Lora. Besides the farming men, there's only half-a-dozen servants, not even a housekeeper to help you keep things in line. I'm afraid it will mean more work than you're used to."

Lora smiled. "I don't mind that, Adam," she said. "It will be nice to be useful for a change. You act as though I were a fine lady, bred up from my cradle never to lift a finger for myself, but the fact is that I had a very good, old-fashioned, practical upbringing. I can balance accounts, and mend and sew, and if I do say so myself, I am a very good cook. Why, I once cooked dinner for the whole Kelsinghurst Hunt at Carrollton!" Lora fixed Adam with a stern look that was wholly belied by the laughter in her eyes. "I assure you, sir, you much mistake the matter if you think I cannot manage without a housekeeper. You have not married a helpless doll, brought up only to dress and do the fashionable!"

"I can see I have not," said Adam, regarding her with an awe that was only half assumed. "You are clearly a woman of unsuspected abilities. I'll admit that it will be a great relief to turn over the running of the household to someone else. But Lora, if at any time you should find the work too much for you, you must promise to say so, at once. I don't want you suffering on in silence. It wouldn't be beyond my means to hire another servant or two, if need be."

"I promise," said Lora seriously. "But I don't think you need worry about that, Adam. Even before I made up my mind to marry you, I had made up my mind that I wasn't going to do any more suffering in silence. The only thing you need worry about now is whether I might not go too far in the other direction and become a perfect shrew!"

"I'm not worried about that," said Adam, taking her hand in his and squeezing it.

Lora smiled at him. "And you needn't worry about the expense of hiring extra servants either, Adam," she said reassuringly. "If I find I really can't manage without a housekeeper, I can perfectly well afford to hire one out of my own pin-money."

"Yes. . . ." Adam gave her a sideways look. "I must confess, I got quite a shock when I sat down with your father to discuss the marriage settlements. I had supposed any income you had was derived from your late husband's estate and would cease with your remarriage."

Lora laughed and looked rather embarrassed. "No, I have my own money, Adam," she said. "My parents are quite well off, and I am their only child. I think that was the only thing that reconciled Lord Carroll's relations to the idea of his marrying me, for my birth certainly wasn't high enough to suit them."

"Well, I am very glad you have your own personal fortune, Lora," said Adam soberly. "It makes it easier for me, knowing you've the means to supply some of the luxuries you're used to that I couldn't afford out of my own income. But at the same time, I'm glad I didn't know about it until a few days ago." He glanced diffidently across the chaise at Lora. "If I had known in the beginning that you were an heiress as well as a countess, I don't think I would have dared go near you, let alone propose marriage to you. I would have been afraid you would think me a fortune hunter."

"Yes, it would have given you something else to be high-minded and self-denying about," said Lora, shaking her head with mock exasperation. "I'm thankful you *didn't* find out, until you were thoroughly committed and had to marry me even in spite of my not being penniless!"

"You know me very well," said Adam, with a rueful smile.

"Yes, I think I do. But there's no reason for you to be self-denying now, you know." Lora gave him a look that was half flirtatious, half reproachful. "We're married now, and yet you haven't so much as kissed me since we got in the chaise. I think you might at least come over and sit beside me, instead of perching on the jump seat as though I had something contagious."

Adam laughed. "I'm not sure you don't," he said, looking at her with sparkling eyes. "Whenever I'm near you, I find myself overcome by an uncontrollable urge to kiss you. And then I start feeling the urge to do other things—and I'm just afraid that if once I ever got started, I'd end up ravishing you right here in the chaise. I've waited this long, I can wait until we're somewhere rather more comfortable, with rather less likelihood of being interrupted."

Lora laughed and began to remove her bonnet with a provocative air. "You may be easy, Adam," she said. "I'll see that you don't go beyond kissing. It will be a chance to show you how assertive I mean to be, right from the start."

"All right, but don't say I didn't warn you," said Adam.

Rising from the forward seat, he came over to sit beside Lora on the bench. She held out her arms invitingly. Adam shook his head dubiously but accepted the proffered invitation. And it did in fact develop, during the ensuing interlude, that Lora was unable to enforce the limits she had set as assertively as she had originally intended. Since the blinds of the chaise were decently pulled, however, no one was the wiser, and she had in any case sufficient warning of their approach to Highleigh House to straighten her hair and put her dress in order before she and Adam were called on to quit the chaise.

The drive that led from the lane to the house was short but wide, newly gravelled and lined on either hand by a fine old growth of oaks and elms. The house itself was of mellow red brick, two stories high, with attic gables, a trellised front porch, and a central cluster of chimneys. Lora was charmed at her first sight of it.

"Oh, Adam, it's lovely," she kept exclaiming, as the chaise drew to a stop in front of the garden gate. "How could you think I would not like it? It's the prettiest house I ever saw. And you say it's been in your family how long?—two hundred years?"

"Yes, and has the inconveniences to prove it, unfortunately. I've been trying gradually to bring the place more up to date, but there's a deal that still remains to be done. However, we'll have a good many years in which to make it all it should be—God willing."

Gripping Lora's hand in his once more, Adam looked down at her seriously. "I can't give you everything Carroll did, Lora, but there's one thing I *can* give you that he couldn't. No matter what happens to me, you will always have a home here. I've already put it down in my will that if I should predecease you, the place will be yours, free and clear."

"Oh, Adam," was all Lora could say. Tears filled her eyes and for a moment threatened to cast a shadow over the happiness she had been feeling. Only for a moment, however, and then the shadow passed, and she saw with the clarity of a vision a long vista of years in which she and Adam might live, love, and be happy together.

"You've already given me everything I want, Adam," she told him, and then added with a daring smile, "Almost everything, that is! Take me inside now, my love, and show me our house."

The sound of the chaise in the drive had already alerted the servants to their arrival. As Adam led Lora toward the house, the front door opened, and a stout woman in an apron and mobcap issued forth, followed by an equally stout manservant in butler's dress, a couple of youthful maidservants, a gangling boy in livery, and a much smaller one in short coat and breeches. Adam smilingly introduced them all to Lora.

"My butler and cook, Mr. and Mrs. Ludlow. And this is Rose and this Rachel, upper and under housemaid respectively—and this is William, who is in training as a footman—and this is John, who does a bit of everything. Pot-boy, yard-boy, and foot-boy, too. A regular jack-of-all-trades," fin-

ished Adam, smiling at the small boy, who grinned and ducked
his head in embarrassment.

The other servants all bowed or bobbed their heads, all except for the maidservant Rose, who swept up her skirts and
dropped to the floor in a curtsy that would not have been out
of place in the court of St. James. "I'm very pleased to meet
you, my lady," she said in a breathless voice.

"Get up, Rose. She's not my lady anymore," hissed Mrs.
Ludlow. To Lora she added in an apologetic rush, "We're all
very glad to meet you, ma'am, and you mustn't mind Rose,
here. She *will* read novels in her off hours, and I'm afraid it
makes her flighty. Indeed, ma'am, I hope you'll find everything
here at Highleigh House to your liking. We've done our best,
and I'm sure we all wish you and the master very happy."

She spoke with so much humility and earnest feeling that
Lora was thrown a little off balance. She had not been used to
being treated by servants with such deference; certainly not by
the servants at Carrollton, beneath whose respectful manners
she had often sensed a deep and abiding contempt. It was obvious that Mrs. Ludlow and the others regarded her in the light
of a great lady and trembled lest they should fail to meet her
exacting standards. Hiding a smile, Lora nodded gravely to each
of them.

"I am very pleased to meet you all," she said. "I trust we
will go on very well together, once we have had a chance to
become accustomed to one another's ways."

While she was speaking, Annie, who had traveled outside on
the box with Sam, had dismounted from the chaise with his aid
and come hesitantly forward. Lora turned to her with a smile.

"And now I must introduce to you my own personal maid,"
she told the other servants. They eyed Annie with a mixture
of interest and uncertainty. In a flash of intuition, Lora saw
that they were wont to regard Annie with the same respect
they had accorded her: a respect that had never been poor
Annie's in all the years she had served Lora, first in Lord
Carroll's household and then in Lady Helen's.

"This is Miss Thompson," Lora told the other servants firmly. They all bowed or curtsied once again. Annie looked a bit dazed by her sudden elevation to the status of a true upper servant, but she acknowledged the other servants' greeting with tolerable composure and held her head a little higher as she carried Lora's jewel and dressing cases into the house.

The front door of Highleigh House opened into a stone-paved hall which led to a square, oaken staircase whose timbers were black with age. On the left of the hall was a good-sized drawing room with a bow window. Behind it was a second drawing room which combined the functions of a study. On the right of the hall was a common parlor and behind it a dining parlor with a round mahogany table and marble-topped sideboard.

Lora admired it all extravagantly. The whole house seemed to her the apotheosis of coziness and comfort. She could scarcely contain her excitement at the prospect of ruling over such an enchanting doll's house. "Do you want to see the kitchen and scullery, too?" said Adam, who had listened with incredulous amusement to these raptures. "And I could show you the woodshed and backhouse, too, if you like."

"No, not right now, thank you," returned Lora, laughing. "I would rather see my own rooms and put off my pelisse and bonnet."

"Aye, but you'll have to come and see the kitchens when you've a spare moment, ma'am," said Mrs. Ludlow, who had tagged along behind them during their inspection of the house. "Very handsome and up-to-date, they are. The master bought me one of them new-fangled closed ranges a few months back, and I'm just beginning to learn the way of it. Heavens, and that reminds me. There's a saddle of mutton roasting this minute and not a soul to tend it. I'll be lucky if it hasn't burned to a crisp while we've been talking."

Mrs. Ludlow vanished in the direction of the kitchen, and Adam led Lora upstairs. "Thank heaven, a moment alone," he said in a low voice. "I was sure she meant to stay at our heels every step of the way. Mrs. Ludlow is a good soul, but you may find her a bit of a despot at times, Lora. I know I do, but it's hard to stand out against such well-meaning tyranny."

Lora laughed. "I know exactly what you mean, Adam," she said.

The upper floor of Highleigh House, like the lower, was divided by a narrow hall. Adam led Lora to a door at the far end of it. "This is your room, Lora. At least, it's my room, too, but I can move to another if you prefer. My parents always shared a room, but I know you're probably used to having one of your own . . ." His voice trailed off diffidently.

Lora looked around the room. It was a large square bed-chamber with a low ceiling, an oaken floor covered with a Turkish carpet, and an old-fashioned four-poster bed. But though the bed was old, it had been newly furnished with counterpane, canopy, and curtains of gay flowered chintz. The floor was polished to a high sheen, and even the andirons that stood in the fireplace glittered from a recent application of crocus and sweet oil. A nosegay of roses and fern stood on the table beside the bed. It was obvious that the servants had taken great pains to make the room look attractive for her, and Lora's heart warmed at this visible evidence of goodwill.

"Why, no, I don't think I should mind sharing a room with you, Adam," she said, turning to smile at him. "This was your room first, after all. And it does look large enough for two."

"You'd have your own dressing room," said Adam anxiously. He opened a door on one side of the room to show Lora a small dressing room with mirror, clothespress, and dressing table. "This is all quite new—comparatively new, at least. It was added on at the time of my parents' marriage, for my mother's use. There's another dressing room right beside it that used to be my father's, which I use now. So I needn't be any bother to you that way, and I had the servants move a daybed in there, so that if there are times you'd rather not have me with you, for one reason or another—personal reasons, you know—"

Adam's diffidence had grown so great by the end of this speech that Lora, by now as much touched as amused, was moved to cut it short. "I understand, Adam," she said. "That was very considerate of you, but I don't think I'll be exiling you to your dressing room very often."

"That's good," said Adam, with an air of not knowing what he said. The two of them stood looking at each other until the sound of Mrs. Ludlow's stentorian voice rang out from below.

"Dinner'll be ready in about thirty minutes. I'm sending Rachel up with a couple of cans of hot water if the two of you want to wash up a bit before you sit down."

"I'd better leave you now, so you can change your dress," said Adam, turning away rather hastily. "I see William's already brought your trunk up—that's good, that's good. I'll just go to my own dressing room now and—er—clean myself up a bit." With which words he vanished into his dressing room.

Lora, shaking with inward amusement, rang for Annie and in a very short time had changed her traveling dress for a dinner dress of white sarcenet. It was very simply cut, as befitted a dinner à deux, and Lora's only ornament was the modest string of pearls which had been Adam's wedding gift to her.

"Will that be all, ma'am?" said Annie, when Lora was fully arrayed in this toilette. "Because if you don't need me any more this evening, I was going to show that girl Rose a few tricks about dressing hair, the same as Lady Helen's woman was showing me a few months back. Rose is very eager to better herself, and if I can teach her to arrange hair, and trim dresses, and a few things like that, she's hoping she might be able to hire out as a fashionable ladies' maid, too, someday."

"That's very altruistic of you, Thompson," said Lora with a smile. "Yes, certainly you may have the rest of the evening off. I shan't be needing you any more tonight."

Annie smiled back shyly. "Thank you, ma'am. Of course I'll be back later to help you undress and all—" She broke off with a blush and then went on in an impetuous rush of words. "Oh, I do think we're going to be happy here, don't you, ma'am? Mr. Wainwright seems such a kind, good-natured gentleman. And his servants all speak very well of him; they do indeed, ma'am." Annie looked at her mistress earnestly, anxious to impress upon her the value of such a recommendation. "I was talking with Sam the coachman on the way here, and he was telling me all about Mr. Wainwright, how he and his family have lived in this house for years and years and how well they're thought of hereabouts. Of course it's not so grand a house as my Lord Carroll's, nor yet my Lord Spelbourne's, but it's nice, isn't it, ma'am?"

"Yes, very nice, I should say, Thompson," said Lora with a smile.

"And the staff all seem very nice, too," continued Annie, in a tone that revealed her wonderment at such a situation. "That Sam seems a nice, pleasant-spoken young man. He was asking me if I might go with him to the Parish festival this day next week, but I said I'd have to ask you first." She looked at Lora anxiously.

Lora, much amused, pretended to give the matter a grave consideration. "I don't see why not," she said judiciously. "Yes, Thompson, you may tell Sam that you will attend the Parish festival with him."

Annie's face lit up with smiles. "Thank you, ma'am. You're very good to me, ma'am, the best mistress that ever was. I'm sure you deserve to be happy if anyone does, you and Mr. Wainwright. And now I'll just take the curling tongs and run up to Rose's room, but I'll be back down here in time to help you undress, never you fear, ma'am. Just you ring when you need me, ma'am."

"I will, Thompson," said Lora. Smiling, she watched the ecstatic Annie flit away toward the backstairs, then put her shawl around her shoulders and went down to dinner.

Nineteen

The dinner, which encompassed two full courses, was served forth with quiet efficiency by the butler Mr. Ludlow and footman-in-training William. Mrs. Ludlow remained in the kitchen to preside over the dishing up; at least, that was her ostensible role, but she still managed to make her presence felt throughout the meal by means of frequent bulletins delivered from the kitchen doorway.

"That's vegetable soup, Mr. Wainwright, the kind you like with our own carrots and late peas. Richards just brought over the first of the carrots today. Mrs. Wainwright hasn't met Richards yet, has she?—nor any of the other outside men. You'll have to have the master take you out to the farm tomorrow, ma'am, and introduce you all around."

"Yes, I'll be sure to do that, Mrs. Ludlow," said Adam in a slightly elevated voice. "Would you be so good as to close the door behind you when you go? We're getting a bit of a draft in here."

Mrs. Ludlow took the hint and vanished back into the kitchen, so that Adam and Lora were able to consume their soup while discussing in a leisurely way their plans for the morrow. With the fish course, however, Mrs. Ludlow reappeared, to give the conversation a different turn.

"How's the mackerel, Mr. Wainwright? It looked like an uncommon good one to me. I just turned it out of the pan this minute, so it ought to be nice and hot. There's more sauce in the kitchen if you need it. Do you prefer your mackerel baked or fried, ma'am?"

"Baked," said Lora promptly, having caught a glimpse of the dish's contents on its way in. Mrs. Ludlow looked gratified.

"That's how I feel, too, ma'am, but a great many people prefer the other," she said, shaking her head over such misguided preferences. "Ah, well, there's no accounting for tastes, as I always say."

Adam, as he helped Lora to fish, gave her a look of most speaking apology. She smiled and shook her head. Mrs. Ludlow, reiterating her offer of more sauce, withdrew into the kitchen while her husband quietly superintended the distribution of that which was already in the sauceboat. When presently the fish was succeeded by a roast saddle of mutton, however, accompanied by gravy, red-currant jelly, asparagus, and potatoes, Mrs. Ludlow felt obliged to put her head into the room once again.

"The mutton's not overdone, is it? I didn't think so, but it's a mercy it wasn't, after the way I went off and left it to itself this afternoon. That's our own asparagus, ma'am, and our own potatoes, too. The mutton's from Granger's farm down the road. We don't raise much mutton here—beef's more our line of country—but this was such a fine joint, I thought it wouldn't come amiss for once."

"That will do, Mrs. Ludlow," said Adam, in a polite but steely voice. "The mutton is very good, and I believe we have everything we need now." His words caused Mrs. Ludlow's head to disappear from the doorway with great celerity.

It did not reappear again until the second course was laid on the table. This consisted of a duckling with green peas, a salad with cucumber and watercress, a gooseberry tart, and a large, elaborately frosted cake.

"Your bride cake, ma'am," said Mrs. Ludlow, appearing on cue. "You can't have a wedding without bride cake, can you? When Mr. Wainwright told me you and he was a-marrying all in a hurry-like, with not so much as a breakfast afterwards, I said to myself, 'Lucy, you'd best be making up the bride cake, then, for it's clear as glass the poor things won't have anyone else to do it for them.' That's my own recipe for bride cake, ma'am, what's been in my family these hundred years. Mr. Ludlow and I had the same cake at our own nuptials thirty years ago—well, not the same exact cake, of course, but one just like it from the same recipe."

"It looks delicious, Mrs. Ludlow," said Lora in an unsteady voice. Adam, who was carving the duckling, gave her a look that nearly upset her gravity, but she managed to keep a straight face as long as Mrs. Ludlow remained in the room. When she and Adam had consumed the duckling, the salad, and a slice of cake each, and had politely refused Mrs. Ludlow's pressing offers of second helpings, the two of them retired to the drawing room.

In the drawing room, Adam sank down on the sofa and buried his face in his hands. "Oh, Lora, Lora," he said. "This isn't exactly how I envisioned our first meal together. You must be wondering what kind of a bedlam existence you've let yourself in for. On my honor, it's not usually so bad as this. I think Mrs. Ludlow is still a bit flustered at the idea of cooking for an ex-countess, that's all. Once she's had time to adjust to the idea, I don't think you'll find her quite so—er—solicitous."

"Oh, Adam, I don't mind," said Lora, laughing. She moved closer to him on the sofa and laid her hand affectionately on his shoulder. "Indeed, I enjoyed the meal very much, Adam. Your Mrs. Ludlow is a good cook, and the other servants seem very competent at their jobs, too. Of course things are bound to be a little disordered at first, with so many changes all happening at once, but time will take care of that, as you say. I have no doubt we shall all do very well together, once the initial period of adjustment is past."

"You are the most forgiving woman in the world," said Adam fervently, taking her hand in his and kissing it. "I do hope you're not regretting marrying me, Lora. I can't help thinking what a comedown it must be for you, going from a palace like Carrollton to a place like this."

"I suppose some people might consider it a comedown," said Lora thoughtfully. "But you know I was never very happy at Carrollton, Adam—and I think I *can* be happy here. I don't know how to explain it, exactly, but everything feels so comfortable here—so right, somehow." She looked around the drawing room, then turned to Adam with a soft smile trembling on her lips. "It's the same way I felt the first time I talked to you that night at the Monroes'. You are right for me, Adam; I only hope that I am right for you."

"Never doubt it," said Adam. Drawing her into his arms, he embarked upon what would undoubtedly have been a very long and luxurious kiss, had not Mrs. Ludlow chosen that same moment to appear in the drawing room doorway with the tea-tray.

"I thought the two of you'd like a cup of tea and a—oh, I beg your pardon, sir! Begging your pardon, ma'am, I didn't mean to interrupt."

With averted face, Mrs. Ludlow set down the tray and hastily withdrew. Adam let go of Lora, leaned back on the sofa, and laughed weakly. Lora laughed, too. "Oh, Lora, I can see it's going to be a long evening. Shall we sing songs? Read sermons? Or would you care for a game of piquet?"

Lora laughingly consented to the last of these suggestions, and they did actually play at piquet for over an hour. Adam several times commented on the slowness of the passage of time and the sun's perverse unwillingness to finish its business and go down.

"Well, of course it's taking a long time to go down, Adam," said Lora, regarding him with amusement. "Today is the solstice, you know."

Adam looked blank a moment, then began to laugh. "Good Lord, I completely forgot," he said. "I would go and get married on the longest day of the year, wouldn't I? Serves me right for boasting about my self-control."

"Well, if it comes to that, Adam, I don't suppose we *have*

to wait for the sun to go down." Lora just glanced at him as she spoke and laid down a red queen with an air of deliberation before continuing, in a dulcet voice. "But of course, if you feel obliged to be high-minded and self-denying for another hour or two. . . ."

Adam folded his cards together with a snap and tossed them down upon the table. "Woman, I regard that as a challenge," he said. "Are you going upstairs now, or will I have to carry you?"

Lora laughed and rose to her feet. "No, that won't be necessary, Adam. But I think it would be better if I went up before you—to get ready, you know. That will give you time to play a game or two of patience while you're waiting. I can see you're very fond of cards." Stooping to kiss his brow, she dropped her cards in his lap and then fled, laughing, to escape the retaliation she clearly saw in his eye.

Upstairs she found Annie already in the bedroom, making the room ready for the night. At Lora's entrance, Annie glanced at the clock with a look of surprise but quickly schooled her features into an expression of studied indifference. "Do you want me to undress you now, ma'am?" she said.

"If you please," said Lora. Annie removed her pearls, dinner dress, and chemise, poured water in the washbowl for washing, and brought out Lora's nightdress. This was no chaste, all-encompassing shroud of muslin such as Lora had worn on her first wedding night, but rather a negligee in the French fashion, heavy with lace and ribbons and frankly provocative in style. Madame LeClaire had presented it to Lora on her final visit, along with a short speech of thanks which had been delivered with actual tears in her eyes. It had been a generous gift, and a completely disinterested one, too, for, as Lady Helen had remarked on the way home, no one but Adam and Annie would ever be in a position to admire it.

That Annie did admire it was evident from her expression

as she brushed out the soft waves of Lora's hair. "You look lovely, ma'am. I never saw such a pretty nightdress before. I suppose you'd rather I left your hair down tonight?"

"Yes, thank you," said Lora. "That will do, I think. Good night, Annie—Thompson, I mean."

"Good night," said Annie. She hesitated a moment, as though wanting to say something more, then with characteristic impetuosity threw her arms around Lora and kissed her. "Begging your pardon for the liberty, ma'am, but seeing as it's your wedding day and all—and I *do* wish you happy, ma'am, I do indeed. There now, don't cry, ma'am, there's no call for tears, is there? Mr. Wainwright won't thank me for making you cry on your wedding night!"

After Annie had gone, Lora remained in the dressing room a moment longer to blot away all traces of her recent outpouring of emotion. She then went into the bedroom and got into bed, propping several pillows behind her back so that she was reclining comfortably against the high oaken headboard. She felt excited but not particularly nervous, the complete antithesis of the frightened girl who had lain cringing in the dark, waiting for Lord Carroll to come to her. The contrast was all the greater because the room in which she lay now was not even dark. Narrow strips of daylight still glowed around the edges of the chintz-hung casements, illuminating the room with a soft, ruddy light.

The memory of that other wedding night could not but recur to Lora now and then as she lay in bed, listening for the sounds that would portend Adam's arrival. With a touch of superstitious feeling, she wondered if the spirit of her deceased husband might even now be hovering somewhere near at hand, silently observing the actions of his former wife. It was not a thought to make Lora very comfortable in her vigil. Fortunately, before she could develop the disquieting idea too far, the door to Adam's dressing room opened, and Adam came into the room. He entered quietly, without fanfare, but the sight of him instantly exorcised from Lora's mind all thought of the late Lord Carroll.

"Hello, Adam," she said, smiling at him shyly.

"Hello, Lora," he said, returning the smile with one almost equally shy. After an instant's hesitation, he came forward to seat himself on the edge of the bed beside her. He had changed out of the clothes he had worn at dinner and was wearing a dressing gown of dark blue brocade, a garment that managed at once to be both sumptuous and severely masculine. Lora reached out to touch the edge of its sleeve admiringly. Adam in turn surveyed her negligee with an appreciative light in his bright brown eyes. "That's a pretty thing," he said.

"Thank you," said Lora. The look in his eye made her feel embarrassed, but excited, too. It was evident that he was feeling much the way she was, not quite knowing where to begin. Lora decided to make it easy for him. Wordlessly she opened her arms, as she had that afternoon in the carriage. This time Adam did not hesitate to accept the invitation. He gathered her into his own arms, running his hands up and down her back and the smooth silk of the negligee.

Lora shut her eyes and burrowed her face against his shoulder. "You smell so good," he murmured in her ear. "Like a flower—no, like a whole garden of flowers, with a touch of a pastry-cook's shop thrown in. Absolutely delicious. And you taste delicious, too." His lips strayed playfully over her neck and ear as he spoke, touching her skin gently with light, teasing kisses. "Delicious."

"Mmm," said Lora. "It certainly *feels* delicious. Oh, Adam, what are you doing to me? I feel as though I were melting inside." With a shiver, she lifted her face to his. "Kiss me, Adam," she whispered.

He kissed her, a long, slow, unhurried kiss that more than ever made her feel as though she were melting inside. Somehow, in the process, Lora found that she had been lowered into a reclining position once more, with Adam on top of her. This suited her very well, for she could stroke his back and shoulders and run her fingers through his hair, conscious all the while of the lean, solid length of his body pressing against hers.

Adam kissed her and kissed her again, letting his lips stray from her mouth to her neck, and from thence to her shoulder. All the while his hands were busy drawing down the shoulder straps of her negligee. Lora trembled a little, but let herself be divested of her negligee by slow degrees. When she opened her eyes, she found Adam looking down at her with an expression of admiration verging upon reverence.

"You're so beautiful," he said. "Oh, Lora, you're so beautiful—so beautiful, my love." And Lora, who had always considered her body rather an embarrassment, found herself suddenly transformed in his vision: felt that she really was beautiful, and was liberated by the knowledge.

"You're so beautiful," he kept saying over and over, touching and kissing her until every nerve of her body felt as though it were on fire.

"Oh, Adam," she said weakly. "Oh, Adam, my love." He seemed to understand the unspoken plea in her words, for he left off his kissing and caressing and drew his body level with hers. Yet, on the very threshold of possessing her, he paused to look down at her.

"I love you, you know," he informed her gravely.

"And I love you, too," said Lora passionately. Putting her arms around him, she drew him to her. "Oh, Adam . . ." And in the moment that made him hers, and her his, she found she had been right: there was no pain, but rather the reverse. It was a pleasure so intense that she wanted it never to end. And yet it did end, only moments later, in a manner completely unexpected to Lora.

"Oh," she said, and then, "Oh! Oh, Adam. Oh, *Adam,*" in a rising voice.

He responded to her voice with a last burst of effort. She heard him draw in his breath sharply, felt him shudder, and knew with complete and utter certainty that he was experiencing exactly what she had experienced an instant before. "Oh,

Adam," she said again, and wrapped her arms around him tightly. He made no verbal response, but stroked back her hair from her forehead and kissed her once, gently, before subsiding into her arms.

For a considerable time they lay there without speaking. Lora, indeed, was so overcome by what had just happened to her that she could not have found the words to speak if she had wanted to. It was enough to feel Adam's body against hers and to luxuriate the deep sense of warmth and well-being that seemed to emanate outward from her very soul. She was not aware she was weeping until Adam, shifting slightly, brushed his cheek against hers.

"You're crying," he said in wonderment, and turned his head to look at her closely. "Why are you crying, Lora?"

"I don't know," said Lora, with a mixture of tears and laughter. "Because I am a goose, I suppose. And because I love you so much. But oh, Adam, I never felt anything like that before—never, never, never."

"No?" said Adam, eyeing her dubiously. "Do you mean you—just what do you mean, Lora?"

In a few simple, straightforward sentences, Lora told him. He looked so astonished, and at the same time so gratified, that she could not help suspecting he, too, had been feeling the ghostly presence of the late Lord Carroll that evening.

"Well, I'll be damned," he said, and then added a moment later, "That's *two* things," in a voice of intense satisfaction. It was a remark that rather puzzled Lora at the time, although later, when she had had time to think it over, she was able to grasp its significance.

At the moment, however, her thoughts were given a different direction by the sound of a clock striking the hour in one of the neighboring rooms. "Adam, do you realize it's only ten o'clock?" she said with a gurgle of laughter. "What must your servants think of us? I shall have difficulty looking them in the face tomorrow."

"Yes, so shall I," said Adam, grinning. "But tomorrow's a

long time away. And seeing that it's still so early, I have a mind to make the most of my opportunities." Whereupon he kissed Lora lingeringly on the lips.

"I love you, Adam," she said, smiling up at him.

"And I love you, too, Lora. It will take me longer than one night to show you how much, but at least I can make a fair start of it."

"You already have, Adam! A very fair start."

As Adam later had occasion to remark, it was a curious but undoubted fact that of all the people who passed that night beneath the roof of Highleigh House, those who had gone first to bed were the last to sleep. From ten o'clock on, he and Lora had lain in each other's arms, talking and kissing and talking some more, and in the intimacy of that interview Lora was able to open her heart in a way she had never dared with any other person, even with Lady Helen. It was not that she made any more dramatic revelations, such as had stunned Adam earlier. They spoke chiefly of small things, made a number of plans for the future both practical and fanciful, and in general indulged in those confidences common to lovers at such a time.

They did not spend the whole of the night in talking, of course. Toward morning, Lora began to sense in her husband's kisses and conversation a certain purposeful direction, which seemed likely to lead to the exchange of more significant intimacies. She waited until the signs grew unmistakable and then, when Adam would have renewed those caresses that had had such a devastating effect on her earlier, she asserted herself strongly, turned the tables on him, and proceeded to do to him very much as he had previously done to her. It was altogether a very satisfying encounter, and as Lora drifted off to sleep in his arms afterwards, she could not help reflecting on the unexpected pleasure to be found in taking one's destiny into one's own hands.

It was late morning when she awoke. Adam was already

awake and appeared to have been studying her while she slept, for his first words after good morning were, "You look incredibly innocent when you're sleeping, O wife of mine. It's hard to believe you're the same houri that seduced me last night."

"I was very brazen, wasn't I?" said Lora with unblushing satisfaction. "You seem to bring out that side of me, Adam. I'm sure I never was before." Yawning, she pulled herself to a sitting position, arranging the counterpane over the exposed portions of her anatomy with somewhat belated modesty. Adam watched her with a somber expression on his face. Observing it, Lora begged to know why he was looking so serious all at once.

"I was just thinking how lucky I am to have you," he said, reaching out to lay his hand on her knee. "It still seems like a dream that I really do. I hope you will be happy here, Lora. I intend to do my best to make you so, but I can't help worrying you might someday regret everything you've given up to marry me."

Lora told him indignantly that she was not so fickle. "I beg you won't talk in that foolish way, Adam. I am very happy to be your wife, and I am sure I shall remain so—although I must confess to having *some* fears for the future," she added thoughtfully.

"What do you mean?" said Adam, looking in his turn rather indignant. "You don't think I shall degenerate into a brute, do you?"

"No, it's not that," said Lora, laughing. "It's only that things have been so perfect up till now that it stands to reason they must start going downhill sometime. Heaven knows they couldn't possibly get any better!"

Adam smiled. "That sounds like another challenge to me," he said. "So things can't get any better, can they? We'll just see about *that,* ma'am."

And when presently he was done with his exposition, Lora was forced to admit that things could, after all, be even better.

Epilogue

Three Years Later

"My love, don't let him tire you. He's getting to be such a great boy, he's almost too heavy to hold on your lap. Arthur, why don't you go see what John is doing?"

Lady Helen addressed these last words directly to her son, who was seated on Lora's lap painstakingly dissecting a rose. "I saw him a minute ago, digging at something down by the gate," she went on, lowering her voice to a dramatic whisper. "Perhaps he has discovered a fox's earth, do you think?"

The three-year-old Earl of Westbrook vouchsafed no answer, but a look of interest appeared on his small serious face. Sliding off Lora's lap, he at once set off down the garden path toward the gate.

At the sight of him, the little girl who had been sitting contentedly in Lady Helen's lap leaned forward with an eager cry and began to struggle to be put down. Lady Helen obligingly set her on her feet, whereupon she immediately toddled off after the earl as fast as her chubby legs could carry her. That young gentleman paused midway down the path to allow her to catch up to him. He then extended his hand to her, and when she had grasped it unsteadily in her own, he solemnly escorted her down the path to the gate, where her brother was conducting excavations with a trowel left behind by the gardener.

"Isn't that a sweet picture," said Lady Helen, looking after them affectionately. "It's quite touching the way young Arthur takes care of John and Helen. He is such a serious, responsible child. I'd almost think he was too good to live, if his goodness weren't leavened with a few human failings. Obstinacy, for instance. His nurse says she never saw a child with such a tremendous will of his own. I can't imagine where he gets it from." She slanted a mischievous look at Lora from beneath the brim of her wide-brimmed Gypsy hat.

Lora laughed. "I can't imagine, either, Helen," she said.

"In any case, I am glad to see your little Helen doesn't take after her namesake in that regard. She is a perfect little angel, Lora. Just like her mother." Lady Helen looked fondly at her friend. "It still touches me that you chose to name her after me. I am quite determined to return the favor and name this next arrival after you, if it should turn out to be a girl." She looked down at her abdomen with an air half contemplative, half rueful.

"Oh, don't do that, Helen! It wouldn't be fair to saddle the poor girl with such a silly name as mine," protested Lora smilingly. She leaned down to brush off her skirt, which the earl had left littered with torn rose petals, then settled back comfortably in her wicker garden chair. "Would you care for another cup of tea, Helen?" she asked.

"No, thank you, my love. I would rather just sit here and admire your garden. Do you tend it all yourself? Adam was saying you had become quite the gardener since coming to Highleigh House."

"I don't know about that," said Lora with a grimace. "I used to do a bit of gardening, but nowadays I'm afraid I leave most of it to the gardener. Since the twins arrived, I find myself rather short of time for other things." She looked with loving pride toward the small boy and girl at the gate, who were digging vigorously under the supervision of the infant earl. "They are a handful sometimes, but Adam is very good about helping me, and I have been very fortunate in my nursemaid, too. Indeed, Adam tells me I ought to let her do more and not take so much upon myself. He never will understand that I don't care to spend my days sitting around in the drawing room, gossiping and drinking tea. Unless of course you are there to do it with me, Helen!"

The two exchanged smiles. It was a beautiful day in late June, and they were seated in the garden of Highleigh House beneath the shade of a spreading elm. All around them bloomed pinks, sweet William, stocks, and a wealth of other sweet-smelling old-fashioned flowers.

"It's so lovely here," said Lady Helen, looking around at it all. "Like a little paradise. And you are the presiding angel, and John and Helen are the cherubs." She nodded smilingly toward the twins at the gate.

Lora laughed. "And Adam the lord of creation, I suppose?" she said, with a shake of her head. "Really, that sounds almost sacrilegious, Helen."

Lady Helen laughed. "Well, perhaps it was a foolish analogy," she allowed. "All the same, you seem very happy here, Lora." With an air half searching, half timid, she studied her friend's face. "Do you remember telling me once that you were resolved never to marry again? Back when you were staying with me in London a few years ago?"

Lora blushed. "Yes, I remember," she said. "But I hope you do not mean to throw my words in my face now, Helen. We are all permitted to change our minds, I hope, when the change is for the better." With an arch look, she added, "Indeed, if it comes to that, I seem to remember you saying some rather stringent things on the subject of childbearing once upon a time! I am sure you as good as swore you would never commit such folly again—and now look at you!"

With a sheepish smile, Lady Helen looked once again down at her swelling abdomen. "I daresay I did say one or two things," she admitted. "But as you say, we are all permitted to change our minds, when the change is for the better." In a more serious voice, she added, "Indeed, I wasn't intending to throw your words in your face, Lora. But I have often thought of the things you said that day—about how miserable you were with Carroll and how sorry you were that you had married him. It came as a great shock to me, for I am sure I never guessed you were unhappy. And so I can't help wondering now if you—"

"Oh, but Helen, you must forget what I said that day," interrupted Lora, looking greatly distressed. "You know that at the time I said all that, I was feeling very bitter and unhappy. I am afraid I expressed myself rather harshly toward poor Carroll, and rather unjustly, too. Not that he was a perfect husband, of course. He was not, but I have come to understand both him and myself much better in these last few years, and I have come to the conclusion that it was my fault almost as much as his that our marriage wasn't a success. If I had known then what I know now, I am sure I would have been a great deal happier with him. Not so happy as I am now, of course, but better than I was."

"Then you are happy now?" said Lady Helen, catching eagerly at her words. Lora did not hear the question, however, for at that moment a hideous outcry arose from that quarter of the garden where the children were playing. In a flash, Lora was up and out of her chair and down the path to the gate. A moment later she returned, smiling ruefully and bearing on each arm a bawling twin, whose dusty fingers had created a new and abstract pattern upon her sprig-muslin gown. Behind her trailed the earl, carefully carrying the trowel in both hands as though it were an object of immense value.

"Mine!" said the youthful John, making an ineffectual attempt to grab the trowel from the earl's hands and sobbing all the louder at his failure.

"Mine," asserted his sister, with sobs equally loud.

"No, darlings, it belongs to neither of you, and if you can't play with it nicely by turns, you shan't be allowed to play with it at all," said Lora firmly. Turning to Lady Helen, she explained, "They were fighting over the trowel. John had it originally, you know, but agreed to loan it to Helen on the condition that she would restore it to him as soon as he asked for it. That was his understanding of the agreement, at least. Apparently Helen had a different understanding. I am afraid she isn't *quite* an angel," she added in a low voice, with a mischievous look at her friend.

Lady Helen laughed. "Perhaps she is more like her godmama than I thought!" She sat watching as Lora rocked and soothed her injured offspring to a state of quiescence. All the while the earl pottered busily underfoot, making scratchings in the gravel with the trowel. "About what we were talking about before," she began at last, hesitantly. "About you and Adam——"

"Oh, here *is* Adam," said Lora, looking up eagerly as the gate squeaked open. Adam and Lord Spelbourne had just entered the garden and were coming down the path toward them. "And Arthur, too. Did the two of you have a pleasant ride?" she asked, as they joined her and Lady Helen beneath the elm.

"Aye, very pleasant," said Lord Spelbourne, nodding to her affably before seating himself in the chair beside his wife.

"Very pleasant," echoed Adam, and dropped a kiss on Lora's brow. Although light, it was no perfunctory caress, and his eyes were warm as he looked down at her. "You seem to have been busy while we were away," he said, surveying the children's tear-stained faces and her own dust-marked gown. "Don't tell me these two have been misbehaving?" He directed stern looks at his offspring, who, far from looking cowed, greeted him with crows of delight. He reached out to unburden her of the nearest twin. "I think a bath is in order," he said, looking that young lady over critically.

"Yes, I was just about to take them into the house," said Lora. Rising to her feet, she took a step toward the house, then stopped suddenly and turned back to Lady Helen. "I'm sorry, Helen, what was it you were saying before? You wanted to ask me something, I know, but I'm afraid I got distracted in all the excitement."

Lady Helen looked at her. The trees and flowers of the garden made a bright background for her as she stood there smiling, holding her son in her arms. Adam, beside her, had hoisted their daughter onto his shoulders so that he might have an arm free to put around his wife's waist. As she waited for Lady

Helen's reply, he leaned down to kiss her impulsively on the cheek. She returned the caress fondly, then turned her attention back to her friend. "What was it you wanted to ask me, Helen?" she asked again.

Lady Helen looked from her to Adam to the children, and the anxiety faded from her face. With a laugh, she rose to her feet, extending one hand to her husband and the other to her son. "Never mind, my love. You've already answered my question," she told Lora. "What I want now, more than anything, is another cup of tea. Come, Arthur—and young Arthur, too—let's all go into the house."

About the Author

Joy Reed lives with her family in the Cincinnati area. She is the author of two previous Zebra regency romances: AN INCONVENIENT ENGAGEMENT and TWELFTH NIGHT. Joy is currently working on her newest regency romance, MID-SUMMER MOON, which will be published in February 1997 and a novella, THE CHRISTMAS BEAU, to be published in Zebra's Christmas regency collection, a CHRISTMAS COURTSHIP (available November 1996). Joy loves hearing from her readers and you may write to her c/o Zebra Books. Please include a self-addressed stamped envelope if you wish a response.

WATCH FOR THESE ZEBRA REGENCIES